Conflict of Interest
Jackson Banks

I0673906

Website: www.writerjacksonbanks.com

Email: writerjacksonbanks@gmail.com

First Edition.

eBook ISBN: ISBN-13: 978-0-9977861-4-9

Paperback ISBN: ISBN-13: 978-0-9977861-5-6

Cover by David Prendergast.

Also by Jackson Banks

<u>Fiction</u>

Alligator River

<u>Non-Fiction</u>

I Put Pants on for This?: Stories in Defense of Staying Home

Author's Note

Conflict of Interest is a thriller novel centered on a lawyer seeking justice for the wrongful death of an elderly man at the hands of a predatory skilled nursing facility. Along the way, this lawyer falls in love and enters into a queer romance outside of his marriage. While entertaining, the story includes elements that might not be suitable for some readers and that others may find triggering. The novel mentions death/illness of a parent, elder abuse, adultery, biphobia, forced outing, external and internalized homophobia, and alcohol use. There are also instances of strong language and graphically described scenes of consenting intimate relations both of a heterosexual and homosexual nature. Readers who may be sensitive to these elements, please take note.

Part I

Discovery

Chapter One

Harry Thomas died alone. Monica, his estranged daughter, never once visited Harry in what was euphemistically called a retirement community after she dumped him in the cheap facility. She didn't care when the nurse from Peaceful Pines called to tell her Harry had passed away. Not until she received the coroner's report, that is. Her father had died from homicide by institutional neglect, and with that ruling came the potential for Harry to have done something good in his daughter's life for once. Monica had immediately called The Law Offices of Everett Stone with thoughts of a large settlement racing through her head.

And now, because of that call, a storm was brewing on the horizon of Everett Stone's life. A life-altering, once-in-a-century hurricane. He thought he was prepared to weather it. He thought he would come out the other side unscathed. The ocean floor is littered with the bones of sailors who thought the same.

The cold snapped the post-sleep fog from his mind. Everett didn't need several cups of coffee each day to get going, like most lawyers. Instead, he drove to the gym and swam in the frigid pool to get his blood flowing and mind working.

Everett enjoyed the solitude more than the exercise in those pre-dawn hours. He acknowledged he could stand to lose a few pounds when he looked in the mirror, but he was reasonably attractive, even if his abs were not as defined as they once had been.

The pool was his chance to think uninterrupted and to prepare for what would come during the rest of his day in his busy law office in downtown Raleigh. It was where he had his best ideas and could focus on the biggest problems in his cases while hearing nothing but the splashing of his strokes. The early hour he rose each day guaranteed he was alone.

His morning ritual had grown especially important since filing the Thomas Estate's wrongful death lawsuit against Peaceful Pines and its owner, Ross Tyndall. It was the biggest case of his career. He was not a famous lawyer by any measure, but in the past decade he had built a reputation as a seasoned and fearless litigator. This case had the potential to make him one of those famous lawyers who get called to be a talking head on cable news. And very rich.

The Big One, as he referred to it around the office, was the case that every trial lawyer dreams of: a sympathetic victim, an evil villain, and an atrocity that would provoke an enormous verdict.

The more he thought about the Thomas case, the more inspired he became and he took his energy out in the water. His strokes quickened and the time it took him to complete his daily two mile swim shortened. This was the case he had gone to law school for. This was the case where he stood to do some actual good rather than just collecting insurance money for people with whiplash.

Everett's black trunks clung to his body as he climbed out of the pool and began drying himself. Once in the empty locker room, he stripped off the trunks and tossed them in his bag with one hand before heading to the shower.

The after-swim shower was almost as important to Everett as the swim itself. This is where he could clear his mind, alone in the large, tiled room, while the steamy water washed away his thoughts.

After he was done, Everett took care in putting on his suit and checking to make sure his tie and hair were just right. He walked out of the gym and into the parking lot.

Everett climbed into his Lexus GX and turned on NPR, ready for the day's headlines. The news out of Washington had him cussing under his breath before he put the SUV into gear.

As he drove away, he never noticed the man watching him from a car parked in the back of the dark lot.

Chapter Two

" Who was this guy?" asked Ross Tyndall. His imposing frame was draped in an orange jumpsuit and he squinted under the harsh fluorescent lights. He was looking at the paperwork lying on the steel table.

"No one special," replied Billy Sloan. Sloan was much smaller than Tyndall, with a bad combover and an ill-fitting suit. His gold watch poked from under his shirt sleeve and was accented by over-sized signet rings on his pudgy hands. He was Tyndall's long-time personal lawyer and fixer, and the only one who visited him in Butner Federal Correction Center.

"What do we know about him?" asked Tyndall.

"Dementia was his primary illness, as with most of the patients. Medicare and Medicaid patient, not independently wealthy."

"Family?"

"There was a daughter. She never visited," replied Sloan.

"How long was he there?" asked Tyndall.

"About a year."

"Who was the nurse?"

"Annie Smith," said Sloan.

"What do we know about her?" asked Tyndall.

"She was new; only there two weeks before the guy died. Single mother."

"Will she be a problem?"

"More than likely," said Sloan. "She slipped through the hiring process — not as easily controlled as the others."

"You try to find the right people, but one always slips through," Tyndall said with a sigh and a shake of his head.

Peaceful Pines had been Tyndall's stroke of genius. In his other ventures there had been witnesses and sympathy from horrified juries. He had hired people who cared about their jobs and their

6

careers, with no motivation to look the other way on some of the shadier aspects of profiting from the sick and elderly. Some of his former patients had testified in the previous trials about the conditions of the facilities and the treatment they received, providing powerful testimony to jurors who thus far had awarded several families millions in verdicts against his former companies.

No longer. Tyndall had set out to establish a liability-proof business with Peaceful Pines. The facility was dedicated only to the care of dementia and Alzheimer's patients. His inspiration for the facility had come in a thought like lightning: *Who could possibly testify against me or be thought believable by a jury if they can't even remember their names or the names of their family?*

There were still state inspections, but those were easily dealt with. Tyndall purposefully put Peaceful Pines in a rural community that had missed out on the explosive economic growth in North Carolina's capital and Research Triangle Park. He knew regulators weren't paid well and were overworked, so he lightened their load by fattening their wallets with cash. The inspector's job was easy when he didn't have to inspect anything other than the amount in the envelope slid across the desk every six months. Fifty thousand dollars annually bought Peaceful Pines a five star rating with the State of North Carolina.

The outside doctor who made her rounds was easy to buy off as well. Charts were easily fudged and problems overlooked when the doctor was barely holding onto her medical license. Dr. Stefanie Tyler was lucky to be paid in the medical field at all after several malpractice lawsuits and struggles with alcohol, let alone double the going rate Tyndall's competitors were paying.

Try as he might though, Tyndall's plan was far from perfect. Every now and then someone with integrity would make it through his screening process. Annie Smith was one of those hires.

"Was everything taken care of afterward?" asked Tyndall. "You know I typically like to oversee that process myself. It makes me anxious that I couldn't this time with being in here. Fucking Feds and their fucking tax evasion bullshit."

"Yes, everything was taken care of how it should be. I made sure of it," said Sloan.

Tyndall let out a sigh.

"Thank you, Billy. I can always count on you," he said. "When I get released from this shithole at the end of the week remind me to buy you dinner and a bottle of that Scotch you like."

Tyndall's brow furrowed after a moment as he considered the situation. There was no need for him to ask why or how Harry had died; he already knew and that was the reason Sloan was here. He looked again at the lawsuit Sloan had brought him. It wasn't the first time he had been sued over the death of a patient, and it wouldn't be the last. This suit was different though.

"Why am I named personally in this lawsuit, Billy? I thought the corporate structure was supposed to protect me from liability on these things?"

"That's where we may have a problem," said Sloan. "But I've already started a plan in motion to solve it."

Chapter Three

❝ I know it's before nine, but this is an emergency," said Dayna.

"It had better be," Everett said as he sipped his coffee behind his desk. The staff knew his rule: no questions or problems before nine, unless it was an absolute emergency. He needed time to muster his people skills.

Everett was always the first to arrive at his office. He didn't like being around people in the morning. His wife, Olivia, hated that he set his alarm for four every morning, but the hours at the gym and few hours alone in the office were always his most productive. Once his staff started to arrive, his train of thought would be derailed with constant interruption throughout the day.

"It's Monica Thomas," continued Dayna.

"Seriously? How many times is she going to call? I've already told her countless times in the three months since filing this lawsuit that these cases take time and it's not a quick fix. Or does she want to complain about something irrelevant again?"

Everett remembered the day he signed Monica Thomas as a client and the disgusted look she had given him and his office when she walked through the door. The only thing special about his office was its location. The Law Office of Everett Stone was located on the twentieth floor of the Capital Center, which provided views of all of downtown Raleigh. Clients were impressed with the view, but not much else. The suite was the smallest available for rent in the high rise and decorated with generic furniture. Still, the location was prestigious and he shared the building with some of the largest and most powerful law firms in the state. Everett might not yet be a heavy hitter, but he at least could share the same building with them. He was sure the location was the only reason Monica had signed the contract.

"No, this time it may actually be a legitimate reason for calling," said Dayna. She walked further into the office.

Everett's private office was strewn with papers and files. The bookcases along the wall were crammed with thick books he hadn't touched since law school and even more files. Stacks of more paper littered one of the two plush leather chairs in front of his desk. If you didn't know Everett and walked into his office, you would have assumed someone had raided it and thrown everything about haphazardly. Everett insisted he had a system and knew where everything was located. His staff had their doubts. Dayna lowered herself into the one empty chair in front of his desk.

Everett stared at her now without saying a word and waited for her to continue.

Dayna had been his assistant for half of his decade in practice. The clients loved her, she was smart, tenacious, and exceedingly loyal. She had been an invaluable asset on many of his cases, but the only case that mattered at the moment was stacked on the floor beside where she sat. There were at least ten banker boxes filled with documents and notebooks, and the file was growing by the day.

"I had a frantic sounding voicemail from her this morning," Dayna said. "She's been noticing a strange car parked near her house and she thinks she's being followed."

Everett rolled his eyes and agreed to take the call. Dayna left his office as he picked up the receiver and hit the button to bring Monica on the line.

"This is Everett," he announced.

"I'm telling you, someone has been watching me," said Monica

"Then don't do anything stupid," said Everett half-jokingly. He had had this same conversation with Monica at least three times already, and was growing tired of his client's paranoia.

"Do you really think this is not a big deal? It's an invasion of privacy!"

"Even if someone was watching you, there's nothing illegal about it. As long as they are not trespassing on your property they are free to set up surveillance and watch you on a public street when you are outside of your house," said Everett. "But, as I said on the phone the other day," he added, "it's unlikely Tyndall's folks are surveilling you. You are not claiming a physical injury. It's usually only in cases of physical injury where people surveil a plaintiff. There would be no need for it in this case."

Monica was insufferable for long periods of time and Everett was sure no one wanted to take on the assignment of watching her every move and trying to eavesdrop on her every conversation.

"Are you sure?"

"I'm sure."

"Then why do I keep feeling like someone is watching me?"

How was Everett supposed to know?

"I don't know," he said. "Have you noticed anything unusual?"

"I keep seeing a car parked down the street. Then when I'm out and about I keep thinking I see the same car?"

"You *think* you are seeing the same car, or you *are* seeing the same car?"

"I'm not entirely sure."

"What kind of car is it?"

"I don't know. I haven't looked that closely. It's some kind of gray sedan, I think."

That narrows it down, thought Everett. *There's probably only a hundred thousand of those in Raleigh.*

"Is it in the same place on your street every time you see it?"

"No, not every time."

"Do any of your neighbors have visitors?"

"I don't know. I don't really talk to my neighbors."

Everett suppressed a sigh. "What about workers? Have you noticed any construction people or anything like that going in and out of your neighbors' houses?"

"No, I don't think so. At least not that I've paid attention to."

Everett pinched the bridge of his nose and said, "Listen, I know you're worried, Monica but I'm sure it's fine. If you're that concerned, then I would pay closer attention. Get a make and model of the car at least, or if you can safely do so a description of the driver and license plate number. Then if you can actually verify it's the same car following you around, you could call the police. But, as I've said, surveilling you wouldn't be illegal on the part of the defense."

"Can't you do something?" she asked.

"Not really, no. Just keep an eye out on your surroundings and try not to worry. I'm sure it's fine."

"I've been trying, Everett, I really have. It's hard not to worry about this though."

"I know. I'm sympathetic, I really am. But you haven't done anything that would paint you in a bad light or jeopardize the case, right?"

"Right," said Monica after a pause.

"Well, there you go then. Nothing to worry about."

The two said their goodbyes and Everett hung up the phone. He wasn't certain his client had told him the truth about not doing anything that could affect the case.

Chapter Four

The phone on the desk began to ring as Everett finished packing his briefcase to head home for the evening. He glanced at the clock and rolled his eyes while taking a deep sigh.

He looked at the caller ID despite his instincts to just leave and let the line continue ringing, and picked the phone up immediately when he read the name.

"What do you have for me?" he asked.

"A witness."

As soon as Monica had called him to take the wrongful death case, Everett had enlisted the services of his private investigator, Randy Montague. Randy had been responsible for obtaining the evidence that had led to some of Everett's biggest successes so far in his career, and Everett knew he would not be disappointed with Randy investigating Peaceful Pines.

Everett sat back down in his chair. "Tell me more."

"Her name is Annie Smith. She's the nurse that was taking care of Mr. Thomas at the time of his death. She was a new hire and had only been at the facility for two weeks," said Randy.

"That's not very long at all," said Everett.

"No, it's not. But, it didn't take her long to discover all the things wrong with the place. I mean, I've seen a lot of fucked up shit in my life, but if what this girl is saying is true it even makes someone like me feel sick."

Everett felt a wave of giddiness run through him. Randy's experience as a military policeman and then a civilian homicide detective had given him a great deal of invaluable skills and experience before he decided to leave government work behind and branch out on his own freelancing assignments from lawyers. He had never once let Everett down on an assignment and the two had become friends over the years.

"Go on," said Everett.

"According to Ms. Smith, Tyndall was still running the show from prison. His right-hand man that was in charge of this facility would call him weekly and do whatever Tyndall wanted him to do. She says she doesn't understand how the staff still has their licenses. They're beyond incompetent and have no business taking care of patients."

"Then how did she get the job?"

"Ms. Smith is actually pretty sharp. She noticed after meeting her new coworkers that they all had similarities. Most have a drug problem. Most live in low-income housing or trailer parks. Most are single mothers.

"She herself is a single mother and while she lives in a decent middle-class place, she drives an old beater. Ms. Smith speculates that Tyndall hires those who are desperate and need the job so they keep their mouths shut and their standards low. All the other staff were hired by Tyndall personally. She was hired by Tremaine, the manager, since Tyndall was an involuntary guest of the Feds. He must not have vetted her as well as Tyndall would have for their standards, if you can call them that."

"I'm hearing a lot of speculation, though," said Everett.

"True. And that was my concern too. Plus, I managed to find her as she was leaving work in the middle of the day. She had just been fired. My concern was her credibility wouldn't hold up; that she would come across as a disgruntled former employee."

"I don't like what I'm hearing, Randy."

Randy let out a laugh. "I knew you wouldn't. But here's the thing — Ms. Smith isn't an idiot. She has proof that Tyndall and his operation were dirty."

Everett's smile returned. "I'm waiting..."

"She says the nurses there all do paper charting because the facility is too cheap to buy them iPads or laptops to use their

Electronic Medical Record system. Apparently, they all use these paper flow sheets and then they're all responsible for uploading the information into the computer system later on. The thing with Mr. Thomas is that his medical records were altered."

"You have a proof of this?" asked Everett.

"I think so. Ms. Smith says she accidentally forgot to turn over the stacks of paper flow sheets she had on Mr. Thomas for filing when she was involuntarily separated from her employment. I'm not sure I believe her when she says it was accidental, but I'm sure not going to push her on that."

Everett let out a chuckle. "Good call, as always."

"So, she tells me all this about the medical records," continued Randy, "of course I immediately ask her if she has any proof she can provide me and she pulls out a thick stack of paper records from her tote bag and hands them over. I'll bet you good money that when you compare these records to the EMR version you got in discovery that the two are going to be very different from each other."

"I'm not taking that bet," said Everett. "Thank you Randy, this is excellent work as always. You never let me down."

"Oh that's not even all of it," said Randy.

Everett listened while Randy laid out the rest of what he discovered, the smile never leaving his face.

This motherfucker is going down, he thought as he walked out of his office after the call ended.

Chapter Five

Everett took a deep breath as he pulled into his garage. Rather than get out, he sat in his Lexus for a few minutes scrolling through X. Coming home was the part of the day he dreaded the most.

The house was a modest two story colonial in the Raleigh suburbs; not his dream home by any means, but comfortable enough. Everett walked through the side door and into an empty kitchen. He found his wife sitting in her usual chair in the den reading a book.

"Hey," Everett murmured as he sat down on the couch and turned on the TV. While his wife like to read, Everett preferred mindless entertainment after long days at the office.

"How was your day?" asked Olivia, barely looking up from her novel. Her blonde hair was perfectly styled and her petite frame was shrouded in a stylish shirt with black Lululemon leggings. She wore Rothy slips and looked ready for a day out, even though Everett knew she probably hadn't left the house all day.

"Fine," grunted Everett.

Olivia and Everett had met at a fraternity party their sophomore year of college and had quickly fallen in love. They married shortly after graduation, and Olivia went to work as a schoolteacher to support the couple as Everett pursued his law degree. She had been a strong, confident woman who came from money and had her pick of men. Everett had been smitten.

The infatuation began to fade over the course of Everett's three years in law school and devolved into constant bickering the summer he was studying for the bar. Olivia quit teaching to be a stay-at-home wife once he got his first job. There were no children; neither of them had wanted the responsibility.

Everett worked hard the first five years to prove himself, and the hours spent at the office left little time to spend with Olivia.

When he started his own firm, the hours grew longer still, and so did the distance between them. Everett couldn't even remember the last time they had made love, at least with each other.

He had discovered her infidelity six months before when she was in the shower. Her phone had dinged, and he glanced at it on the bedside table and saw the text from the younger man who did their landscaping. The suggestive message had been accompanied by a picture of his shirtless torso.

How cliche, he thought at the time.

Everett considered confronting her. He thought better of it when he considered what a divorce would entail, and more importantly, what it would cost. She could have her fun; he didn't care.

Now, all these years later, what started off as a hot-and-heavy romance had become stale and obligatory.

"How was your day?" asked Everett while looking at the TV.

"Fine," replied Olivia staring at the pages of her book.

"What did you do today?"

"Just some stuff around the house."

Everett knew that was code for "nothing." Although, to give Olivia credit, it looked like she had at least pushed the start button on the Roomba.

"I also went for a walk around the neighborhood," she continued.

"Oh?" Everett by this point was fully consumed in Netflix.

"Yeah, it was weird because for the second day in a row I noticed someone parked up the street in a gray BMW. The driver kept looking toward our house and then at his watch. Do you think that's weird?"

Everett was too engrossed in an old episode of *Breaking Bad* to have heard the question. He didn't notice Olivia staring at him waiting for a response, or hear her breathe a small sigh before returning to her novel.

The remainder of the night went like every other night. They ate a frozen dinner together on the couch while Olivia continued reading and Everett continued watching TV. Neither said another word to the other.

Later, they undressed in the bedroom and were naked in each other's presence only long enough to pull on their pajamas.

For another hour of near silence they lay in their king size bed, next to each other yet still far apart. Olivia was still reading, and Everett was staring at his phone scrolling through X absent-mindedly.

As Everett turned the light off and glanced out the window of their bedroom, he saw a gray BMW pull away from the curb down the street.

Chapter Six

Everett was back in the pool the next morning, eager for his swim. Shortly after beginning, he was startled by a disturbance in the water.

A shadow passed in the lane next to him, and Everett caught a glimpse of the other swimmer. It was a man who appeared to be in his mid-twenties.

Everett turned his attention back to his lane and kept lapping the pool. After completing his swim, he climbed out and glanced into the water while walking along its perimeter toward the locker room.

The stranger was still swimming his laps. Everett noticed his underwater observations were correct: the younger man was slender and toned with blonde hair. He was wearing a Speedo, which Everett thought unusual for his age.

Once in the locker room, Everett walked into the empty and slightly cool cavern that was the tiled shower room and chose his usual spot in the middle of the row of nozzles. He turned the faucet on and let the hot water run until steam filled the room, and then stepped under the head and let the water wash over him and relax his tense muscles.

Eyes closed, Everett allowed his mind to stray toward nothingness when he was interrupted by the sound of feet patting on the wet tile behind him. Glancing over his shoulder, he noticed the stranger from the pool.

A chiseled jawline framed a handsome face. The man's short blonde hair was still wet. Everett's eyes drifted downward as the stranger continued to walk. Everett thought the man must have spent a good amount of time using the squat rack on the fitness floor. The stranger stopped and turned on the faucet three down from Everett.

Everett turned back toward the wall but kept glancing at the stranger out of the corner of his eye. Looking at men in the shower was a bad habit he tried to hide, lest a conflict occur. What if he stole a glance at the wrong guy who took offense? Everett presented himself as straight and lived his life that way, but had fought against his true self since his teens.

Sometimes he wished he could go back and live his life differently. He often imagined what it would be like if he had felt comfortable being who he wanted to be all those years ago, without the fear of reprisal from his family or being ostracized by his peers. Would he have ended up with Olivia anyway? Would he have found love with another woman? Or would his soulmate have turned out to be a man? Everett wondered most of all whether he would be happier, or whether it would have turned out all the same given his most committed relationship had always been with his career and ambition.

He finished his shower and toweled off. Once at his locker, he got dressed and ready to head into the office. As he walked down the rows of lockers, Everett noticed the stranger was no longer there and he was once again alone. He wondered if he would see more of him in the future, and a small portion of Everett hoped he would. While he had always enjoyed having the pool to himself over the years, perhaps this handsome change in routine would make his days a little better.

He walked out of the gym just as the sun was beginning to crest over the horizon. A Subaru drove past him in the parking lot and he noticed the stranger from the pool was behind the wheel. As his gaze followed the Subaru, he noticed a gray BMW in the back of the lot.

I swear I've seen that car somewhere before, Everett thought to himself. He watched for a few moments longer, then dismissed the thought and climbed into his Lexus.

Chapter Seven

Everett threw the last stack of medical records into one of the banker boxes sitting next to his desk.

"You ready?" asked Dayna.

"As ready as I'm going to be," replied Everett.

His shirt sleeves were rolled up and his hair was slightly disheveled from running his hands through it all day. Everett rubbed his eyes and downed the last of his Starbucks. It was his sixth cup of the day.

"You need anything else?" asked Dayna.

"I don't think so. Just some rest. I'm sick of this case. I love it and hate it all at once."

"You and me both," chuckled Dayna.

The fifteen boxes of records lining the floor of his office represented the discovery responses of Peaceful Pines and Ross Tyndall. It was a classic document dump by the defense, delivered at the last minute and not organized in any particular manner. The defense hadn't even undertaken the courtesy of bates numbering the thousands of pages of documents to make them easier to organize and reference. The tactic had been designed to make his life difficult and increase the chance he would miss important details that could help the case.

Dayna had been in his office most of the day organizing the file and helping Everett pull what he needed for the upcoming deposition of Ross Tyndall. She had given the other support staff strict instructions to let them be so they could focus. In a perfect world, they would be able to help with the task, but there were other cases that needed attention too and it was a small firm. Everett had spent the long day analyzing the documents and planning the questions he intended to ask. It was important to develop a strong strategy, given the stakes of the case. He wasn't about to half-ass the deposition of the main witness.

Everett shut the cover of his laptop and pushed in his chair. He picked up the last stack of documents on his desk and slid them into his briefcase.

"Do you have them all?" asked Dayna.

"Yes, I have all the exhibits. We should be good to go."

"Do you want me to go ahead and supplement our discovery responses?" she asked.

Once Everett saw that the defense intended to make the litigation as frustrating as possible, he had made the decision to detour from the high road. If Tyndall and his army of lawyers wanted to play games, then he could too.

Inside Everett's briefcase was a stack of evidence that could potentially ruin Tyndall since those left in charge of Peaceful Pines during his recent prison stay had been sloppy. Everett had an obligation to turn that evidence over, but not necessarily right away. Randy had been slow in getting it to him, and it wasn't ready to send when Monica's discovery responses came due. It didn't matter to Everett that Randy had been slow, because he had instructed him to hold the evidence. The law only required that Everett supplement the materials within a reasonable period of time, whatever that meant.

"No," he said to Dayna. "They're probably prepping him for his testimony right now. There's no reason to give them an advantage by sending it to them. The deposition starts at ten in the morning. Set the email to go out about two hours in. They won't be able to do anything about it by that point. It will ruin their entire day once they see what it is."

Dayna stepped aside as Everett walked out of his office.

"Have fun," she said.

"You know I will."

Chapter Eight

The law firm of Wright & Reynolds occupied the entire floor ten stories above Everett's small office suite. Stepping off the elevator, visitors were greeted with a lobby lined in mahogany paneling, marble flooring, custom furniture, and chrome accents. The entire office was designed to do two things: 1) impress clients, and 2) intimidate the opposition.

The largest law firm in the state, Wright & Reynolds had over two hundred fifty litigators and countless support staff. Ten of those lawyers sat in the spacious conference room overlooking the state capitol for a meeting with Tyndall.

Kenneth Wright, the managing partner, was at the head of the table. Sitting opposite was Tyndall. All the lawyers were wearing expensive, tailored suits. Tyndall was wearing jeans and an old sweatshirt. He looked at once bemused by so much attention from so many lawyers, and annoyed at having to attend the meeting. He checked his watch for the tenth time since arriving an hour before.

Tyndall stared down the long conference table at Wright. Wright was in his early sixties with gray hair. He gave off an air of self-importance and over-confidence typical of so many trial lawyers.

"Ross," began Wright, "we need to get you ready for your upcoming deposition. It is very important you perform well to give us the best chance at trial. What I want to do today is first go over the ground rules for a deposition, and then ask you some questions I think you'll likely be asked for practice. My team will also jump in as needed and provide feedback on your presentation and responses.

"Speaking of which, as far as presentation, and as a reminder, this deposition will be videotaped and the video could later be played at trial. You should look your best to enhance your credibility with the jury. I would suggest..."

Tyndall raised his hand to cut Wright off from speaking.

"I'll wear whatever I'm comfortable in. As you gentlemen know, I spent the past few years wearing the same prison uniform every day and no one is ever going to tell me what to wear again. I don't like wearing suits and I'm not going to wear one. I find them restrictive and pompous."

Wright shifted in his seat and his brow furrowed. Several of the other lawyers looked at their tailored suits with sheepish expressions on their faces.

"First, let's go over the rules," continued Wright, a gruffness slipping into his tone. "The first rule of a deposition is obvious: always tell the truth. You are under oath."

Tyndall rolled his eyes. "Are you listening to yourself? Or have you given this speech so many times before that your mouth is on autopilot. Lecturing a client to tell the truth is unnecessary. Stop wasting my time."

Wright's jaw clenched and he set his pen down on the table. He drew a deep breath before continuing.

"The second main rule of a deposition is to never guess at an answer," instructed Wright. "If you don't know something, or don't remember something, just say so. Guessing leads to problems and could create credibility issues in front of a jury. Credibility is everything at trial."

Wright continued with his rehearsed rules. Halfway through his speech Tyndall raised his palm again.

"Do you have a question?" asked Wright.

"I want to know why we're wasting our time, and so much billable time at that, going over these rules? Let's cut to the chase. All of you are familiar with my background by now. You know this isn't my first time being deposed, and probably won't be my last. I don't need reminders. Let's move on."

Wright shifted in his seat again and frowned. He gripped the arms of his chair, turning his knuckles white. One of the associates at the table looked down at his lap and tried to suppress a smile when he saw his boss's reaction.

"Ross, whether you like it or not I'm going to do my job," said Wright. "I know you didn't hire me—your insurer chose us—but you're stuck with us as lead counsel if you want coverage for this loss. So, you're going to have to listen. If I were in your shoes, I'd take this seriously. You're being defended under a reservation of rights since there's a question as to whether some of the alleged acts and omissions that caused Mr. Thomas's death are covered under the policy. Your policy only covers accidental deaths through negligence, not intentional acts, which is what homicide is. Even assuming there is insurance coverage, there's a chance the verdict could exceed your insurance coverage limits, and we've already discussed how your corporate structure may not be enough to protect you from personal exposure. So I'd at least pretend to care about what is going on."

Tyndall glared across the table at Wright as his cheeks flushed and he clenched his fists. He began to lean forward, but a pudgy hand tapped his arm and pulled him back against his seat.

"Let's just move on and get this over with," said Sloan, who was seated to Tyndall's right. "He knows the drill on depositions, get to the questions you want to practice with him."

Wright's jaw clenched, and the remaining attorneys turned toward Sloan with varying levels of contempt on their faces. Whenever Sloan spoke, their faces always looked like they had been assaulted by a foul odor.

The questioning began with standard banal background questions. Tyndall rolled his eyes to each inquiry and continually checked his watch, but Wright continued unbothered and shifted into the more critical questions that were anticipated.

"Was Mr. Thomas provided with his medications during his time at Peaceful Pines?" asked Wright.

"Of course."

"Was he bathed?"

"Yes," replied Tyndall.

"Did you document his treatment in medical charts and records?"

"Yes, we did," replied Tyndall.

"Have you had a chance to review the medical records of Mr. Thomas provided in discovery?" asked Wright.

"Yes, I have."

"Are they accurate?"

"To the best of my knowledge, yes," answered Tyndall.

"Did your staff follow the applicable standards of care?"

"Yes, we did. As we do with all patients," responded Tyndall.

"Do you have any opinion as to why Mr. Thomas's death was ruled a homicide by institutional neglect?" asked Wright.

"No, I don't," lied Tyndall. "All I can say is that we followed the standard of care. Mr. Thomas was fed, bathed, given his medication, and generally taken care of in the manner that one would expect of a five-star rated facility. I cannot speak to what the medical examiner was thinking, but the evidence contained in Mr. Thomas's records doesn't seem to support the conclusion."

Wright stared down the table at Tyndall for a few moments, tapping his pen on the legal pad in front of him. He turned toward one of the other lawyers at the table who nodded his head. "I think that response will work well, Ross. It's definitely a question I expect Stone will pose to you during the deposition, so remember that response."

Tyndall continued fielding questions from Wright. After ten minutes, he once again interrupted and told Wright to get the point.

"You've got at most thirty more minutes before I leave and get on with my day. I have a business to run," he said.

Wright flushed at being interrupted a third time. Most of the lawyers flanking the conference table sank lower in their seats and checked their watches or phones.

"I don't think you're taking this seriously, Ross."

"I'm not, Ken. It's a waste of time."

"I don't think you understand the ramifications of this case. You may think your assets are shielded and you can hide behind the corporation and the insurance policy..."

"It's worked for me before," interrupted Tyndall.

"It may not work this time. How many times have we been over this? There's a doctrine of law called piercing the corporate veil. Stone has alleged you created Peaceful Pines by committing a fraud, and if he can prove that, then he can get past the corporate structure and go after you personally."

"Then I'll declare bankruptcy."

"Maybe. That would stop some of the bleeding, but Stone can probably still get a large portion of your considerable assets. You have a lot of money, Ross, and you probably can't discharge all your debts outright. The bankruptcy would also have dire consequences for your ability to start more businesses in the future or getting the credit to do so."

"He's got to get me to that point first," said Tyndall.

"This is not a good case for us, Ross. The evidence is frankly not good."

"It will be fine."

"How can you be sure?" asked Wright.

Tyndall said nothing in response.

"No one has a crystal ball, Ross. I've been involved in a lot more cases than you have and actually tried them instead of just sitting there in the defendant's seat. All the lawyers in this room—except maybe Sloan—have tried dozens of cases each. We can give you a hypothesis, but none of us can predict the results of a trial with certainty. At the end of the day it's the same as throwing a pair of dice down on a craps table in Vegas."

Tyndall crossed his arms over his chest and didn't say anything in response.

Wright began asking his questions again and Tyndall answered with derision in his voice and a few eye rolls. He kept checking his watch.

After thirty minutes, Tyndall abruptly stood and began walking toward the conference room door. Sloan followed.

"We're not done, Ross," said Wright with his voice raised.

"Yes, we are," said Tyndall.

"You're making a mistake," said Wright.

"Whatever," said Tyndall as he crossed the threshold and left.

"It'll be fine," whispered Sloan as they walked together toward the elevator. "I've made sure of it."

Chapter Nine

All of the Wright & Reynolds lawyers were hunched together on one side of the massive conference room table. Tyndall was seated in the middle of his lawyers, with Wright just to his left. Sloan occupied the seat to his right.

Along the other long side of the table was a row of empty chairs, just one of which would be occupied by Everett. The court reporter sat at the head.

Tyndall's lawyers all had dour looks on their faces, except Sloan, who appeared content and disinterested. Wright scowled at Everett as he crossed the threshold. Everett managed a small smile despite the butterflies in his stomach and his knees feeling shaky under his off-the-rack suit.

Sloan and Tyndall stared back at Everett with smug expressions on their faces. How Sloan was even in the room Everett didn't know. The opposition research Dayna had put together revealed Sloan had been in trouble with the State Bar so many times during his two-decade career it was a wonder he still had a law license.

"Good morning," Everett said to the group.

A small murmur of acknowledgement came in return.

"Morning," Tyndall said loudly with a smile on his face.

That smile won't be there for long, Everett thought.

• • • •

Once everyone was situated and ready, the court reporter placed Tyndall under oath.

"State your full name for the record."

"Ross Eugene Tyndall."

Everett knew Tyndall would have been prepared thoroughly for his deposition and knew Tyndall would be expecting Everett to begin with the easy background questions.

Everett didn't care about Tyndall's background, however. He cared about Harry Thomas. He cared about justice.

"Please explain your understanding of why Harry Thomas's death was ruled a homicide by institutional neglect."

"Objection," said Wright.

"This is a deposition. You can answer the question," Everett instructed Tyndall, ignoring Wright.

"I don't have an understanding on that," answered Tyndall.

Wright glanced at his client's short response.

"Is that because you were in prison at the time and not there?"

"Partly."

"For tax evasion, correct?"

"Yes, that's true. We all make mistakes."

"What's the other part?" asked Everett.

"What do you mean?" replied Tyndall.

"You said your stint in prison was only part of the reason you don't have an understanding on why Mr. Thomas's death was ruled a homicide by institutional neglect. What's the other part?"

"I can't read the medical examiner's mind, counselor." Tyndall let a snarky smile cross his lips.

Wright rubbed his temples.

"Did you not ask your staff what happened?"

"Of course I did," replied Tyndall.

"What did you learn?" asked Everett.

"That Mr. Thomas had been looked-after, just like all our residents. He was treated according to our policies and procedures, and the standard of care. He was fed when he was supposed to be. Bathed when he was supposed to be. Administered medications on schedule. I don't know why the medical examiner ruled the way they did, as we didn't find any evidence of neglect. His medical records do not seem to support that conclusion."

"What steps, if any, did you take to investigate his death internally?" asked Everett.

"We did what I just said," replied Tyndall. "In addition to speaking to all the staff, we also verified what they told us by meticulously going through his chart to corroborate their accounts."

"Who is 'we'?" asked Everett.

"Bill Tremaine, who runs the facility on a day-to-day basis. Once the lawsuit was filed around the time I was released from prison, I personally asked the staff questions and read Mr. Thomas's medical records. I'm always concerned when one of our patients passes away, but I was especially concerned in this case given the circumstances. I wanted to satisfy myself that the medical examiner had made an error, which I believe they did."

Everett paused and let the statement hang in the air before continuing.

He pulled a stack of documents out of an accordion file on the table next to his seat. "I'm marking these as Plaintiff's Exhibit 1. Please take a look at these."

Tyndall flipped through the stack of documents briefly.

"Are those Mr. Thomas's medical records?"

"Appear to be."

"Are those true and accurate copies of his medical records from your facility?"

"Appear to be."

"I want to ask you a series of questions concerning the content of these records."

"Suit yourself."

For the next two hours Everett painstakingly went through the printed records and highlighted the treatment Harry had received at Peaceful Pines. Tyndall read from his staff's notes and recited the facts on the pages: regular baths, regular changing, flawless medication administration, and regular feedings.

All of it was a lie.

A round of cell phone chimes went off around the table as Dayna's email containing the supplemental discovery responses was delivered.

"Did you ever alter these records?" asked Everett.

"No," testified Tyndall.

"That was a bad question on my part since you were locked up at the time. Did you ever instruct anyone else to alter these records?"

"No."

"Do these records exist in the same version they have always existed in?"

"As far as I know."

Everett took a sip of coffee and held Tyndall's gaze. Tyndall's eyes seemed to burn with contempt and defiance.

An uncomfortable silence built in the room as the two continued to stare each other down. Wright was scratching the side of his face and Everett thought he might be contemplating retirement. Sloan was scrolling through his phone, looking not the least bit interested in the proceedings.

"Would you agree that not giving patients their prescribed medications can lead to their death?" asked Everett.

"It depends on the medication, but generally yes that could be a consequence," replied Tyndall.

"Would you agree that not changing a patient's diaper can cause horrible, painful sores?"

"In some cases."

"Would you agree that not bathing a patient for long periods of time can cause adverse health effects in the patient?"

"Yes, I would agree to that."

"Did all of those things happen to Harry Thomas at your facility?"

"No."

"Did you know all those things were happening to Harry Thomas your facility?"

"I just said they didn't happen."

"Did your staff regularly feed Harry Thomas?"

"According to the records, yes."

"Do you believe you were responsible for the death of Harry Thomas?"

"No." A smirk formed on Tyndall's face.

Everett didn't quite know what to make of the expression. He caught Wright glancing in his client's direction and saw his lips turn downward.

"We've been going for several hours," said Wright. "Why don't we take a break?"

"I don't need a break," said Tyndall.

"Ross..." began Wright.

"I said I don't need a break, Ken. Let's just get this thing over with so I can get back to my business."

Everett looked at Wright and thought the man must have wanted to throw his client out the windows behind him. A part of Everett would have enjoyed seeing that.

"I want to circle back on the subject of the medical records we've been talking about. I know you testified that you reviewed Mr. Thomas's medical records..."

"That's correct," interrupted Tyndall.

"As I understand it, your facility uses an Electronic Medical Record system?"

"Yes."

"Do you use paper records as well?"

The smug look on Tyndall's face diminished ever so slightly. "Yes, we do. We use flow sheets, which then are inputted into the EMR system."

"Did you review the flow sheets for Mr. Thomas?"

"Yes, I did," said Tyndall with confidence.

"I did not see those flow sheets in the discovery responses your attorneys produced. What happened to them?"

Tyndall smiled before responding. "Unfortunately, we stored the paper records on site and a water line broke in the storage room. It flooded all the records and we lost them. Fortunately, they had already been entered in the computer system."

"I see," said Everett.

Everett held Tyndall's gaze for a moment before smiling himself. He reached into his briefcase on the chair beside him and pulled out a thick stack of records.

"I'm marking these as Plaintiff's Exhibit 2," said Everett as he slid the stack of documents across the table. "Can you please glance through those and tell me if you recognize them?"

The cocky smile disappeared from Tyndall's face as he flipped through the records. Wright, who had been looking over his client's shoulder, turned red in the face.

"Objection!" said Wright.

Everett never broke eye contact with Tyndall, who was glaring at him from across the table.

"These were not produced in discovery," continued Wright.

"Yes, they were. Check your email," said Everett.

Wright glanced at his phone before slamming it back down on the table.

"Sending these during the deposition hardly counts as producing them in discovery."

"Mr. Wright, you know as well as I do that the rules merely require us to produce them in a reasonable amount of time after we received them. We only recently received these records, and produced them as quickly as we could."

"Everett..." began Wright.

"You've made your objection and the court can deal with that later. Right now, I have a right to continue my examination and that's what we're going to do," interrupted Everett.

"Now, Mr. Tyndall..."

"Where the fuck did you get these?" snarled Tyndall as he cut Everett off.

"I take it you recognize them? That was going to be my next question."

Tyndall said nothing in response.

"Mr. Tyndall, I've posed a question to you and unless you want me to move the court for sanctions for refusing to answer a valid question you need to give me a response."

"Go to hell," said Tyndall in response.

"Is that a yes?"

Sloan nudged his elbow into Tyndall's side. "Yes," replied Tyndall.

"Do these appear to be flow sheets from your facility?"

"Yes."

"Do these flow sheets pertain to Mr. Thomas?"

"Yes."

Everett spent the better part of the next hour highlighting some of the more glaring inconsistencies between the paper flow sheets and the printed EMRs. The entire defense team, except Tyndall and Sloan, seemed to sink lower in their seats as Everett went on in detail about lack of medication administration, lack of bathing, and numerous other gross violations of the standard of care. By the time Everett was finished, Tyndall looked like he wanted to murder him despite the room full of witnesses.

"Do you regret Harry Thomas's death?" continued Everett.

Tyndall let out an exasperated sigh.

"Do I regret it? His death was not a result of anything we did. So I regret it only insofar as I'm not making money off the poor bastard any longer."

The brazenness of the reply caused Everett's jaw to drop. One of the defense lawyers let out a small gasp. His neighbor shot him an admonishing look. The rest of them looked like they wanted to die themselves, including Wright.

"You've done nothing wrong? Despite the records in Exhibit 2 you maintain you've done nothing wrong?" asked Everett.

Tyndall pushed the exhibit away from him and toward Sloan. "Like I said, these appear to be flow sheets pertaining to Mr. Thomas from my facility. But, these are not the flow sheets I recall seeing. I don't know where you got these, because our flow sheets were accidentally destroyed, as I've testified, before discovery commenced in this case. I don't believe these are accurate copies based on my recollection. The EMRs are an accurate record of Mr. Thomas's treatment at Peaceful Pines."

"Did a nurse named Annie Smith author the records in Exhibit 2?"

"It appears so," replied Tyndall.

"Have you asked Ms. Smith about the care of Mr. Thomas?"

"Ms. Smith was no longer employed by Peaceful Pines by the time I had the ability to look into Mr. Thomas's death."

"What happened to her?"

"I'm not sure."

"Do you have any way to get in touch with her?"

"We have tried, but her address and phone number are no longer valid. You've been provided with her previous contact information," replied Tyndall.

"What have you learned from this incident?" asked Everett.

"There was nothing to learn. We did everything by the book. Our records show that. My staff confirms it. I don't know why he had the sores he did. I don't know why he was so emaciated. I'm not a doctor, but my limited understanding is those conditions can be caused by multiple things. The fact is Mr. Thomas was quite advanced in his age, and unfortunately suffered from several chronic and severe diseases. Sometimes old people just die, Mr. Stone."

"No more questions," said Everett.

Wright leaned forward and cleared his throat, as Everett expected. He would want to try to rehabilitate his client as best he could and clean up some of the more harmful testimony.

"No questions," said Billy Sloan before Wright could speak.

The rest of the defense team looked at him, appearing astonished he would have the nerve to say anything at all during the deposition, let alone pass on their opportunity to ask questions. Everett smiled at the sight.

"Have a good rest of the day, gentlemen," Everett said as he collected his briefcase and walked out of the conference room.

· · · ·

Everett traveled down the ten floors to his suite and shut the door to his office. He walked around his desk and collapsed into his chair, letting out a long breath as he settled.

"Got you, you motherfucker," Everett said to himself.

The smile began to fade from his face as he thought more about the case and deposition.

That went almost too well, he thought. *Why was Tyndall so cocky? And why did Sloan cut off the questioning?*

Everett thought about the deposition more as he gazed out of the window at the city lights. *It's nothing,* he concluded. *Tyndall and Sloan are just being over-confident. They've gotten away with things for far too long and no longer know a real threat when they see it.*

Still, Everett's gut was uneasy, though his conscious mind couldn't articulate the reasons. He tried to think through his anxiety and determine the exact source, but couldn't come up with one. By all accounts, working up this case had been easy.

That was exactly the problem. The case had been progressing far too easily. What was he missing?

Chapter Ten

The stranger was already doing laps in the pool.

As Everett stretched his arms to prepare for his laps, he watched the stranger moving through the water with a steady freestyle stroke.

He climbed into the lane next to the stranger and gripped the edge of the pool, brought his knees up and planted his feet on the side. Everett was ready to push off into the water, and push the Thomas case out of his head for a little while. He took several deep breaths and thrust himself forward. Everett brought both arms in front of him and overlapped his hands as he glided through the water for a quarter-length of the lane before stroking and kicking into his own rhythm.

For most of the next hour, Everett and the stranger were side-by-side as they made their way down their respective lanes; rhythm and pace seeming to sync.

Everett had to admit he enjoyed the company. He liked the fact he was keeping up with the younger man's brisk pace.

Toward the end of the session, Everett's age began to catch up with him and the stranger started to pull ahead. Everett stopped once he had reached the equivalent of two miles in distance, removed his goggles, and pulled himself up from the ledge until he was standing on the pool deck. He stood there at the end of the lane toweling off and catching his breath, watching the stranger take another lap.

Everett heard the sloshing of water from the other end of the pool deck as he opened the door to the locker room a few moments later. He could hear the stranger's wet footfalls behind him.

The stranger walked past his row of lockers as Everett spun the combination dial. He stole a glance and felt a tinge of nostalgia for the time when his skin and muscles were as firm as the younger man's. He started for the showers.

Everett saw the stranger emerge from a row of lockers as he reached the threshold to the shower room. The stranger walked confidently past Everett and went inside the tiled room. His body was still wet from the pool and water dripped from his short blonde hair. The stranger hadn't bothered wrapping himself in a towel and had shed his Speedo.

Everett walked into the shower and found his normal place in the center of the nozzles. He turned the handle to hot. The water began to flow and steam began to fill the shower room.

Halfway through his shower, Everett felt someone staring at him. He turned his head from the tiled wall to his right and saw the younger man looking directly at him. More than that, he had turned so that his whole body was facing Everett. Everett's breath caught.

Everett looked at the man but didn't speak. It wasn't often he couldn't find words. He heard his heartbeat in his ears, and saw a smile cross the stranger's face. Everett's biggest secret, and fear, collided as he felt himself becoming aroused.

He was about to ask the stranger what he thought he was doing, but the stranger took two confident strides toward him before Everett could open his mouth. The man stopped directly in front of him.

The two stood eye-to-eye and inches apart in the steamy tiled room; the only sound was that of the water raining down on the floor.

Everett's heart quickened further and he felt a flutter in his stomach. His hands vibrated with nervousness. He held his breath. His mind stopped processing information.

For all Everett's confusion and nerves, the young man seemed calm and was looking at him with a sly expression on in his face. His blue eyes were locked directly onto Everett's hazel ones.

Everett opened his mouth to begin to speak, a protest planned, but before he could get out the first syllable the stranger leaned forward and kissed him.

Everett knew he should step back and say something. He didn't. He thought he should push the stranger away and extricate himself from the situation. He didn't. Instead, Everett remained there, returning the kiss. Butterflies pounded in his stomach, his pulse was drumming rapidly. Everett could feel himself getting harder as his conscious screamed at him to stop. The logical side of his brain begged Everett to be faithful to his wife and marriage. To not give in to something he had worked hard to hide from himself and the world. Everett refused to listen. This was something he had fantasized about for far too long.

Everett knew most men in his position would have reacted differently. Perhaps they would yell out. Kick. Punch. Exclaim, *"What the fuck?"* and clarify, angrily and emphatically, they were not *that way.*

His mind continued to howl at him to stop what was happening at once, but he gave in to long-denied desire. How easy it was to throw away his vows and promises to Olivia.

Everett groaned as the stranger continued kissing him with soft lips. His knees weakened as the minutes went by. Everett ran his hands through blonde hair as the two embraced.

The stranger stopped suddenly and pulled away. He stared Everett directly in the eyes.

Everett returned the man's gaze. A smile formed at the stranger's lips, and he began to walk out of the shower.

Everett turned to follow the stranger's path, admiring him as he walked.

"Wait," Everett said as the stranger reached the threshold.

The man paused and looked over his shoulder.

"What's your name?" asked Everett.

"Jake," the man said after a pause.

"I'm Everett."

Jake smiled, then walked out of the room.

Chapter Eleven

D*on't you dare do this,* Everett thought. *Stop. Do not go any further. You absolutely have to let this go.* Everett's logical side fought violently with his arousal and long-repressed desire. Eventually, his heart won out.

Everett raced back to his locker, whipped the towel from around his waist, and completed drying himself off.

After yanking his duffle bag from the locker and tossing it on the wooden bench behind him, he unzipped it and dressed as fast as he could. He didn't bother with his tie. Everett ran his fingers through his hair and left it partly disheveled.

He grabbed his duffle off the bench and fast-walked down the locker room until he came to the row Jake had walked down. His heart raced and the butterflies returned to his stomach as he turned the corner.

Jake was gone.

Everett went to the parking lot as fast as he could without breaking into a run. There were a small handful of cars, including a BMW far in the back he thought looked familiar. All the cars appeared to be empty. Everett felt the crush of disappointment.

Everett climbed into his Lexus and took a deep breath before turning on the ignition. He glanced in the mirror and finished fixing his hair, then put the SUV into gear and drove to his office.

• • • •

The disappointment of Jake leaving so quickly without so much as a word—or a phone number being exchanged—put Everett in a funk by the time he arrived at his desk.

He sipped his coffee and his anxiety began to spike as he thought of the events that morning.

What the hell are you doing, Everett? he asked himself. *You're married.*

Drinking his coffee, Everett stared out his window trying to rationalize his actions. *It was a one-time thing. Everyone makes mistakes. She'll never know. It's not like our marriage is happy. You two are more like roommates than anything else at this point, and she's been having her own affair.*

Pouring his second up of coffee, he tried to get his mind to focus on his day's work. Monica's deposition was coming up, and he needed to get ready to prepare her for her testimony. It would be a lengthy meeting, and there was a lot of work he would need to do to turn that piece of coal into a diamond. But first, he checked his emails and began going through some paperwork in his inbox once he was seated at his desk, but the words didn't register. His mind drifted back to Jake.

"Are you okay?" asked Dayna a few hours later.

"Yeah, why?" Everett replied.

"You don't seem yourself today. It's like you're distracted."

"Oh... um, I guess I am a little," said Everett. "But I'm fine."

"Did the deposition not go well?"

"What?" asked Everett.

"Tyndall's deposition. How did it go? I was sort of expecting you to say something about it earlier today, but you haven't said anything."

"It went well. It was almost too easy. The timing of those records was perfect, by the way." Everett turned his attention to his monitor.

"That's good," replied Dayna. She dropped some paperwork into his box and left his office, giving him a quizzical look on her way out.

Everett decided to call it quits around four that afternoon. The mental energy he had expended trying to keep his mind off Jake had made him more tired than usual. He thought about heading around the corner from his building to The Raleigh Times Bar but decided against it. The distraction caused by Jake was not what he needed at the moment with the Thomas case heating up and becoming more active, and alcohol would only make matters worse. He headed home instead.

"Why me though?" Everett asked as he looked at himself in the rearview mirror. It was the question that had been bothering him most of the day. He wasn't in his twenties anymore, or nearly as fit as the stranger had been. Everett looked like your average guy, while the younger man looked like something out of a fitness magazine.

Who cares? It was wonderful. Stop analyzing everything all the time.

He thought about Jake some more and the smile returned to his face. Everett realized that he didn't even know the man's last name.

This would be nothing, he eventually decided. It was just a little making out. No one needed to know. It didn't need to happen again; he could resist if Jake tried coming onto him. No one needed to know his bigger secret either.

• • • •

Everett sensed Olivia taking stock of him and wondered if she suspected. He wondered if he cared whether she did. He walked over to Olivia and kissed her on the cheek. The look of confusion was obvious on her face.

He didn't blame her. The kiss may have been overkill. Everett couldn't remember the last time he had greeted her like that.

"What's gotten into you?" Olivia asked. "And why are you home so early?" Her eyes narrowed slightly.

"I just had a good day, and I wanted to see you." It was not the first time he had lied to his wife, and it would not be the last.

"Work going well?" Everett thought the question didn't make sense, considering he just told her he had a good day. Then again, she never really listened to him. She was probably just relieved he didn't catch her with the yard guy and thinking about how to schedule their rendezvous if he was going to be breaking his regular habits.

"Very well." Everett said.

"I'm glad. I know you've been working hard on that case."

"The Thomas case, yes. What's for dinner?" Everett asked out of habit, trying to sound normal..

"I don't know. What would you like?"

This was the same question-and-answer exchange they had every night. It annoyed Everett. Why did he have to decide what to have for dinner after making hundreds of decisions throughout the work day? What did she have to worry about while he was slaving away at the office? It never mattered what he wanted anyway, as she was a terrible cook. Whatever she chose to make would be borderline edible at best.

He brushed the questions off and refused to let them annoy him for once. Tonight was different. He had been thinking about Jake all day. Jake in his Speedo. Jake's naked body. Jake's mouth pressed to his.

Everett smirked at his wife as the thoughts of Jake stirred his arousal. "You. I want you for dinner."

Everett grabbed Olivia by the hand and pulled her gently off the couch.

"What are you doing?" she giggled.

"You," Everett said with a smile.

Everett led Olivia upstairs to their bedroom and pushed her onto the bed. He undressed himself and then removed her clothes as she smiled. Olivia clearly appeared surprised but seemed to welcome the unusual show of affection from her husband.

They made love as if they were young and enamored with each other again. They fell asleep in each other's embrace.

Everett drifted off to sleep thinking about Jake.

Chapter Twelve

E verett's excitement grew as he approached the gym, and his stomach fluttered when he pulled into the parking space. A broad smile crossed his lips, and he was giddy for the first time he could remember in his adult life. He couldn't wait to get to the pool.

Everett knew he shouldn't be so happy. He should be disappointed with himself and feeling guilty. He should hope he never sees Jake again. But Jake had given Everett an experience he had denied himself his entire life. Everett promised himself he would not let things go further than they already had, but he didn't see the harm in seeing Jake at the gym as long as he kept it platonic going forward.

Everett glanced down each row as he made his way through the locker room and toward the pool. Jake wasn't there. Maybe he was already in the pool.

Everett stripped out of his clothes and pulled on his trunks, slamming his locker door behind him.

Opening the door to the pool deck, Everett's heart dropped and the smile disappeared from his face. No one was there.

I just got here before him, that's all, he thought.

Everett climbed into the water and began his laps. Stroke after stroke, he glanced into the lanes next to him hoping to see Jake.

Everett remained alone for the entire two miles. His mood had soured as he finished his swim, pulled himself out of the water and removed his goggles.

Everett walked back into the locker room and stripped off his trunks. He walked to the shower and chose his usual spot. As he turned on nozzle and the hot water began to run, he glanced around with some small amount of remaining hope, although the rational part of his mind knew Jake would not be coming.

Everett tried to clear his mind and focus on work but all he could think about was what happened the morning before. He felt himself becoming aroused at the memory, and turned the water to cold before turning it off altogether and grabbing his towel.

He was in his office within the hour, not noticing the gray BMW that had been following him since he left his house that morning. Everett sat down at his desk, took a sip of coffee and logged onto his computer. He attempted once more to push Jake out of his mind.

It was a one-time thing. A chance encounter. There's no need to think about it anymore. You have more important things to do than live out some fantasy.

The Thomas trial was rapidly approaching, and he needed to prepare. Everett didn't have time to be distracted by some guy in a pair of Speedos.

Chapter Thirteen

Monica arrived at Everett's office early for what would be a lengthy meeting. She needed to be prepared to testify in her own upcoming deposition. A team of lawyers was just waiting to tear her to pieces, despite being an allegedly grieving daughter.

It's the "allegedly" part that worried Everett. It was no secret to anyone involved in the case or in her life that Monica had been estranged from her father for a long time before his death.

A social worker had brought Harry Thomas back into her life. A neighbor had found Harry wandering down the street confused and yelling at everything that moved: squirrels, birds, the toddler down the street. It was strange behavior, but the yelling was not out of character, at least according to Monica's recollection. There had been a quick diagnosis of dementia once Harry was admitted to the hospital.

The doctors told Monica that Harry would need extensive care. It was better for his condition to be somewhere familiar and with people he knew surrounding him. They suggested she may want to consider taking him in to live with her since she was the only family he had left. Her mother had died of cancer years ago.

Monica sipped her coffee with shaky hands as she tried to recall all of Everett's admonitions about how to testify and what they had already discussed over the past several hours. The first thing he had said to her was that a deposition can make or break a case.

Everett had spent a great deal of time going over Monica's testimony regarding the details of the case itself. They had been running through the questions, and carefully scripting answers that were truthful, but not necessarily the whole truth. Everett viewed his client's job as answering the questions that were asked, but that didn't mean she needed to volunteer information or state every detail. It was an attorney's job to ask questions to get the information they needed.

"Why did you choose Peaceful Pines?" asked Everett for what must have been the fifth time since they began. He had lost count somewhere around the third round of practice testimony.

Moving in with her was out of the question, she had said originally. The day before he was discharged from the hospital she had sat at her kitchen table Googling facilities. Everett had almost gasped when she had told him that in less than ten minutes, she'd found Peaceful Pines and never gave her father a second thought after dropping him off two days later.

"It was advertised as a specialized care facility. It seemed to have good reviews. It felt like the best place for my father," said Monica now. Everett smiled at the refined response.

"Did you meet with Ross Tyndall when you moved your father into the facility?"

"Yes. We discussed the facility itself and the care my father would receive. He assured me it would be top-notch. He said they hired only the best staff. That they had skilled and respected doctors come in and treat the residents in-house. It seemed like a clean and well-run facility."

This is what Tyndall told her, Everett knew, but he also knew she had doubted, even then, the veracity of the statements. She had told Everett something always struck her as off about the man. He had the qualities that made him seem like a car salesman. She had brushed it off at the time, and had signed the admission paperwork in less than thirty minutes after she arrived at the facility. Everett had told her these were details she didn't need to mention unless specifically asked.

"Did the staff provide you regular updates on your father during his time in Peaceful Pines?"

"Yes, they called once a month and said everything was fine. He was doing well and was healthy."

That was true. The staff called Monica once a month to give her updates and reports on her father. What Everett had told her not to elaborate on was that she never answered the calls. Brief synopses were left in voicemails, most of which were not listened to until after her father's death.

"Did you ever go visit your father?"

Monica drew in a breath.

"No."

Everett paused for a moment and considered this response. This was the biggest weakness in the case and the main way Tyndall's lawyers would be able to advocate for a smaller amount of money at trial. The answer needed explanation, but the fact that father and daughter had been estranged for so long bothered him. Would a jury care to give Harry Thomas's daughter the full amount of justice if she hadn't spoken with her father in so long?

It was possible. The horrors Tyndall had reaped on the residents of Peaceful Pines were plentiful, and a jury would want to make the award large enough to deter the behavior. But, with the right answers from Monica — the answers that made her look sympathetic — the size of the deterrence, and his contingency fee, could be significantly larger.

Everett considered his options. Letting Monica launch into a narrative explanation of the reasons why she never visited her father would be too risky. She might jumble her words, and open the opportunity for more questions from Tyndall's lawyers.

Everett knew from his time working with Monica that there was a good reason she had never visited her father. But, Monica had quickly shut down and become vague when he tried to find out the details behind the estrangement.

"Was it because it was too painful?" asked Everett. He had to be careful with his wording so as not to provide the testimony for her, and hoped his client could read between the lines.

Monica paused before answering. "Yes."

This was good. A jury may believe it was painful because of his dementia and deterioration, not because of the family issues.

"Do you regret not visiting your father?"

Monica hesitated. She had told Everett before she had not regretted it in the least. She never wanted to see the man again once she left home in her late teens, and she had no intention of ever going back to Peaceful Pines after she signed the admission paperwork. She had told Everett she hadn't even gone when her father was transported to the facility by the hospital to settle him in.

"Yes," she replied. She glanced away quickly and avoided Everett's gaze.

Everett caught the eye movement and her body language, but decided the answer was sufficient. It was the answer they needed.

"Do you regret not being able to reconcile with your father before his death?" asked Everett.

"Yes," Monica replied, still avoiding eye contact.

Everett continued his mock interrogation for a while longer and after several more hours had finished going through Monica's expected testimony. He had explained to her at the beginning her testimony needed to be short as it was the weakest part of the case, and she had followed directions beautifully.

Everett returned to his office after releasing Monica from the conference room. Shutting door behind him, he said another prayer that she wouldn't mess the case up for him. The case was near-perfect and Monica was the only thing that could jeopardize it.

Chapter Fourteen

A week after Monica's deposition, Tyndall was called once again to the spacious conference room of Wright & Reynolds to have his army of lawyers give him bad news.

Tyndall was sitting at the head of the large table, flanked on either side by his team of lawyers. Wright was in his usual position at the opposite end. Sloan was sitting directly to the right of Tyndall, and his presence once again seemed to annoy every other lawyer in the room.

Sloan was the only person Tyndall trusted. He had been Tyndall's fixer for going on two decades and had been with him through thick-and-thin. He was paid in cash each year, in hefty amounts, to keep him loyal and overlooking the ethical rules and, at times, even the law.

The truth was Sloan had no choice but to be loyal to Tyndall. He had almost failed out of college due to his propensity for drugs, and had gained admittance to a third tier law school by the sheer fact they were desperate for students to fill their seats at fifty thousand dollars a year. Even at a school more concerned with profit than academics, Sloan met the standards to graduate by the skin of his teeth, and didn't pass the bar exam the first time. Or the second. Or even the third. The fifth time turned out to be the charm.

It wasn't that Sloan lacked smarts—he was actually quite cunning—he just had no ambition for academics. He preferred solving problems the old fashioned way: threats and blunt force. He was a perfect match for Tyndall. Since Tyndall was his main client, Sloan had managed to stay under the State Bar's radar for most of his career, excepting a few minor reprimands and censures as a result of opposing counsel's complaints.

Tyndall had felt Sloan was the only lawyer he needed, but his insurer disagreed, so here he sat. To hear the lawyers of Wright &

Reynolds talk, Tyndall was surprised the large national firm hadn't flown in other experienced litigators from their offices nationwide. They acted as if the sky were falling.

In contrast to his legal team, Tyndall acted as if it were a beautiful day and the case was a pleasant walk.

Kenneth Wright was finishing up his summation of the problems in the case, including the deposition testimony of Monica. He relayed to Tyndall that she had presented exceptionally well, and had near-perfect answers to every question posed to her.

Tyndall couldn't help but wonder how, with all the education in the room, his lawyers hadn't been able to shake a money-grubbing plaintiff like Monica Thomas. He often thought that she cared less for her father than Tyndall himself had. At least for Tyndall, Harry Thomas had been bringing in a steady stream of revenue each month.

The court had ordered a mediation to take place, and it was scheduled for the coming week. Wright was explaining the process to Tyndall, and the challenges involved with trying the case. The words "significant" and "record-breaking" were used to describe the potential verdict.

Tyndall and Sloan both sat at their end of the table with smug looks on their faces, giving Wright the occasional roll of their eyes as he worked his way through the well-rehearsed apocalyptic speech.

"I don't think you understand the risks that this case poses to you," Wright said. "The evidence in favor of the plaintiff is quite compelling. I can easily see a jury finding against you." Tyndall by now had lost count how many times Wright had told him this over the course of the case. His patience for it was wearing thin.

"We have evidence too," replied Tyndall. "We have the state inspections and ratings. We have the fact that old people just die sometimes - that's a fact of life. We have records showing flawless medication administration and care for this guy. Dr. Tyler will back that up, she treated him during his entire stay."

"Ross, I'm frankly surprised you got those ratings. The records are problematic because of the inconsistencies with the paper flow sheets that Stone got ahold of. As for Dr. Tyler, that's a whole separate problem. She was barely holding onto her medical license and is not someone a jury would find credible. More importantly, she moved out of state and refuses to cooperate with us."

"This case presents potential financial ruin," said another well-groomed suit. "To your company, and possibly you."

"Well then figure something out. That's why you're paid several hundred dollars an hour," Tyndall barked. "I knew the risks before the first twenty times you've told me over the past months. That's what the insurance is for."

"It's not that simple, Ross," said Wright. "As we've discussed, your insurer may not cover any judgment and, even if they do, your coverage limit may not be enough to cover the verdict."

"They can't get to my assets. The business is protected as an LLC," replied Tyndall.

"Not necessarily," continued Wright. "As we have also discussed many times, Mr. Stone has enough evidence that the business was set up outside the bounds of corporate law that the protections of the LLC may disappear."

"I think we need to discuss settlement options," the other senior litigator said.

"No, we do not need to do that. We're not going to settle," Tyndall said.

"Sir, I really don't think you understand," said a third suit. "We are likely going to lose this case, it's just a question of how much. It's in your best interest to try to make a deal, one that limits your personal exposure."

"Fuck that," Tyndall said.

"Ross..." began Wright again.

Tyndall raised his hand and silenced him. Wright's brow furrowed and his face flushed red.

"I'm done talking about this," Tyndall said. "Are you finished? Have you said what you called me in here to say? I'm tired and ready to leave. If you want to discuss settlement you can save your breath because I'm not interested in settlement and never will be."

Several of the lawyers looked like they were about to protest, but stopped themselves when Tyndall and Sloan both stood up to leave.

"Listen to me, gentlemen, we have nothing to worry about. Everett Stone is not going to win this case at verdict. I guarantee it. He'll settle this case for the insurance money like all ambulance chasers do and consider it a win, and all of us will walk away from the whole thing," said Tyndall.

All the Wright & Reynolds lawyers assembled looked astonished by the ignorant and brazen statement. Several looked down at their legal pads and seemed to question why they had ever chosen this profession that brought them so often into contact with people like Tyndall. Others looked like they wondered if their client perhaps needed psychiatric help based on his delusions. None of the lawyers looked happy.

Except for Billy Sloan.

Chapter Fifteen

Every morning he walked to his usual locker. He stripped off his clothes and pulled on his trunks, then walked into the pool deck. Everett was nothing if not a creature of habit.

He had settled back into his normal routine and cynicism. Everett had not seen Jake in the gym for several weeks and had given up hope of ever seeing him again, resigning himself to the idea that the previous encounter had been a one-time thing, never to be repeated.

There was only a week to go until trial and work stress was ramping up. Monica had done well in her deposition, exceeding his expectations, and mediation was in a few days. If the defense were smart, they would have Tyndall open up his bank accounts and dump them on the conference room table. But, Everett wasn't sure he wanted them to settle. He wanted his record-setting verdict. He wanted the fame. He wanted the money. Everett wanted justice.

His relationship with Olivia had been better immediately following his encounter with Jake, but now they'd also fallen back into their old routines and sullenness. Everett questioned how much longer the marriage would last.

He took a deep breath and steadied himself as he lowered himself into the water. Everett's breath caught at the chill, and he slipped on his goggles.

He braced himself against the wall and then pushed off, beginning his swim. As with every morning for the past few weeks, no one else came and he remained alone.

Lap after lap, Everett thought about Jake and what it meant for him now. He had never allowed that side of himself to surface outside of dark nights alone and his own private thoughts.

Was I not good enough? he thought as he wondered why Jake had never returned. *Am I a bad kisser?*

Maybe he realized I'm too old.

His arms began to ache as he neared the end of his workout, but he kept powering through.

Maybe I should download Grindr. Give that a try.

Olivia floated into his mind.

It's wrong. I should feel guilty. But, I don't. I'm not sure I love her like I used to. I'm not sure she loves me. If she can have her fun outside of the marriage, in supposed secret, why can't I?

• • • •

In the shower, he turned on the water and watched the steam build, lathering soap in the process and rinsing the chlorine from his body.

Eyes closed, he let the hot water run over him and relax his tense muscles.

Sensing movement from behind, Everett opened his eyes. His pulse quickened. He turned his head to the right.

Jake was smiling at him. It was a coy smile, one that seemed to say, *Bet you never thought you'd see me again.*

Everett's eyes wandered from Jake's young face down his neckline and over his chest and well-defined abs before he knew what he was doing. His eyes stopped below the waist. Everett felt himself getting aroused but tried to tamp it down. He felt a certain measure of shame and he felt his cheeks warm. His heart was racing with excitement and butterflies beat against his stomach.

Jake's smile widened and he took a step closer to Everett. The two were almost touching.

"I'm glad to see you too," Jake said. "Hope you don't mind my not joining you in the pool recently. I decided to work out on the weight floor upstairs."

The surprise and elation cleared. Everett suppressed his smile, but not without a great deal of effort. He raised his hand, not quite touching Jake's chest but close. He had wanted this moment so often over the past few weeks, but his practical side regained control of his senses.

"I'm married," said Everett softly.

"Why should I care?"

"I'm also too old for you."

"That's really for me to decide, isn't it? I'm attracted to older men, and there's nothing wrong with that."

"Are you calling me old?"

"I'm calling you sexy."

Everett smiled, but still resisted his urges.

"This just..."

"Just what?" said Jake with that cute smile of his.

"It's just very random. I've been coming here for years and no one has ever been in the pool as early as me. Then you show up, and just happen to be attracted to me?"

Jake took a step closer to the point their feet, and other appendages, were practically touching. "I just moved to the area, and needed a gym. I chose this one because it's the closest to my apartment. The rest of it? Serendipity."

Everett didn't know how to respond. Before he could think of something to say, Jake's hand moved and Everett felt it close around him. Everett moved his hips slightly forward.

What the fuck am I doing? he thought.

Everett closed his eyes and cast aside any thoughts of protesting. He let out a quiet moan as Jake kissed his neck under the hot water.

Jake pulled away. He smiled that coy smile again and walked out of the shower. Everett watched him the entire way, trying to catch his breath and regain full strength in his knees.

Everett turned to face the shower wall again and closed his eyes.

Stop. Stop. Stop, he repeated to himself.

After another minute, he turned off the water and left the shower, at once gleeful and ashamed.

The locker room was empty. Disappointment crept over him.

Turning down the aisle where his locker was located, Everett noticed a small sheet of paper sticking out of the crack between the door and frame. He removed it and read the messy handwriting.

It was an address. An invitation.

Chapter Sixteen

Everett didn't sleep that night. His profession was the usual culprit of sleepless nights, but tonight his thoughts were consumed once more by Jake. Everett had all but resigned himself to never seeing him again before Jake showed up in the locker room that morning.

Everett couldn't quite wrap his head around what was happening between the two.

What does Jake, someone so much younger, see in me?

If he is into me, why did he take so long before returning? The weight floor couldn't wait?

How did he know I would be okay with it?

Everett could find no clear answer to any of the questions that were running through his head as he stared at the wall in his dark bedroom. Olivia slept quietly on the other edge of the expansive king-sized bed.

When he wasn't trying to be discern some rational intent behind Jake's advances, Everett thought about how good it felt to be wanted again. How young and special it made him feel; something he hadn't felt in a long time. He caught himself smiling and becoming aroused under the sheets.

Everett glanced at Olivia in the darkness and watched the soft rise and fall of her breathing. She had a peaceful look on her face.

Everett wondered, not for the first time, where it had all gone wrong between the two. Had he ever really loved her? Or did he simply love what she provided him: companionship, stability, and an air of normalcy?

Everett's mind raced through their life together. Yes, he decided, on some level he still loved her; but Jake was different. Jake offered Everett something Olivia never could. He offered validation for a part of Everett that he always hid from himself and the world. A space where he could be himself and not be ashamed of it.

Can it work? Can I see Jake, have fun with him, without it blowing up in my face?

Everett let out a sigh and closed his eyes as he considered the risks and debated himself.

I don't see why not. You've kept that side of you hidden all your life. If you're careful, why would anyone find out?

It's too risky. Olivia probably felt the same thing before you found out, only she's the type of care and create a scene about it.

You've already taken the risk on some level. If you didn't intend to pursue this, why didn't you push him away either time?

You can't.

But, maybe you can. It happens all the time. A fun little fling here and there outside of the marriage, and no one has to be the wiser.

It could destroy your life.

So could continuing to suppress this side of myself.

Everett looked at the clock on his nightstand and saw he had only three more hours before his alarm would sound. He closed his eyes once more and tried to clear his mind.

It didn't work. Instead, he debated what he was going to do when his alarm went off.

· · · ·

Everett got ready and packed his gym bag while butterflies beat furiously against the walls of his stomach.

He had made up his mind right before his alarm went off. It was the first morning in years that the gym would not be his destination.

Everett's mind raced as he climbed the stairs of the apartment complex in the pre-dawn hours, the chill of the winter air caressing his face. He glanced around with each step he took. His heartbeat in his ears, and he felt for a moment like he might throw up.

Thoughts raced through Everett's head, trying to compel him back to the car.

What would happen if Olivia found out?

What would happen if others found out?

Why am I risking so much for someone I don't even know?

He was tired of these thoughts. They had been bouncing around his head all night. Everett pushed them aside. He had made a decision and intended to stick to it.

Everett reached Jake's door and drew a deep breath. He raised his hand and hesitated. He knocked.

There was no answer.

He could feel his heartbeat quicken even more as he knocked the second time.

There was still no answer.

Everett reached in his pocket and checked the address written on the note Jake had slipped into his gym locker. He confirmed the apartment number on the door. Everett was in the right place.

Everett started to knock a third time, but thought better of it.

This is crazy. What am I doing here?

He turned to walk back toward his car. Just as he did, Everett heard a lock click and glanced over his shoulder to see the door crack open.

Everett turned fully around and saw Jake standing in the threshold of the now-open door. Jake was wearing only his boxer briefs. A slight smile crept across Jake's face, and his blonde hair was a mess. It looked like he had just gotten out of bed.

Everett started to speak, but no words came out. He wasn't sure what to say.

"I was hoping you would skip the gym and come here this morning," Jake said.

Everett smiled.

"Come in," Jake invited.

Everett crossed the threshold into a still-dark living room that was sparsely furnished. He could see a large flat screen TV with a PlayStation on an entertainment center that looked like it was from IKEA. The only other furniture in the room was a cheap-looking coffee table, an old couch and an even older recliner. Everett again wondered about Jake's age.

Jake closed the door behind him.

"I'm glad you invited me over," began Everett, his speech a bit fast and shaky. "I would like to get to know..."

Jake stepped out of his underwear and stood before Everett.

Everett stumbled mid-sentence and couldn't find the rest of his words as he took in Jake's body.

"Did you really think I invited you over to talk?" asked Jake.

Jake stepped forward and grabbed Everett's shirt. He began leading Everett down the dark hallway toward the bedroom.

"Why me?" Everett managed to blurt out as he allowed himself to be lead down the hall. "We don't even know each other."

"Why not you?" Jake asked with a smile. "I liked what I saw that first swim. That's all there is to it."

Jake was silhouetted by the light coming from the small bedroom. He led Everett into the room and turned to face him. Everett looked at him in the soft light and saw that Jake was already aroused. Everett was too.

Jake released Everett's shirt and moved his hands lower. One hand undid Everett's belt while the other zipped down Everett's fly. Jake undid the button at the waist, gripped either side of Everett's pants, and pulled them to the floor. Jake next removed Everett's shirt and tossed it in a messy pile.

They both stood facing each other. There was hunger in their eyes. Jake reached up and grabbed the back of Everett's head, pulling him in for a kiss.

Everett was awkward at first, a product of his nerves and fears, but then he wrapped his arms around Jake and pulled their bodies together as they continued to kiss.

Everett moved his hand between them and touched Jake; lightly at first, and then gripping him tighter. Jake pulled back and moaned before leaning forward again to kiss Everett's neck. Jake's hands grasped his ass.

Jake pulled back a step and the two smiled at each other as they made eye contact. Jake placed his hands on both of Everett's shoulders and re-positioned him so his back was now toward the bed.

Jake playfully shoved Everett backward, and he fell onto the mattress. Its old springs creaked under the weight.

Everett rose to his elbows and began drawing his legs toward his chest so he could get back up, but he was stopped by Jake's weight as he climbed on top of him.

Everett froze and then closed his eyes as Jake began to gently kiss his neck and playfully run his fingers through Everett's hair.

Jake moved down to Everett's collar bone and then began kissing his way down the length of Everett's torso. Everett writhed from the slight tickling sensation Jake's lips made as they moved down the length of his body.

Jake took Everett in his mouth and he let out a moan. The moans grew louder in the minutes that followed.

Everett was breathing heavily, his eyes closed. His hips were undulating gently, and the fingers of one his hands were running through Jake's hair.

"I'm close," whispered Everett.

Jake stopped.

"Tease," Everett chuckled, his eyes still closed.

Jake stood and grabbed Everett's legs, throwing them over his shoulders and pulling Everett's thighs so that his body came to the edge of the bed in one smooth movement.

Everett's eyes came open at the surprise movement.

Jake smiled down at him, his blonde hair even more of a mess from Everett's tussling.

Everett felt a brief moment of pain as Jake entered him. There was a pause, and Jake bent down and kissed him.

Jake stood once more and began thrusting back and forth; slow at first and then picking up speed.

As Jake continued deeper and faster, Everett closed his eyes as the pleasure grew.

Everett felt Jake's hand come between his thighs and grab ahold, stroking up and down. Slow at first, then fast, then slow again; the movement of Jake's hand matching the rhythm of his hips.

Everett never wanted the moment to end, but he knew it would... and soon.

"Come with me," whispered Jake.

Everett moaned and he felt himself getting closer as Jake thrust back and forth inside him with newfound speed and intensity.

They both moaned, louder and louder as they came closer to closer to climax. They released in unison.

Jake collapsed onto the bed next to Everett and the two lay side by side for several moments, panting and staring at the ceiling.

"That was... nice," Everett said.

"Yeah, it was," Jake replied.

Jake got out of the bed and walked out of the room toward the kitchen.

Everett raised himself up on his elbows and watched as a still naked Jake left the room.

When Jake was out of sight, Everett lay back down and crossed his hands behind his head.

"Coffee?" asked Jake as he came back in the room carrying two mugs.

"That would be great," said Everett.

Jake handed him a mug and then climbed back onto his side of the bed.

The two finished their coffees and sat in awkward silence.

Everett felt a mix of emotion. Happiness was overpowering the shame and guilt. He wondered what Jake was feeling, if anything.

How many times has he done this?

Everett was just about to say something when Jake finished his coffee and set his empty mug on the nightstand. He looked at Everett and leaned over to kiss him. Everett eagerly met his lips.

Jake pulled back from the kiss and took Everett's mug from his hand, placing it next to his.

A look of mischief crossed Jake's face and Everett could see him getting arouse again.

"Turn over and get on your hands and knees," commanded Jake.

Everett did so without a word.

Everett and Jake stayed in bed with each other well into the afternoon.

Everett's phone vibrated non-stop from the pocket of his pants on the floor.

He didn't care. The office could wait.

The only thing he cared about today was Jake.

Chapter Seventeen

❝ I don't think you understand."

Tension filled the conference room as Wright glared down the table at Tyndall. The other attorneys flanking either side of the table looked down at their legal pads trying to avoid being drawn into the crossfire.

"I understand perfectly," said Tyndall.

"With all due respect, that seems doubtful if you just sat through the same presentation we did," said an adjuster with Tyndall's insurance company.

Tyndall glanced at the adjuster and rolled his eyes. He returned his withering gaze back to Wright, who sat unflinching in the confidence of his position.

"I don't care what that prick Stone said," replied Tyndall. "This case is not going to turn out the way all of you anticipate. I've been through jury trials before. I've lost before. I won't lose this one."

"The evidence says otherwise," said Wright. "There are many mediations where we come back in this room and I can tell the client not to worry about much of what the plaintiff's lawyer said in opening session. This is not one of those times."

Everett had spent the better part of an hour during the mediation's opening session laying out his case in excruciating detail. On the video screen, he displayed medical records detailing the poor treatment Harry Thomas had received in Tyndall's facility, records he could prove had been altered. He also detailed Tyndall's abysmal history, and gruesome photographs from Thomas's autopsy.

Many attorneys on the defense team had looked uncomfortable during the hour. The mediator looked at Tyndall with apparent disgust. The insurance adjuster had cried.

When the parties left the session to go to their breakout rooms, the mediator started in Everett's room. The defense team did not have to wait long for the demand. The mediator had not argued with Everett for a more reasonable number. After the openings, there seemed to be no number too unreasonable for plaintiff and their position.

"If you want to settle this so bad," continued Tyndall, "then get it settled for the insurance money. That's what insurance is for."

Wright breathed a deep sigh. "Ross, we're going to offer the full policy limits. Unfortunately, your policy only had five million dollars in coverage. That doesn't come close to meeting the demand, and Stone is not going to accept the five million and walk away. He just said as much—convincingly."

The fifteen million dollar demand Everett sent to the defense team was astronomical by most local standards, and more than the mediator or the defense had ever seen in a mediation.

"Then you should have done a better job in the opening session of providing a defense," said Tyndall.

Wright bristled and his face grew red. His hands clenched into tight fists. Another partner sitting next to him leaned forward slightly in his chair, apparently afraid Wright may get up and assault Tyndall for the remark.

"Provide a better defense?" spat Wright, "With what, Ross? We have no defense. I've been practicing for decades and this is the worst case I have ever seen. Hell, there are centuries of combined experience in this room, and it is the worst case any of us have ever seen. We have a deceased elderly man with horrific bedsores. Altered records for Christ's sake! The only thing we have on our side is Monica Thomas's relationship with her late father, and a jury frankly is not going to care about that when they see the rest of the evidence."

Wright took a deep breath before continuing.

In a more even tone, he said, "I again recommend you strongly consider offering an amount above the insurance limits. There is likely room to negotiate here. If you settle today, you could be saving yourself much greater exposure at trial."

"Absolutely not. I will not offer a dime of my own money to settle this case."

"Ross, I don't understand your position. You have the money to offer. You're a very rich man. If this case goes to trial, that could change very quickly. Stone could get a verdict that could wipe you out financially."

"That is not going to happen."

Wright stared down the conference table at Tyndall. "In all my years of practice I have never seen a client so stubborn in their refusal to accept their fate and the chances their case presented in front of a jury."

"I don't give a shit," replied Tyndall. "I'm right."

"How can you be so sure?" asked Wright with a sigh.

Tyndall did not respond and stared down the table at Wright.

"You don't know anything, Ross. Yes, you have been sued before. Yes, you have lost and lost big before. But in those other cases where the verdict was above the insurance limit you were sheltered. You were able to hide behind the corporate entity and keep your money."

"And I'll do the same in this case, if it comes to that."

Wright let out a laugh. "It will certainly come to that. I'm telling you now this verdict will be substantial. It will exceed the limits. It will likely exceed the demand Stone is making here today. It will likely far exceed what this case could settle for if you would just negotiate at a reasonable level. The problem here, Ross, is this time for whatever reason you decided to form this corporation by forging your son-in-law's signature on the documents. The entity is fraudulent. It will be dissolved by the court."

Tyndall sat there with a smug smile. He made no response to Wright's pleas.

"Will you please reconsider and offer some money above the insurance coverage?" begged Wright.

"No," said Tyndall without hesitation.

Wright turned his attention to Sloan who was seated to Tyndall's right. "Will you please weigh in here? I know you understand our position. Can't you try to talk some sense into our mutual client?"

Wright's face flinched as he spoke to Sloan, as if speaking to him as an equal pained him.

Sloan looked up from his smartphone and stared directly into Wright's eyes. He shook his head and glanced back down at the screen.

Tyndall leaned back in his chair and glanced up at the ceiling, appearing bored and uninterested.

Wright clenched his fists.

The partner next to Wright lightly touched his arm.

Wright unclenched his firsts, but his jaw remained tight.

Uncomfortable silence filled the room.

"Go get the mediator," barked Wright to one of the junior associates nearest the conference room door.

The associate jumped up and left the room.

A few minutes later the mediator entered, trailed by the associate.

"Well, what do you have for me in response to their demand?" asked the mediator without taking a seat.

"We're prepared to offer the policy limits of five million dollars, that's the first and final offer," said Wright.

The mediator looked up from his legal pad. He stared at Wright in stunned silence, and then opened his mouth to speak.

Wright raised his hands before the mediator could get a word out. He and the mediator had worked together hundreds of times over the years and knew each other well. No words were needed to convey what was left unsaid between them. *Difficult client; a real pain in the ass. Not my decision.*

The mediator let out a sigh and turned to leave the room.

"Wait," said Tyndall.

Everyone in the room turned to face his direction.

"We can do a little better than five million dollars."

Everyone in the room except Sloan cracked a slight smile and for a moment the tension in the room dissipated.

"Yes?" asked the mediator.

"We can offer five million and one dollars. Not a penny more. Final offer. Today only," said Tyndall. "Are you happy now, Ken?"

The smiles disappeared around the conference room table. Wright pushed his chair back from the table and strode quickly to the large window overlooking downtown Raleigh with rage written across his face.

Everyone understood the dollar for what it was: a middle finger extended to Everett and his client.

The case was headed to trial.

Chapter Eighteen

" You're kidding, right?" asked Dayna.

"Nope," Everett said with a chuckle.

The two sat in Everett's office discussing the mediation that had just ended. Everett poured them both a glass of whiskey to celebrate the end of a long day, and achieving their objective.

"Only one dollar?" asked Dayna.

"Just a single buck," confirmed Everett.

Dayna let out a laugh. "What a bastard."

"A stupid bastard," corrected Everett. "I know Wright counseled him to offer decent money above the policy limit. He'd be stupid not to on a case like this. And the thing is, with Monica being who she is, if he had put a reasonable amount on the table she probably would have taken it for the simple fact that it would be a quick payday. But, by offering only a dollar— basically a fuck you to her—he's all but guaranteed this case will be tried to verdict."

"Do you think he'll come back on the eve of trial and offer more money? You know how the defense loves to do that."

"Maybe he will, maybe he won't. Even if he does, Monica was so pissed at the end of mediation today I doubt she'll take it anyway at that point."

They both raised their glasses and clinked them together before taking a sip.

"Congratulations," said Dayna. "You got the trial you wanted."

"Yes, I did," Everett said with a smile.

• • • •

Everett stayed in the office for another hour after Dayna went home catching up on emails and a few of his other cases. The sun had set and his stomach was reminding him that he needed to eat.

73

Once in the parking deck across the street from his office building, Everett pulled out his cell phone and texted Olivia. *On my way home. What do you want me to pick up for dinner?* He continued walking to his car as he waited for a reply.

His phone buzzed as he unlocked his car and threw his briefcase into the backseat. Everett read the message from Olivia: *"I don't know. Is there anything you want?"*

"So fucking predictable," mumbled Everett.

He decided to stop and get Thai as he climbed into the driver seat and closed the door. *She hates Thai*, he thought with a chuckle.

Everett put the Lexus in reverse and began easing off the brakes. The quiet in the cabin was disrupted by a high-pitched beeping and the sudden jarring stop of his back-up sensors automatically halting the vehicle to avoid hitting something behind it.

"What the fuck!" exclaimed Everett.

He glanced in his review mirror and saw a gray BMW stopped directly behind his Lexus. He waited a few seconds and watched the BMW, which seemed to have no interest in moving.

"Move asshole," Everett said inside his car.

He honked his horn when the BMW still made no effort to get out of the way. The windows were tinted and he could not make out the driver.

After a few more moments of enduring the stalemate, Everett threw his Lexus in park and opened his driver side door. He began walking toward the BMW, but stopped when the driver got out of his vehicle as Everett reached the rear bumper of his SUV.

Everett stared wide-eyed at the massive man who emerged from the sporty sedan. He was easily six-foot-three-inches and upwards of two-hundred-fifty muscular pounds. His close-cropped hair and ram-rod posture suggested to Everett that he may have been former military.

"Can I help you?" asked Everett, trying to keep his adrenaline in control and his voice from shaking.

The man stared at him for a moment before replying. "No, I don't think so. But you can help a friend of mine."

"Who's your friend?" Everett suspected he already knew.

The man smirked in return, but said nothing. He began walking around the front of his car toward Everett.

Every part of Everett wanted to return quickly to the inside of his vehicle but he forced himself to stand his ground. If his suspicions were correct, he was not going to give this man's so-called "friend" the satisfaction.

The man stopped a foot away from Everett. He towered over Everett and his shoulders were almost as wide as the space between the Lexus and the car parked next to it. He casually slid both his hands into the pockets of his dark jeans.

"I think you're going to want to help my friend," said the man.

"I don't know what you're talking about," replied Everett. "I don't know who you are or who your friend is."

"Don't insult me. We both know you know who my friend is. And who I am doesn't matter. All that matters is I know who you are, Mr. Stone."

"A lot of people know who I am," said Everett. Despite his efforts his voice had started to shake.

"Not the way I do, Mr. Stone. They don't know where you live. They don't know that you leave for the gym most mornings by five in the morning. That you get home most nights to your wife by six thirty. Go to bed by eleven thirty. That your wife's name is Olivia. She's quite the looker, by the way."

Everett's mind raced and he recalled Monica complaining about being followed. The gray BMW suddenly looked familiar to him, and he realized he had seen it at both the gym and on his street.

How long has this guy been following me? he managed to think despite the stress building within him. *And where has he followed me to?* He could barely breathe as he thought through the possibility that this man had seen him and Jake together.

Everett swallowed and discreetly slid his right hand into his pants pocket. He placed his thumb on the Lexus's key fob and hovered it over the panic button.

"I wouldn't do that, Mr. Stone," said the man nodding to Everett's pants. "We wouldn't want to draw attention to ourselves. We're just having a friendly conversation. I'd hate to have it turn ugly, especially since it's unlikely anyone would get here in time to help you."

The man closed the distance between he and Everett to only about six inches and withdrew a knife from his own pocket. The steel glinted under the fluorescent lights of the parking deck.

"I want you to listen to me carefully, Mr. Stone. My friend is going to make a generous offer sometime soon. You have the opportunity to come into quite a bit of money by most peoples' standards, and you're going to take the money that is offered to you without any complaints. It's a win-win situation for both you and my friend in that my friend will get to keep most of his money, and you'll get rich by taking what he is going to offer. Do you understand what I'm saying?"

Everett nodded.

"Good. I knew you were a smart man, Mr. Stone."

"What... what happens if I don't agree?" asked Everett.

The man shook his head. "Well, Mr. Stone, unpleasant things will happen."

Everett flinched at the sound of hissing coming from his Lexus's tire where the man had stabbed it with the knife. "Catch my drift?" he asked Everett.

"I could go to the police."

The man chuckled as he withdrew the knife from the rubber. "Yeah, you could do that. But what evidence do you have that would help or even make them pay attention?"

Everett didn't reply. Both of them knew the answer to the question.

The man walked back to the BMW and stopped to look at Everett once more after opening his door. Just before climbing in and driving away he gave Everett one more piece of advice: "Do the right thing, Mr. Stone."

Everett watched the man leave and then climbed into the relative safety of his Lexus. He gripped the steering wheel to try to steady his shaking hands and he took deep breaths to lower his heart rate from its dangerous level.

Does he know about Jake? The thought terrified Everett to his very core. *Could there be pictures of us together?*

Everett closed his eyes and tried to think back and remember details he hadn't paid attention to at the time. He felt confident that the man had never been in the gym, he would have noticed someone with such an imposing stature. Everett and Jake had never walked out of the gym together, so he was safe from that angle as well.

What about the apartment?

Everett felt like curling his knees to his chest and crying, but he forced himself to think. *If he had anything on me and Jake, he would have used it. There's no way Tyndall would have sent this man to intimidate me into taking whatever offer is coming if he had evidence of Jake and I being together. He would have used that evidence instead if he had it.*

"It's going to be okay," Everett said to himself. He kept repeating the phrase until he felt himself beginning to believe the words.

Chapter Nineteen

I t had been weeks since Everett was last in the pool. He instead spent each morning in Jake's apartment, followed by full days at the office preparing for trial.

Everett's days in the office grew longer. He needed to focus, but there was chaos all around him; banker boxes filled with documents and exhibits lined the halls and his staff was working overtime. He often closed his eyes and pictured the headlines in the newspapers he hoped would come from the verdict.

Wake County Jury Awards Record-Setting Verdict.

Merchant of Death Put Out of Business with Huge Verdict.

When he wasn't imagining the headlines, he was picturing a beach house and new Range Rover.

Everett was neglecting his other cases, and angering the clients. That didn't matter to him. The Thomas case was worth more than all the others combined.

He was having the time of his life despite the long hours of hard work. He felt as if he were actually about to accomplish something; to help solve a real problem and make an actual difference.

As much as he looked forward to the trial, a part of Everett was disappointed the defense hadn't offered a larger settlement. Every jury trial came with its risks. Not to mention the negative health effects he was sure to experience after sustaining himself almost exclusively on coffee during the day and bourbon at night, which was his ritual during trials.

Jury selection would begin in a week and Everett found himself once again standing in front of Jake's door. He knocked softly.

"Please let this go well," he whispered in prayer. He could feel his heart beating fast and strong, and there were butterflies in his stomach. He felt like he did the first time he had knocked on this door.

Jake opened within seconds. His hair was disheveled from sleep. He hadn't bothered to put on any clothes. There was no point in doing so at this stage in their relationship.

Everett stepped inside his spartan apartment, Jake shutting the door behind him. Jake began walking down the hallway to the bedroom.

"Wait," Everett said, still standing in the living room.

Jake turned to face him. "Do you want to do it on the couch instead?"

"No," Everett said. "I actually just came by to say that I need to take a break."

Everett had agonized about the conversation he was about to have all morning on the drive over, and hoped Jake would understand.

"Why?" Jake asked, his smile fading.

"It's this case I'm working on. Trial is coming up and I need to focus on it. You distract me too much... but in a good way." Everett smiled at Jake.

"Surely an hour of um, 'exercise,' a day won't hurt? We've been doing this for weeks now."

"I really need to focus, Jake. Jury selection begins in a week. I've been working long hours. I need to get back in the pool and keep my head clear. This is a huge case with a lot on the line and I can't let our fun interfere with my work."

"You want to get back in the pool?" asked Jake. "I could use a swim myself. Like when we first met."

Everett grinned as he recalled the post-swim showers with Jake.

"That won't take nearly as long as our mornings here. We have to be quick in the locker room," Jake said with a smirk.

"You make a good argument, counselor," Everett chuckled.

"Well, my parents always said I was good at arguing and should go to law school," Jake quipped.

"As tempting as that is, I really can't. It's still too much of a distraction. But I promise after the trial I'm all yours again."

"After the trial?" asked Jake, raising his eyebrows. "How long will that be?"

"I know it seems like a long time, but it's really not. I promise as soon as its over I'll come straight here, regardless of what happens. I won't go home to Olivia. I'll say I'm celebrating with the office staff and you can have me all that night and into the next morning."

"I suppose I can live with that," said Jake with a smile.

"Thank you for understanding. I was worried you wouldn't and I would ruin things between us."

"No, I really do understand. This case is important to you. If you need to focus, you need to focus. It's kind of flattering that I'm what you're thinking of most days and I can derail your train of thought on something so important."

"It's because you're important to me, too."

Everett walked toward Jake and kissed him long and slow.

"I need to go," he said as he pulled away from Jake's lips. "Thank you again for understanding. It means so much to me."

"Wait," Jake said as Everett turned to leave. "I got up early just for you, and you're just going to leave me like this?"

Everett turned back around and smiled at Jake's arousal. He took a step closer and lowered himself to his knees.

After Jake was finished, Everett left the apartment and got in his car to begin another long day.

He checked his phone before pulling off and saw several missed calls and texts from Randy.

Chapter Twenty

" I had a busy night last night," said Randy as he walked into Everett's office and sat down.

"Tell me all about it," said Everett.

Randy took a dollar bill out of his pocket and placed it on Everett's desk. He slid it forward.

Everett smiled and took the bill. "Consider yourself represented," he said. "This will buy a one-hour consultation. What you say stays between us as attorney and client." Everett and Randy had worked together long enough that they trusted each other and knew each other was above-board. Sometimes, however, a line was tight-walked and an extra level of protection was necessary.

"I've been following that gray BMW you mentioned since your meeting with the guy the other night. It was actually pretty easy—it's clear he knows nothing about counter surveillance."

"Were the hours bad?" Everett said while thinking of Randy's bill.

"No. The guy's lazy too. He'd leave your street by the time you go to bed but wouldn't get up until mid-morning or so."

Everett relaxed in his chair. He had been worried his assailant might have discovered him going over to Jake's.

"Anyway, last night he deviated and stopped watching you. I guess he thought he had made his point in the garage the other night," said Randy.

"So what's he been up to?"

"Good old fashion witness tampering."

"Shit. Which witnesses?" asked Everett.

"Annie Smith I know for sure. I don't think he got to any of your other witnesses, but I would recommend calling them before trial just to make sure."

"I'll do that," said Everett. "So, what happened?"

"I followed him to Annie's house and watched from down the street as he parked in her driveway and went up to her front door. She didn't answer at first, but he was insistent and kept pounding. She opened up with the door ajar, but he pushed it further open with his hand. I couldn't hear what they said, but her eyes went wide and her face went ashen. I grabbed my camera and got a shot of the guy while he yanked Annie's phone out of her hand. Turns out she was going to call 911."

"And then?" asked Everett.

"Well, you know how I can't abide men who beat up on women, especially single mothers with their kids in their house."

Everett nodded. A few of Everett's past clients had been involved in some unfortunate domestic situations, and Randy had taken care of the problem pro bono.

"So I snuck up behind him and decked him with a hard right hook. The son of a bitch fell right off her porch and into her yard. He starts to get up and I see him reaching into his waistband, so I kick him in the stomach and draw down on him. He and I had a nice little conversation about how he was going to leave Ms. Smith alone, and you and Olivia alone, and basically anyone connected with this case."

"Did he agree to that?"

Randy nodded. "I told him I used to be law enforcement and have plenty of friends still in the profession who owe me favors. That part was the truth, obviously. But, I may also have intimated that I have several other guys who work for me that aren't afraid of bending the rules and getting their hands dirty that would be keeping an eye on him for an indefinite period of time."

Everett smiled and encouraged Randy to continue.

"He got up, and I made him apologize to Ms. Smith for frightening her. He then started to drive away."

"Do you think he got the point?"

"I think so," chuckled Randy. "His tires peeled as he sped off."

Everett laughed before asking, "Did you find anything definitive to connect him to Tyndall? While I know you can be persuasive, it would be helpful to have that in our back pocket in case we need it."

Randy shook his head. "Unfortunately, no. He's using a burner phone so I couldn't get into any of his accounts to trace him. He's smart and never met with anyone from Tyndall's outfit while I was trailing him. No direct connection that we have evidence of, but I don't think you're going to have to worry about it. I've come across tons of these guys, they work through intimidation but don't have the balls or the smarts to competently follow through. And I'm sure even a piece of shit like Tyndall isn't stupid enough to actually order and pay for something overtly physical and risk it being tied back to them."

"I agree. I think that likely solves the problem. How was Annie?"

"She was shaken, but once she and I spoke she calmed down considerably. She sends her regards and is looking forward to testifying."

"That's great, Randy. You never cease to amaze me."

Randy and Everett both stood and shook hands. On his way out of the office, Randy turned and gave Everett a piece of parting advice. "If I were you, I wouldn't let your guard down. I think this took care of the issue but you never know what Tyndall might do if he gets even more desperate."

"I will, Randy. I've been on alert and more careful. Plus, I keep my concealed carry in my briefcase in case something goes awry."

Randy nodded his approval. "Good. I just don't want my best customer getting hurt."

"I won't," chuckled Everett. Part of him wasn't so sure.

Chapter Twenty-One

Everett was exhausted. The night air felt crisp while he sat on his back porch sipping whiskey and puffing on a cigar.

The past week had left him feeling ragged, and exerting himself in the pool to burn off his pre-trial stress and anxiety only served to make him more tired. The weeks spent in Jake's bed instead of the lap lanes had taken a toll on his fitness.

Everett was looking forward to the weekend. The Thomas case was fully prepared for trial and he was ready to begin on Monday. A lot of lawyers Everett knew spent the weekends before trial in their offices, holed up and going over the details one more time and finishing up their preparations at the last minute. That had never worked well for Everett; he preferred to take the weekend before trial off so that he could be rested and at his sharpest when the big show began.

Many trial lawyers have their superstitions, like athletes before a big game. Some carry lucky objects into courtroom battles, while others have certain rituals they like to perform. Everett was in the latter camp, and usually enjoyed a hike and a good book the weekend before he began a trial.

The back door opened and Olivia walked out with a glass of wine. She was in a pair of tight jeans and one of Everett's old sweatshirts, with her hair pulled back into a ponytail. It was a tomboy look Everett had always found attractive on her.

"How was your day?" asked Olivia.

"Long. Just like every other day recently," replied Everett.

"Was it at least a good day?"

"I suppose it was. I'm ready for trial finally."

"That's good," said Olivia. She sipped on her wine.

Everett puffed on his cigar as she continued to look at him across the patio table. He knew she had something on her mind, so he asked out of obligation more than anything else.

"How was your day?" asked Everett.

Olivia prattled on as Everett stared at his whiskey and feigned interest, nodding every now and then and saying "uh-huh" at appropriate intervals to make it appear as if he was actually listening to what she was saying.

"Is there anything you would like to do this weekend?" Olivia asked after she was done with whatever story she was telling.

"The pre-trial usual," Everett replied. "I'd like to go for a hike up in Umstead State Park, but other than that I wasn't planning on doing too much of anything. What about you?"

"Oh, I don't know. I have some errands to run. I thought maybe we could go out to dinner somewhere?"

"I suppose we can do that. Anywhere in particular you want to go?"

"I don't know. What about you?"

Everett always had to decide where they would eat for dinner, usually after Olivia rejected the first half-dozen suggestions he made.

"I'll think about it," he said. He would waste no time or energy doing so.

The two sipped their drinks and stared off into the night.

Everett took another sip of his whiskey and his thoughts turned to Jake. It had been a week since he had last seen him, and it had been hard to push him out of his mind the first day. Fortunately, Everett had always been good at compartmentalizing his personal feelings in favor of his work, so he hadn't really given Jake much thought the rest of the week.

Part of him couldn't wait to see Jake again. Everett hadn't yet been able to understand how he was so lucky that Jake had just happened to walk into his life and take an interest in him.

It just doesn't seem plausible, thought Everett. *Why would someone like him come on to someone like me in the shower? I'm at least ten years older than he is. I don't have the physique he does either. Why would he all of a sudden just start showing up at the pool?*

"Maybe we could see a movie after dinner?" asked Olivia, bringing him back into the present.

"What?" replied Everett.

"I suggested that maybe we could see a movie this weekend after we go out to dinner," repeated Olivia with a sigh.

"Yeah, sure. Anything you want to see?"

"I'll take a look."

Everett's thoughts drifted again as Olivia pulled out her phone.

Is this some kind of set up? That doesn't seem plausible either. How would anyone possibly know that I'm attracted to men as well as women? I've always been very careful, and have never acted on my attractions with another actual person. No, that can't be it. Maybe he just likes older guys like he says? His story is certainly believable—moved to the area, chose a gym, and saw an older guy he liked. Maybe fate brought us together. Why do you have to be so cynical and suspicious all the damn time when something good happens?

"How about that new *Jurassic World* movie?" asked Olivia.

"Eh. The second one wasn't very good I'm not sure the third will be any better. But if that's what you want to see that's fine."

I bet Chris Pratt reminds her of the yard guy. I wonder how that affair started. Did she come on to him, or did he come on to her? Did she have the same doubts I'm having?

Everett's mind drifted from his practical thoughts about the relationship to more fun subjects. He couldn't deny how Jake made him feel; the way his heart raced when he saw him, the feel of Jake's warm skin against his in the mornings, and the lust that kept Jake at or near the front of his mind most of the time when Everett wasn't at work. *I'm not sure why I care why he started this,* he thought.

"What are you thinking about?" Olivia asked.

Everett came back to the present and realized he was smiling. Part of him wanted to confess and tell her exactly what he was thinking about merely for the satisfaction of seeing the look on her face. He knew he couldn't. Olivia was having an affair, but she would deny it if he cared to confront her about it. It was traditional. His affair was with a man and it would make it more scandalous. Olivia came from a conservative upbringing and she wouldn't react well to the nature of his own extra-marital relationship. She would leave him, and her petty side would require revenge despite her own hypocrisy. The legal community is small and the results would be catastrophic to Everett, who had no intention of coming out. Gossip would swirl like leaves on a gusty autumnal day.

"You," Everett said. "Out of those clothes."

Olivia smiled at him and blushed. "I'd love to but I'm quite tired."

"I know," said Everett quietly and with a slight smile. *You're always allegedly tired when I try to get some, no matter the time of day,* he thought. *But that's okay. I have Jake now.*

Part II

Trial

Chapter Twenty-Two

" All rise!"

The bailiff's jarring voice echoed in the courtroom, bouncing off its institutional beige walls and sparse furnishings on the tenth floor of the Wake County Courthouse.

Standing when the judge entered was one of those antiquated traditions that the law clung to like a vise. It was a show of deference to the court. Lawyers, court personnel, parties, and witnesses rose in unison at the pronouncement. Except one man. Tyndall remained seated in the second row, with contempt written on his face.

"*Oyez! Oyez! Oyez!* This Honorable Court for the County of Wake is sitting for the dispatch of its business! The Honorable Josiah Clement sitting and presiding. God save this State and this Honorable Court. Please be seated and make sure all electronic devices remain silent."

The bailiff moved from the center of the courtroom to his post beside the bench. Josiah Clement shuffled from his chambers into the room with a customary grimace of annoyance on his face.

Judge Clement was a local legend in the legal community. At almost seventy, he was deeply wrinkled and his hair was completely white. He walked with a slight hunch due to chronic sciatica. Before being elected to the bench, he had been one of the most well-known trial lawyers in the state and had made a fortune representing big businesses.

His temperament was what most people knew him for, however. Judge Clement suffered little patience for tardiness and unpreparedness in his courtroom. He was known to practically snarl at young lawyers just starting out and unsure about themselves and their ability. A poor young lawyer a few years back had once forgotten to place his cell phone on vibrate and Judge Clement put in him jail for contempt for three days—one day for each ring that sounded around the courtroom before the lawyer could silence the call. He proudly told people at cocktail parties that he consistently won the award for the most ornery judge in the state.

His Honor took the seat behind the bench, and everyone in the room quickly sat.

"I'm going to call the calendar," began Judge Clement. "When you hear your case, announce your presence and forecast how long your matter will take."

The crowd sat uncomfortably on the hard wooden pews that filled the courtroom gallery. One by one, each lawyer stood and answered the call. Everyone's back hurt by the end.

Judge Clement disappointed most of the people in the room as he announced which cases would be taken up in the courtroom that week. The Thomas trial had priority, so the half-dozen other cases ready for trial would have to wait until another session. Everett knew some of those lawyers were relieved; hoping for a session when Judge Clement wouldn't be presiding. He almost wished he were one of them.

Everett, Monica, and the defense team were told to report back to the courtroom that afternoon to promptly begin jury selection. Judge Clement emphasized the word *promptly*, in such a way that conveyed that even a second of tardiness would result in severe consequences.

· · · ·

Everett and Monica were sitting alone in the courtroom. It had long cleared out and the only people filing back in were related to to the trial. Their wooden table was cheap and roughly the size of a standard executive office desk. There were two chairs at each counsel table, one for the lawyer and one for his client. This suited Everett and Monica just fine.

On the other side of the courtroom Wright was seated on the end closest to Everett's table. Beside him was Tyndall, who wore a cocky smirk.

A chair had been added to the end of the table to fit Billy Sloan. He looked hungover and greasy, which was not out of the ordinary. The remainder of the defense team had been relegated to the uncomfortable benches behind the bar, or had been ordered by Wright to stay put in their spacious offices and bill on other matters until they got a text message to carry out some trial-related task.

At precisely two o'clock, the bailiff announced Judge Clement's return.

"Call in the jury, madam clerk," commanded Judge Clement.

His Honor didn't bother asking the lawyers if they were ready to proceed. If Judge Clement was ready to begin, then you were expected to be ready as well.

Everett took a deep breath as everyone waited for the prospective jurors to file into the courtroom. The tension in the air was palpable. Judge Clement hated waiting on anyone and radiated anger.

The doors to the courtroom opened after a long twenty minutes, and a herd of approximately forty Wake County citizens strolled through the door with frowns on their faces and trying to avoid eye contact with everyone.

Some carried books, and others had laptop cases in an attempt to make the day of waiting at least somewhat productive. Many carried nothing to occupy them at all, which didn't seem wise considering the hours of waiting they had to do. Then again, Everett had always told people on his most cynical days as a lawyer that a jury is nothing more than twelve people too stupid to figure out how to get out of jury duty.

Everett glanced around once the venire was all seated and those he could see seemed largely okay. He had already identified a few that he would immediately dismiss if they were called into the box:

several overly educated-looking men or obvious businesspeople. These types of jurors weren't a fan of awarding large sums of money in his experience.

The back row of the gallery was almost invisible behind the sea of other heads from the lawyers' vantage point. Everett couldn't see any of their faces with any clarity, and it appeared as if one was hunched over retrieving something from a bag.

Once all the prospective jurors were seated Judge Clement looked out at them with a stern face.

"Ladies and Gentlemen," he began, "welcome to this session of Wake County Civil Superior Court. You fine people have had the good fortune of being selected for jury duty this session and twelve of you will hit the lottery and fill this box to my left.

"Here in a few minutes, the clerk will call twelve of you into the jury box. The lawyers will then have the opportunity to ask you questions to see if you can be a fair and impartial jury for this case.

"But, before we get to that point, I'm going to tell you a little bit about this case and introduce the people up here behind the bar."

Judge Clement proceeded to tell the jury the case was a wrongful death case in which the plaintiff was seeking money from the defendant and his nursing home for the death of Harry Thomas. Everett was introduced, along with the long list of defense counsel. Judge Clement also read off a list of witnesses who were expected to testify later in the trial.

"Do any of you know any of these people or lawyers?" asked Judge Clement. No one raised their hands.

"Do any of you feel you already can't serve as fair and impartial jurors?" asked Judge Clement. A few hands went up.

"Now," continued Judge Clement, "for those of you who raised your hands I'm going to ask each of you in turn why you feel this way. Let me caution you now: jury duty is a part of civic responsibility. Our system cannot function without citizens like you doing their part. I will excuse those of you with legitimate reasons for not being able to serve as fair and impartial jurors. However, if I get the sense any of you are bullshitting me and trying to get out of jury duty for the sake of shirking your responsibility as citizens, I will hold you in contempt and you will have an all-expense paid hotel stay courtesy of the Wake County Detention Center. Now, if you have a legitimate excuse, please keep your hand raised and I will be with you shortly."

All of the hands raised in the gallery went down in unison.

"That's what I thought," snarled Judge Clement. "Madam clerk, call the first twelve names, please."

The clerk began reading off the names of the first twelve unlucky people. Everett watched and scrutinized each of them, trying to glean any insight as to whether they were good or bad for the case.

The clerk announced the last juror: "Jeremy Phelps."

Both lawyers turned to look at him as he rose from the back row wearing blue jeans and a hoodie. He had his hood up over his head and he shuffled into seat number twelve and looked down at his lap. Everett hadn't been able to clearly see his face.

Once the clerk was done reading off the names, Judge Clement looked up from his computer and turned his attention to the jury box. His brow immediately furrowed when he saw the man wearing the hood. He glanced at his bailiff who was scrolling on his iPhone and his brow furrowed some more and his jaw tightened.

"Mr. Phelps!" yelled Judge Clement. "You will remove that hood this instant and keep it off your head for the remainder of your time in this courtroom, or you will find yourself in contempt!"

Jeremy Phelps removed his hood and everyone saw his face clearly for the first time.

Everett felt like he was about to faint.

Chapter Twenty-Three

Judge Clement called a five-minute recess as soon as he was done yelling at Jeremy about the hood and asked the bailiff to join him in his chambers. There was no doubt the bailiff was about to receive a dressing down for missing the twelfth juror wearing a hood and not asking him to remove it immediately.

Everett literally ran to the restroom once he was in the hallway.

He locked himself in a stall and doubled over, placing his hands on his knees. His breathing was shallow and he could hear his heart pounding in his ears. The room seemed to tilt in his field of vision.

Judge Clement had asked: *Do any of you know any of these people or lawyers?* All jurors are asked this question to ensure there is no bias and appearance of impropriety during the trial. No one had raised their hands. But one of them lied.

Everett recognized Jeremy Phelps the second he lowered his hood. That wasn't the name he knew him by, however. Everett knew him by the name "Jake." The man he had been having an affair with for weeks.

Why didn't he tell me his real name? Everett thought.

Everett's stomach wretched as the next question came to his mind: *What am I going to do?*

Jake, or Jeremy, or whatever the hell his name was, was sitting in the box holding the prospective jurors for the biggest case he had ever tried. How in the hell had this happened?

Why didn't he say anything?

He should have said something.

I should say something.

Everett's stomach wretched again at the last thought. He was sure he was having a panic attack.

"No," Everett whispered to his shoes. "I can't do that. Or maybe I could. What if I just say I saw him at the gym?"

No! Absolutely not! he screamed in his head. *If I do that, that will open the door to more questioning. Then what? He says, "Yes, in fact, because one thing led to another and..."* Everett almost threw up again.

Everett forced himself to take several deep breaths and stand up straight. He closed his eyes and took several more breaths to try to get his heart rate back down to normal.

When he calmed down, Everett checked his watch. It had been almost five minutes, and he was expected to be back at counsel's table.

Fuck!

Everett knew he was supposed to inform Judge Clement that he was acquainted with Jeremy Phelps.

The thought of this sent Everett's heart rate skyrocketing again and a cold sweat began to dampen the back of the shirt under his suit jacket.

He could see what would happen as if it were a premonition. Judge Clement would first ask why Everett hadn't immediately told him when the juror's name was called. He would surely threaten Everett with contempt, at a minimum.

Even worse, knowing a lawyer doesn't automatically disqualify a person from serving as a juror. The defense would be allowed to inquire of Jake how it was he knew Everett so they could ascertain whether Jake could still be fair and impartial to both sides in the trial. After all, if Everett had been a friend-of-a-friend or some casual acquaintance then that likely would not affect a prospective juror.

Casual was not the word that defined Everett and Jake's relationship. Acquaintances don't see each other naked and make love over their morning coffee every day.

Jake would be forced to disclose that he and Everett were lovers, and if he didn't—if he perjured himself—Everett would be required to bring the truth to the court's attention. All while Everett sat there with his client in a room full of people. While Everett sat there with his wedding band on his finger, and a picture of his wife set as his iPhone's background.

Everett vomited.

Taking out his handkerchief and wiping his mouth, he forced himself to think.

"He's already lied by omission," Everett whispered to himself. "What makes you think he's going to start telling the truth now? You really think a guy who sleeps with a married man gives a shit about being honest?"

No, Everett concluded, if Jake hadn't spoken up by now there was no reason to believe he would.

"What? You're going to tell Judge Clement you've been having an illicit gay affair with juror number twelve?" whispered Everett to himself.

One of things Everett learned early on in his career, something that every lawyer is told as early as the first day of law school, is that their reputation is the most important commodity they have.

It may feel like in a city the size of Raleigh that you can't throw a rock on a street corner without hitting a lawyer, but the legal community is small and most everyone knew each other or at least knew of each other. And that community was filled with gossip.

If Everett revealed his secret, then there was no doubt in his mind that virtually every lawyer in the city would know by the end of the day. Some of his friends and colleagues, the more progressive ones at least, would be fine with the homosexual nature of the relationship, but they would not be as accepting of the affair.

Others, like Judge Clement, would probably look at him with disgust and refer to him with slurs behind his back for the remainder of Everett's career.

Most would simply excitedly talk about the scandal until the shock wore off and fresh gossip came along.

There was also Olivia to think about. She would find out at some point today as the gossip made its way to her. Everett doubted she would forgive him, especially with how strained the marriage had been. There would be a divorce, with a painful splitting up of the marital assets.

Most importantly, there was the Thomas case itself. How would the other jurors react? How would his client react? Everett couldn't afford to do anything to jeopardize the case. Anything further, at least.

Everett glanced down at his watch and saw that only a minute remained of the recess. He tried to collect himself one last time and adjusted his tie in the bathroom mirror as he walked out toward the courtroom.

Everett sat down at counsel table just as Judge Clement was returning to the courtroom. The bailiff trailed behind him looking like a puppy who had just been smacked with a newspaper for taking a shit on the carpet.

Everett straightened up in his chair and turned toward the jury to get ready for jury selection. His expression and demeanor looked to others as if nothing was wrong. It was a well-practiced poker face developed over years of litigation.

Inside, Everett wanted to die rather than face what was about to happen.

Chapter Twenty-Four

Jury selection began after a few introductory comments from Judge Clement regarding the process and what he expected of jurors' behavior if they were selected.

Everett had the burden of proof, so custom and procedure dictated that he begin the interrogations.

Everett was always nervous at the start. It wasn't that he was inexperienced; it was a just a natural reaction to having to make quick friends of twelve strangers that wanted nothing to do with you and your client. He always told himself and other lawyers that if you weren't nervous, then it probably meant you no longer cared and it was time to find a new line of work.

This time it was more severe. Everett felt more than the flutter of butterflies in his stomach. His heart was beating fast, his mouth was dry, and his palms were sweaty. Sweat collected under his arms and dripped down his back.

He began asking questions. He always found the process monotonous and interesting at the same time. On one hand, he asked the same questions over and over to twelve different people, and then again to some of their replacements. On the other, he learned a great deal about the people he was talking with and it was a challenge to try to ascertain who would be a good juror and who wouldn't through a mixture of logic, intuition, and just plain luck.

Judge Clement had told the jurors in his opening remarks that the process was designed to allow the lawyers to figure out who could be fair and impartial. That was lie, of course. Neither side wanted a jury that was fair and impartial. They wanted a jury that was in favor of their side.

Everett never went in order by seat number with the jurors. Instead, he always asked whether anyone wanted to volunteer first. Public speaking and being asked questions by a lawyer is intimidating to most people and they wanted nothing to do with the process. He was looking for the person who didn't mind speaking up and going first. Everett was looking for the leader; the person most likely to be the foreperson and in control of deliberations at the end of the trial so he could make sure that person was right for his side of the case right off the bat.

Juror Number Three raised their hand and volunteered to go first. Everett began with basic questions about what the juror did for a living, whether they had family, whether they knew anyone involved in the case, and other questions designed to break the ice and get the juror talking.

He then moved down his list of more relevant questions. Had a loved one ever been in a nursing home? Did the juror trust that facility? Was that trust ever betrayed? How do you feel about awarding money for pain and suffering?

Everett moved on to the next juror and then the next and then the next, asking for volunteers between each juror. Everyone was volunteering except Juror Number Twelve. Jake.

Everett usually had laser focus selecting a jury. It was important to pick the right people. It wasn't just about listening to what the juror said, it was about listening to what they weren't saying. It was about making eye contact and building a rapport. The lawyer needed to pay attention to the juror's body language too.

Jake's presence was making all of this difficult. Everett had a hard time concentrating on what the other eleven people were saying. He kept glancing toward Jake, trying to make sense of him being there and what he thought of the situation the two had found themselves in. Jake stared straight ahead the entire time with an expressionless face.

A mark was placed next to each juror's name on Everett's legal pad as he went one by one. A checkmark meant that they could stay, an "x" meant Everett would excuse them when the time came. After the first juror, Everett had already gone ahead and placed an "x" next to Jake's name. He had calmed down enough at that point to come to the logical conclusion he should have developed at the recess. Everett cursed himself momentarily for having let his emotions knock him off his game and into a panic.

Although he knew he was going to excuse Jake, he still needed to keep up appearances and go through his questions with him. Everett drew in a deep breath as he began his interview.

"Mr. Phelps?" stated Everett. "Where in the county do you live?"

Jake looked at Everett dispassionately as if they were meeting for the first time. "Here in Raleigh."

"Are you married?"

"No."

"Any children?" Everett's heart was beating fast yet again.

"No."

"What do you do for a living?" It was the first time Everett had asked him that question.

"Um... I'm a consultant in the information technology sector." Everett wasn't sure what to make of Jake's hesitation in answering the question, nor was he expecting that answer. Jake never struck him as the nerdy tech type.

"What do you like to do in your spare time when not at work?"

Everett held his breath. He hadn't wanted to ask that question, but he needed to ask all the same questions as he had the other jurors. He prayed silently that Jake wouldn't say something crude about how he had been spending his mornings. A *"you"* would probably cause Everett to have a stroke.

"Nothing special," said Jake.

Everett's anxiety briefly flashed to anger and then disappointment.

So I'm nothing special?

Now came the tricky question, and the question that sent Everett's blood pressure back up through the stratosphere.

"Do you know anyone involved in the case?"

"No," Jake answered without even the slightest bit of hesitation.

Everett paused in his questioning and looked at Jake, meeting Jake's eyes with his own. Jake looked back at Everett unblinking. *Don't linger*, Everett reminded himself.

Everett quickly recovered from the pause before it became too long and too awkward and drew the attention of Judge Clement.

He moved on to his other questions regarding the case and the issues involved.

"Thank you, Mr. Phelps," he said at the end. Everett let out a deep breath. The worst of it was over.

"Just a moment, Your Honor," Everett said.

"Make it a quick moment, Counselor," Judge Clement retorted.

Everett glanced at his notes. He could use up to eight challenges to excuse any juror he wanted for any reason, and so far he had identified four, including Jake, that would be going home after the first round. Everett was pleased that the other eight seemed like they would be good for his case, but knew that several of them would go home after the defense was done.

Everett stood and began reading off juror numbers. He always liked to look at the jurors as he did this as a way of showing respect for their time.

"Your Honor, at this time we would like to thank and excuse Jurors Number 4, 8, 11, and..."

Everett glanced quickly at Jake.

Jake in return gave an almost imperceptible shake of his head and there was a subtle furrow of his brow.

"...and..." Everett gave Jake a puzzled look.

Jake gave another shake of his head, this one a bit more animated but still not enough to be noticed by anyone casually watching. Jake seemed to warn Everett with his eyes.

"And what, Counselor?" demanded Judge Clement.

"And... that's..." Everett was still hesitating when Jake leaned slightly forward in his seat and gave his head another quick shake. "...that's all, Your Honor."

What the hell was that? thought Everett.

Chapter Twenty-Five

When the lunch recess began, Everett walked out of the courtroom as calmly as he could manage.

His heart was pounding again and his hands trembled riding the elevator down the ten floors. Everett walked outside onto a busy noontime downtown Raleigh street.

Why had Jake seemed so insistent on staying on the jury? Why did he appear to not want me to dismiss him? Who is this man? He didn't even tell me his real name!

He called Dayna at the office while walking the two blocks to a local coffee shop.

"I need you to do me a favor," said Everett.

"Sure thing, what do you need?

"I need you to run a background check and internet search on a prospective juror. I want everything: criminal background, social media, driving records, anything you can get."

Since Everett had already passed the jury to the defense, he was stuck with Jake no matter what at this point. Dayna didn't need to know that. What Everett needed to know was more about his lover, who could very well end up as Juror Number twelve if the defense didn't dismiss him.

"Okay, is everything all right?" asked Dana.

"Yeah, I think so. I just have a funny feeling about this guy. He's saying the right things, but my gut is telling me something is wrong."

"Can't you just use a peremptory?"

"I don't want to waste one if I don't have to," Everett lied again. "I'd rather get him kicked off for cause if I can."

"With Judge Clement?"

"I know it's a long shot, but it's been known to happen."

"What's the juror's name?" Dana asked.

"Jeremy Phelps."

"Does he live here in Raleigh?"

"Yes, and works in IT."

"Okay. I should be able to find him."

"Email me when you complete the search. Make it quick, please."

Everett walked into the coffee shop and ended the call. After ordering a large black coffee, he went to an open seat in a deserted corner and waited.

Everett took a couple of deep breaths and a sip of the comforting drink to try and calm his nerves. He tried to distract himself from his thoughts by scrolling through the morning's headlines, but his mind kept drifting back to Jake.

What the hell am I doing? Everett thought back to the shake of the head Jake and given him. *I should have dismissed him. Now I may be stuck with him, and if anyone finds out I'm screwed.*

After a few minutes he began to do his own searching as impatience took over. Everett opened Facebook and entered "Jeremy Phelps" into the search bar. There were a lot of results. Everett quickly scrolled through the profiles with his thumb while sipping coffee. After a few minutes, he had located the right profile.

The profile picture was one of Jake standing shirtless on the beach. His blonde hair was windswept and he was smiling behind a pair of aviators. His well-defined pectorals, biceps, and abs were deeply tanned. He had a cocktail in his hand as the sun set in the background.

Everett felt fleeting lust take over for the anxiety and dread that had consumed him all morning. His mind drifted to the times he and Jake had spent in the shower and in Jake's bed. He felt the smile creep across his lips. *I do like the prospect of seeing him every day at least. Hell, he's made me feel happy again for the first time in a long time.* Everett shook away the thoughts after a few moments.

The profile was set to private and Everett couldn't see anything else. The same was true of Jake's profile on the other major social media sites.

Everett checked his watch. There was still almost forty minutes left in the lunch recess. He continued to drink his coffee and scrolled through the morning's emails as he waited.

The iPhone chimed a few minutes later and Everett opened the message from Dayna. He hesitated for a moment before clicking on the attachment.

Everett quickly scanned the report and his mouth fell open.

Jeremy Jacob Phelps, aged twenty five years and owner of a Subaru, had been busy in the public record.

Everett read, and then re-read, the list of criminal charges. Insurance fraud. Assault and battery. Various computer-related crimes. Multiple counts of prostitution. Somehow all the felonies had been dismissed, but there were still misdemeanor convictions. His stomach dropped and his head spun.

I'm sleeping with a fucking male prostitute!

Everett rubbed his temples and then slipped his phone into his pocket. He stood from his seat and rushed to the coffee shop's restroom, where he threw up for the second time that day.

Chapter Twenty-Six

Three replacement jurors were seated in the box as soon as the lunch recess ended. Everett's questioning of these jurors was different than those before lunch. His hands shook, his inquiries were disjointed, and his voice had a slight quiver.

Although Everett was trying to focus on the substance of what the three new prospective jurors were saying, he could not help thinking about Jake's criminal history.

It's so much worse than I thought, he said to himself more than once while stealing a glance at Juror Number twelve.

He considered his moral and ethical transgressions. Everett pondered how it was he didn't suspect he was sleeping with someone who sold his body for money after how they met. He worried about sexually transmitted disease, or criminal charges even though no money had ever changed hands between the two. *What will happen if Olivia finds out?*

The Thomas case was meant to cause Everett's reputation in the legal community to shine, and now it threatened to ruin it. Everett passed the three new jurors in the box to the defense table with that cheerful thought.

Kenneth Wright began asking his questions of each of the jurors in order of their respective numbers. It was a textbook examination, which meant it was boring and repetitive for anyone who is not a law school professor.

Wright seemed to be barely listening to what the jurors had to say and was instead focused on taking notes. Everett noticed Wright's focus on his notes made him miss important verbal and body language clues into how the prospective jurors may decide the case. For as much money as he was billing per hour, he wasn't a particularly charismatic or effective lawyer at building rapport with the jurors.

Everett managed to calm himself down some during Wright's mediocre performance. Worrying was replaced with praying. Praying that Jake wouldn't say anything to out Everett. Praying that Wright would solve this problem and dismiss Jake from the jury.

Wright continued on with his monotonous questioning for what felt like forever. Everett repeated his prayers no less than a million times during the same period.

"Just a moment, Your Honor," said Wright.

Wright glanced down at his notes. Everett held his breath.

Ross Tyndall and Billy Sloan both leaned close to Wright and the the three whispered to each other as they decided which jurors should go, and which should stay.

"Counselor," said Judge Clement, "is there a reason this is taking so long?" It had been three minutes.

Wright, Tyndall and Sloan continued their whispering and ignored the judge.

"Counselor!" bellowed Judge Clement.

Wright shot out of his seat, clearly startled, to address the court. He excused five of the twelve prospective jurors. None of those excused were Jake.

Everett was sure he didn't actually pass out when his prayers went unanswered, but only because he came back to consciousness with Judge Clement barking at him to question the five new jurors instead of the bailiff standing over him or administering CPR. Everett did his best to ask questions of the five new people in the box, but he frequently stumbled over his questions and couldn't concentrate on what they were saying.

"You Honor," began Everett, "we accept all of these jurors."

"You do not challenge any juror?" asked Judge Clement.

Everett let out a deep sigh as he glanced back down at his legal pad, which had the five names of the new jurors written down but was otherwise blank.

"No, Your Honor, we do not challenge any of the new jurors." He would just have to hope these people were not too bad or could be won over during the trial.

"Very well," said Judge Clement, appearing somewhat confused. "We will pick two alternate jurors from those remaining in the galley, and then we will resume trial with opening statements in the morning. Ladies and Gentlemen in the box, welcome to the jury."

"Did that go okay?" asked Monica as Everett was packing his things into his briefcase after the alternates had been selected and the day was done.

"Yes, it did," lied Everett.

Monica was smiling, no doubt also thinking about the money. "I'll see you tomorrow."

"See you tomorrow, Monica."

Everett pulled out his phone to text Olivia once he walked out of the courthouse and onto Fayetteville Street.

He typed a text: *Done for day. Need to work late at office to get ready for tomorrow. It may be an all-nighter. See you later.*

K, was the reply.

Everett walked the two blocks to The Raleigh Times Bar and ordered a bourbon. He had no intention of going into his office, and no reason to. He was already prepared for the next day, and the day after. Everett prided himself in preparing for every contingency he could think of well in advance of the start of any trial.

He just never thought he would be having an illicit affair with one of the jurors.

Everett took the first sips of his bourdon as he thought about Jake. Part of Everett was furious with the situation. The ethical problems it presented were grave. The thought of everyone finding out about his affair, with a man no less, scared the hell out of him. There was a small part of Everett that still felt duty-bound to bring the issue to Judge Clement's attention. The other part of Everett laughed incredulously at the idea and wanted to avoid jail and public humiliation.

Everett considered all of the possible courses of action as the amber liquid calmed his nerves. He could always tell Judge Clement that he knew Jake, and that Jake was just a friend. Of course, if he did that Judge Clement would be furious he did not speak up sooner and Everett would likely be sanctioned. Judge Clement was also notoriously loath to dismiss a juror and at the very least would allow Wright to question Jake about their "friendship." That was too big a risk.

He thought about Jake's criminal record, especially the prostitution charges and the random way the two had met. Could someone be paying Jake to be having this affair with him? Everett quickly dismissed the idea. He had buried his true sexuality his entire life. No one knew that he was bisexual and he had never had a physical relationship with another man. It was impossible anyone could know.

Everett considered to weigh his options. If he came forward and did the right thing, both ethically and legally, he would certainly face the wrath of Judge Clement and may possibly risk outing himself and bringing his affair into the light. If he stayed silent, he would betray his obligations as an officer of the court and risk far greater consequences if anyone ever found out the truth. What to do?

Everett made his decision after the third bourbon.

Chapter Twenty-Seven

Everett had been pounding on the apartment door so long without an answer he was beginning to wonder whether Jake was even home. He was just about to give up and leave when it opened.

Jake was standing there in a white v-neck t-shirt that showed off his collar bones and chest, as well as a pair of tight jeans.

"Hello," Jake said with a smirk.

Everett brushed past him without bothering with a response or waiting for an invitation. He knew that being here was a mistake, and against the Court's rules, but he no longer cared. He needed answers and he intended to get them.

Jake closed the door behind him.

"What the hell do you think you're doing?" Everett asked.

"I was sleeping," said Jake.

"In jeans?"

"It was a long day. I guess I didn't have time to change into my PJs. Why are you here so late anyway? It's almost ten o'clock. Shouldn't you be home with your wife?"

"Shouldn't you be out picking up a John?" Everett's eyes held Jake's with a scowl.

Jake's coy smile vanished. "I'm not sure I know what you're talking about," he said.

"Bullshit you don't. You don't think once I learned your real name I didn't check up on you to find out what else you have been lying to me about, Jeremy?"

"Technically, you didn't ask me about that."

"Don't be an ass."

"I thought you liked my ass," Jake said as his smile returned.

Everett turned away from Jake and tried to collect himself. He felt like screaming, or punching something. Someone.

Still, Jake was a member of his jury now whether he liked it or not, and he needed to be careful. He shouldn't even be talking to him, let alone standing in his living room. If Everett didn't handle this confrontation well, it could jeopardize everything.

"Why are you on this jury?"

"Because I was summoned, and it's my civic duty. Apparently, you lawyers thought I could be fair and impartial."

"I'm not an idiot. I saw you shake your head and give me nonverbal cues when you knew I was about to dismiss you. Why did you want to stay on this jury?"

"So I could watch you work your magic. To see if you're as good in the courtroom as you are in bed. So I could spend all day with my sexy lawyer boyfriend."

Everett bristled again. He wasn't Jake's anything. He was Olivia's. This was nothing more than a judgment lapse on his part that had gotten way out of hand.

"You know what we're doing is wrong, right? You know that if anyone ever found out that we know each other and didn't inform the court, then not only is it a mistrial, but Judge Clement is likely to throw us both in jail—for a long time. How can I possibly trust you to keep this a secret when you've been lying to me this whole time?"

"Spending the extra time with you would be worth it," said Jake. "Maybe we could even be cell mates and share a bunk."

Everett smiled despite how bad the joke was.

"Look, Everett, I know you're upset. But I haven't lied to you, I just didn't volunteer information you didn't ask about. As far as why you should trust me, ask yourself why you shouldn't. What would happen if I told anyone? Like you said, we'd both be screwed. I've been to jail and don't plan on going back. I've gotten my life together and have a real career now. Have I threatened to expose you to Olivia? Have I demanded money to keep quiet? Have I done anything except want to spend time with you?"

Everett stood there considering what Jake had said.

Jake removed his shirt after a few minutes of silence between them.

"I'm not here for that," said Everett. "I came here to talk and figure out what we're going to do."

Jake unbuttoned the waist of his jeans. "I have some ideas," he said.

"Jake, we can't sleep together when you're on my jury. And you're on this jury until we can come up with a way to fix this situation."

Jake unzipped his jeans.

Everett stood there trying to control his impulses. It had been a while since he and Jake had made love, and his heart and body wanted badly to embrace Jake, to taste the salt on his skin, to feel Jake inside him.

"Maybe you can fake an illness? Or some other emergency that will get you excused? We could fill your seat with an alternate juror," said Everett.

Jake stepped out of his jeans.

"Jake, Jeremy, or whatever... what is your name actually?"

"Jeremy Jacob Phelps. I go by Jake."

"Why didn't you say anything when you were asked in jury selection whether you knew anyone involved in the case?"

"Why didn't you?" asked Jake.

"I... I was afraid the truth about us would come out," admitted Everett in a voice just above a whisper.

"I understand that," said Jake. "But I wouldn't have outed you no matter what. I'm not that kind of guy. When I came out it was awful and I would never put anyone in a situation like that they weren't ready for. Like I said, I didn't say anything because I was curious about your case. I want to see more of you, even if we can't have any obvious contact. Just being in the room with you is enough for me."

Jake closed the distance between the two of them and kissed Everett long and hard.

He took Everett by the tie and led him down the hallway to the bedroom, where he undressed him.

Jake gently shoved Everett backward toward the bed and grabbed his ankles, pulling his legs up onto his shoulders and positioning Everett's waist on the edge of the mattress. Jake thrust himself inside. Both of them kept their eyes locked on the each other as Jake moved his hips back and forth, going deeper with each thrust.

When Jake was done, both men lay on the bed staring up at the ceiling lost in their own thoughts. They eventually drifted off to sleep.

• • • •

The next morning Everett was awakened with a vigorous shaking. He noticed the smell of coffee before he fully opened his eyes.

"Come on, Counselor," Jake said. "We need to get showered and ready to go. We're going to be late for court."

Chapter Twenty-Eight

They showered together and the closeness under the hot water was too tempting to resist. They made love again, wasting more time neither had before the second day of trial.

Everett and Jake dressed quickly and ran out of the apartment. Jake followed Everett to his SUV and began to climb into the passenger seat before Everett stopped him.

"You need to drive separately," said Everett. "We can't be seen together."

"Do you really think anyone will notice? Raleigh's a big city."

"It's not big enough. We can't take the risk. Judge Clement will put both of us in jail if he finds out about us."

"Jail's not so bad," Jake said with a smile.

Everett's good mood vanished, and he felt a flush of embarrassment and anger. He knew Jake was joking, but the remark brought back the reality of Everett's predicament and the risks he was taking.

"That's not funny. At all," said Everett.

Jake seemed to realize he had crossed a line and nodded his head, closing the passenger door of Everett's SUV and running toward his own car.

• • • •

Everett was out of breath when he fast-walked into the courtroom with only three minutes to spare. The elevators in the courthouse were slow, so Everett had run up ten flights of stairs to the courtroom. He could feel the sweat soaking through his shirt underneath his suit jacket.

"Good morning," Everett said to Monica as he sat.

"Are you okay?" asked Monica.

"I'm fine," Everett replied while taking a deep breath. "Had some car trouble and took the stairs. Didn't want to be late."

Monica didn't have time to respond again before the bailiff called the courtroom to order and everyone stood. Everett took deep, slow breaths to calm his heart rate and steady himself while Judge Clement shuffled into the courtroom and assumed the bench.

"Do you have all my jurors?" Judge Clement asked the bailiff.

"We are still waiting on one juror, Your Honor."

Everett's heart rate shot back up and his stomach felt queasy.

"Which juror?" asked Judge Clement

"Mr. Phelps, sir," said the bailiff.

Judge Clement cleared his throat and scowled around the courtroom before turning his attention to the wall clock.

The bailiff's radio squawked and another bailiff who had been posted at the jury assembly room informed them the last juror had arrived.

"Bring them in. Now," said Judge Clement before the bailiff could relay the message they had all heard through the radio anyway.

The bailiff radioed to send the jury in as commanded.

The doors to the courtroom opened a few minutes later after the jurors had been lined up like school children and walked down the short hallway from the assembly room. They shuffled across the back of the courtroom and up the side aisle toward the jury box, filing into their seats one-by-one.

Jake was the last to be seated.

"Mr. Phelps," said Judge Clement before Jake was even settled. "I understand you were the one that made us all late getting started today."

Jake looked at Judge Clement and then looked at the clock in the back of the courtroom. It was only three minutes past the time court was set to begin.

Oh, no, thought Everett when he saw Jake's movements. *Please don't be a smart ass or argue.*

"What do you have to say for yourself?"

Jake began to speak and then paused. Everett could see the whiff of defiance leave his face as his instincts overrode his youth.

"I'm sorry, Your Honor. I didn't plan for traffic well enough. It won't happen again."

"It better not. I have my eye on you. Don't think I forgot about the hood yesterday, young man. And now this. If you step out of line one more time, you will spend this weekend in the detention center."

"Yes, sir."

Judge Clement stared a Jake a few moments longer before sitting back in his large leather chair.

"Ladies and Gentlemen, welcome to day two of this trial. In a few minutes the attorneys are going to give their opening statements. Opening statements are not evidence in the case, and should not be treated as such by you. Rather, they are a forecast of the evidence that each attorney contends you will hear. Mr. Stone, please begin your opening statement."

Everett rose from his table and walked the few feet to stand before the jury box. He had tried many cases in his career, but his heart still raced and butterflies beat furiously in his stomach each time he was about to begin his case with a new jury.

Everett stood for a moment and looked at each of the jurors before he began.

"The sores on Harry Thomas's body were so severe, the flesh turned black with rot. His once sturdy frame withered like a dying tree into nothing more than skin and bones. One-by-one, his organs started shutting down as he lay in his bed covered in his own filth. Harry Thomas's body began decomposing before he was buried in the ground, while he was still alive, feeling every moment of it."

Everett paused. He had the jury's complete attention. Some appeared horrified, some angry. None of them looked disinterested, which is exactly what he wanted.

"The condition of his body was so bad, the medical examiner ruled his death a homicide by institutional neglect. Harry Thomas was ignored by those he trusted most. Those charged with the care of this elderly and vulnerable man. They let him lay in his own feces and urine, day in and day out. They starved him. Deprived him of his medications."

Everett half-turned toward the defense table and pointed. "They killed him with indifference."

Everett allowed the slightest of smirks to cross his face as he met Tyndall's callous eyes.

Everett continued with his opening statement, one of the longest he had ever given, and detailed the parade of abuses at Peaceful Pines that confronted Harry Thomas up to the time of his death. He detailed the cover up Tyndall had tried to undertake, and his sordid history with operating other nursing homes.

"He turned these homes into death factories. The commodities were vulnerable bodies, left to die with minimal care and supervision for the sake of reaping large profits," continued Everett.

"Peaceful Pines was the latest iteration for Ross Tyndall, and perhaps his cruelest yet. He learned a lesson from the past judgments and lawsuits. From the fines levied by regulators. But, it wasn't the lesson intended. What Ross Tyndall learned was not that he needed to live up to the promise he made to these people and the families who trusted him. No. What he learned was that he needed fewer witnesses. Fewer people who could testify against him. So he opened Peaceful Pines and specialized in Alzheimer and dementia patients, those who wouldn't remember the atrocities he would go on to commit against them, and wouldn't be found credible due to their disease.

"But, as you now know, thanks to good people who refused to let Tyndall bury the truth, his plan didn't work. At the end of this trial, you have the chance to send Ross Tyndall a message and teach him the right lesson with a number he can't ignore and recover from."

Everett paused and looked at the jurors as a whole one last time. All of them looked angry now, and more than a few had their arms crossed and were glaring at the defense table.

This is my jury, Everett thought, *we've already won.*

Everett turned and walked back to the table. The courtroom was silent as he did so, thick with tension. Even Judge Clement seemed to be looking at Tyndall with more disdain than usual.

Once Everett was seated, Judge Clement turned his attention to the defense table.

"Mr. Wright, the jury is with you."

Wright stood from his chair and walked across the courtroom to stand in front of the jury box. He didn't appear nervous at all, and Everett suspected it was because he likely no longer cared about this case. He seemed to be going through the motions, providing an adequate defense as he was required to do, but to Everett it was clear Wright lacked a passion for his client's cause and there was certainly no love for Tyndall within the man. Wright's only goal, Everett assumed, was to staunch the bleeding from a very large wound and try to save his client from financial ruin.

Wright's opening statement was almost as long as Everett's as he attempted to explain away the indefensible. The five star rating from the state was a big portion of his theme. Much more of his time was spent attacking Monica personally and attempting to paint her as a greedy daughter who cared only about the money.

None of the jurors looked at Wright as he spoke, and even more crossed their arms across their chest.

Everett had to fight hard to suppress a big smile as Wright concluded his statement and walked back to counsel table, his face betraying his feelings of defeat.

Chapter Twenty-Nine

W right sat red-faced with a furrowed brow as Everett called his first witness.

Charles Reed was Wright's witness, and one of the few that had a chance to do him some good in the defense's case-in-chief. Everett was calling him as an adverse witness, however, and this rarely signaled something good.

Reed looked confused and glanced to Wright for help as he began his walk from the gallery up to the imposing witness stand. Wright stared down at his legal pad.

Reed climbed onto the stand and began to sit before being scolded by Judge Clement to remain standing while the clerk swore him in. Reed swore to tell the truth while looking unsure of himself in front of the jury. His voice cracked and wavered like a teenager's as he said, "I do."

"What is your occupation? asked Everett after getting him to state his name for the record.

"I'm a facilities inspector for the North Carolina Department of Health and Human Services."

"What does your position as a facilities inspector entail?"

"I travel to various nursing homes and skilled care facilities in my assigned geographic region and conduct routine inspections, as well as investigate any complaints against a facility."

"How often do you conduct those routine inspections?"

"At least quarterly."

"So at a minimum four times a year?"

"Yes, sir."

"And is it fair to say you will go to a facility more than that if there are complaints from a patient or another individual, such as a family member?"

"Yes, that's correct."

Reed seemed to start to relax on the stand and his tone sounded more confident. He made sure to turn to the jurors to answer Everett's questions like Wright had coached him to do when they spoke before trial.

"How thorough are these inspections that you conduct on a quarterly basis?" asked Everett.

Reed launched into a long narrative of the items inspectors are supposed to observe and evaluate. The list included items like the state of housekeeping and furnishings, building equipment, and aspects of a patient's actual care.

"Do you actually review medical records when you're at the facilities?"

"Yes," replied Reed.

"Do you review records for all patients?"

"Sometimes. Usually we do a spot check on the records."

"What types of things are you looking for?"

"We're looking for many things. For example, whether doctors' orders are being carried out and whether medication is being administered properly."

"Given the nature of these facilities, would you agree that this is one of the most important aspects of your inspections?"

"Yes, I would agree with that."

"Is Peaceful Pines one of the facilities you inspect?"

"Yes, it's one of my facilities."

"What was its star rating at the time of Harry's Thomas's death?"

"It was a five star facility."

"And do facilities earn stars based on your inspections?"

"Yes."

"What is the range?"

"Zero to five, with five being the highest."

"How long had you been inspecting Peaceful Pines?"

"Since they opened ten years ago."

Everett was granted permission by Judge Clement to approach the witness, and he lifted a large stack of documents from his table and carried them to the stand.

"Are these the records of your inspections for the time you have been overseeing Peaceful Pines?"

"They appear to be."

"It looks like in the first three years, the star rating never climbed above two and was often zero, is that correct?"

"Yes, that's accurate."

"And then about seven years ago the facility received its first five star rating."

"Yes, that's correct."

"And the rating has remained five stars every quarter since that time?"

"Yes."

"Can you explain that?"

"The facility worked hard to bring themselves into compliance with our regulations, and has continued working hard to stay in compliance. They've done a great job managing the facility and caring for the patients."

"Uh-huh," replied Everett.

Everett paused to allow the jury time to digest what Reed had just testified to before continuing.

"Have there been complaints against Peaceful Pines in the last seven years?"

"Yes," replied Reed.

"Have you investigated those?"

"Yes, I have."

"And how many complaints have you had in the past seven years?"

"Ten."

"Ten? In a seven year period?"

"That is correct."

Wright shifted in his seat. Tyndall and Sloan appeared to be daydreaming and not hearing anything Reed was saying during his testimony.

"One patient complained of an insect infestation. What happened with that complaint?"

"I inspected the facility and didn't find any evidence to corroborate the complaint."

"Another patient complained that their pain medication was being withheld. What happened to that complaint?"

"I again inspected the facility, looked at the patient's medical records and also performed a pill count from their prescription bottles, and again could not find any evidence to corroborate the complaint."

"A third complaint was from a patient's family member who reported unusual bruising to the patient and indicated they suspected abuse."

"Yes, and again I investigated and there was no evidence to corroborate those complaints."

"In fact, out of the ten complaints in seven years, not a single one was corroborated?"

"Yes," replied Reed.

"You're familiar with why we're here today: the death of Mr. Thomas?"

"Yes, I am."

"Are you familiar with the circumstances of his death?"

"Yes, I am."

"Did you investigate his death after the medical examiner ruled it a homicide?"

"I did."

"And what did you find."

"What happened to Mr. Thomas is unfortunate, but I again found no evidence to corroborate the medical examiner's report or that there was any wrongdoing on the part of Peaceful Pines."

"Was this investigation thorough?"

"Yes, sir. Very. I take all my investigations and inspections very seriously."

"I see," said Everett. "Did you talk to a nurse named Annie Smith?"

Reed shifted in his seat and glanced at the defense table.

Wright gave him a slight nod of encouragement. This topic had been covered in depth in their pre-trial conversations.

"I did."

"Did she report to you her concerns with Mr. Thomas's care?"

"She did."

"And?"

"I reviewed the medical records and spoke with the other nurses and could not find any evidence to corroborate her allegations."

"Did Ms. Smith mention concerns that the records had been altered?"

"Ms. Smith did mention that, but I had no evidence that they had been altered, or by whom."

"Did you have access to all of Mr. Thomas's medical records?"

"Yes."

"Including the paper flow sheets?"

"Yes."

"You didn't find any discrepancies in them?"

"There were a few, mostly the records authored by Ms. Smith. My understanding was she was a new employee who had only been there two weeks so it appeared to me based on the remainder of his records from before Ms. Smith arrived and other aspects of my investigation that she made errors on the flow sheets and corrected them when she inputted them into the Electronic Medical Record system."

"Those were pretty severe and substantive errors, were they not?"

Reed glanced at the defense table again. Wright was looking down at his legal pad. This time it was Sloan who gave Reed an almost imperceptible nod.

"The flow sheets were taken from an old form template. You have to understand that almost all charting nowadays is done electronically and has been for years. Ms. Smith was a newer nurse, and likely wasn't trained in how to use the paper forms correctly."

"How carefully did you review those records?" asked Everett.

"I took the medical records to my office to perform an audit."

"That doesn't really answer my question."

"I'm not sure, sir. I read them as thoroughly as I could. We are frankly overworked and understaffed."

"I see," said Everett. "Well, no matter. The jury will hear more about those records later on. Since the death of Harry Thomas, the facility has continued to get five star ratings?" asked Everett

"That's correct."

"And your inspections, even after Mr. Thomas's death, have remained very thorough?"

"Yes, absolutely. Especially in light of his death."

"No more questions, Your Honor."

Judge Clement looked at Wright for cross examination. Everett watched as Wright looked to Reed and to his legal pad. It was unusual for a lawyer not to ask any questions on cross examination, but Everett suspected that he wouldn't as the direct had gone as well as Wright could hope for and was probably consistent with what they had planned.

"No questions, Your Honor," said Wright.

"Mr. Stone, call your next witness."

Everett smiled as he watched Reed leave the witness stand and thought of what was coming later in the trial.

Chapter Thirty

E verett tried to read the jury's faces. Some appeared sympathetic. Others angry, though he hoped that was over Tyndall and not anything Monica had said. Jake and Everett made eye contact briefly, and the corners of Jake's mouth upturned ever-so-slightly. Everett quickly turned his attention back to his witness, but took it as an encouraging sign.

Everett had been leading Monica through her direct examination for almost two hours. She had been careful in her responses in both her wording and how she presented. They had rehearsed her direct examination and testimony so many times she had it memorized as if she was an actress in a play. But, it wasn't enough to say the words; Everett had told her she needed to sell them. She needed to believe them, and appear authentic in delivering them to the jury. Everett thought she was doing a fine job following his instructions, despite what he had assumed were low odds in the beginning.

Relief appeared to wash over her as Everett told Judge Clement that he had no more questions.

Now came the hard part.

Everett's anxiety about Monica's cross-examination abated when Judge Clement called a recess before cross began. He watched as Monica descended the witness stand with shaky legs and stole a glance at Ross Tyndall who gave her a wink. Kenneth Wright was looking at her like a wolf looks at prey.

• • • •

Everett closed the door to the small conference room in the hallway right outside the courtroom.

"Are you okay?" he asked.

"I think so," replied Monica. "How do you think I did?"

"You did excellent, Monica," replied Everett. "I could not have asked for a better direct examination from you. The jury was responsive to your testimony, and you did beautifully explaining everything we talked about."

"It didn't sound rehearsed?"

"Not at all."

Monica appeared to relax for the first time since Everett had announced her as his next witness.

"Are you ready for what comes next?" asked Everett.

"I think so," Monica replied with a shaky voice.

Everett looked at her for a moment, taking stock of his witness. The one witness in the entire trial that worried him the most in terms of their ability to derail the case.

"Monica, that doesn't sound convincing."

"I'm trying, Everett. I really am. But I'm as scared as I've ever been in my life."

Everett reached across the conference room table and took Monica's shaking hand in his own. He was not the best at comforting people in their time of need—an ironic trait for a personal injury lawyer—but he had mustered all the patience and empathy he possessed with Monica over the course of the case to ensure his victory.

"Monica, listen to me," he said.

Monica looked him in the eyes.

"You are going to do fine, do you hear me?"

Monica shook her head ever so slightly.

Everett took a deep breath and tried to quell the rising frustration.

"Monica, you will. I promise you will be fine," he said.

Monica fixed her gaze on the conference room table and didn't respond.

"Look at me," said Everett. The comforting tone was replaced with his customary authoritarian way of speaking.

Monica met his gaze, close to tears.

"You need to pull it together," said Everett shifting his tactics to tough love. "Cross examination is not going to take long, and then I can rehabilitate you if I need to on redirect. Wright won't go long with his questions, he'll get in and get out as he knows a jury will not forgive a boring cross examination. They're conditioned by television and movies to expect high drama and a knock-out, not a ten round match."

"That's what worries me. That I'm going to be knocked out."

"You needn't worry, Monica. You're prepared for this. We've spent hours upon hours going over this. You performed exactly as we rehearsed on direct. You're ready for cross examination. You're prepared to block those punches. I know you can do this."

"I'm glad one of us does," said Monica.

"Monica, you need to get your confidence back. I'm not sure how to do that for you. There's no reason for you to doubt yourself after how well you just performed. If you don't get your head in the game then you're jeopardizing the case. You're putting your ability to get justice at risk."

Monica gave a small nod of acknowledgment.

Everett wasn't satisfied. He knew he needed to appeal to something that mattered to her. Something more than her sense of justice. Something more than Tyndall's accountability for her deceased father's death.

"Monica," said Everett. He continued once she met his gaze. "If you do well on this cross examination, just like we rehearsed, then the case is pretty much in the bag after that. The rest of our case is just as strong. We are virtually guaranteed to be very, very rich after this."

Monica seemed to consider what Everett had just said.

"How rich?" she asked.

"Record-breaking verdict rich."

Monica's spine straightened and her demeanor changed in an instant. The abruptness almost startled Everett.

"Let's go get this motherfucker," Monica said.

It was now Everett who felt nervous, but he couldn't quite pinpoint why.

Chapter Thirty-One

W right leaned forward and took in Monica as she sat on the witness stand. He could sense the nervousness in her, but she was doing well at hiding it from the jury. Monica met his gaze with a neutral expression, but Wright could feel the contempt she held for him.

Wright allowed a slight smile to cross his face. He was going to enjoy this.

"Ms. Thomas," he began, "I am very sorry for your loss and once again offer my condolences. You understand it is my job to ask you some questions now?"

"Yes," replied Monica.

"Your father was in Peaceful Pines for three years before his passing, correct?"

"Yes."

"And during that time you voiced not a single concern about his care to Mr. Tyndall."

"That is true."

"You also did not voice a single concern about his care to any of the staff at Peaceful Pines."

"Yes, that's true."

"You didn't file a single complaint about his care with the State either, did you?"

"No, sir. I did not."

"Never voiced any concerns with his physicians?"

"No, sir, I did not."

"Did you even know who his physicians were?"

"Objection," stated Everett. "Argumentative."

"Overruled," said Judge Clement.

"Let me ask my question again: did you even know who his physicians were?"

"No, sir. I did not."

Wright stole a glance at the jurors. Some of them appeared less sympathetic toward Monica than they had a little while ago during direct examination. Some of the older members were looking at the floor rather than at her.

"In fact, Ms. Thomas, you placed your father in Peaceful Pines three years before his death and not once during that period did you visit him?"

"No, sir."

"Not on his birthday."

"No."

"Not on Easter."

"No."

"Not at Thanksgiving."

"No, sir."

"Christmas too."

More of the jury was beginning to look away from her.

"That's correct."

"Would the staff periodically call you during that three year period to give you updates on your father or bring medical issues to your attention?"

"Yes, sir, they would."

"How many times did you return those calls."

"I can't recall."

"You can't recall? Let me see if I can help you out: is the number zero?"

Monica pursed her lips and gave a slight scowl in Wright's direction.

"Was the number zero, Ms. Thomas?"

"That's correct."

"Let's move on from the staff. How many times did you call your own father in the three years that he lived in Peaceful Pines?"

Monica looked down at her hands, which were folded in her lap.

"Ms. Thomas? Can you please answer the question for the ladies and gentlemen of the jury?"

Monica looked toward the jury. All but a few of them were looking down at the floor or away from her now. The faces still looking toward her were far from friendly.

"I didn't call my father."

"You didn't call your father? Not once in three years?"

"No, sir."

"When is the last time you even saw your father?"

"Shortly before he was admitted to your client's facility. When he was diagnosed with advanced dementia."

"That was a bad question on my part. What I meant to ask was this: when was the last time you spent any meaningful time with your father?"

"I don't understand the question," said Monica.

"I apologize for asking a confusing question, Ms. Thomas. Let me try to make this clearer. Correct me if I'm wrong, but as I understand it just before you placed your father in Peaceful Pines he had been discovered walking down the street in a confused state and he subsequently was diagnosed with advanced dementia. You went to to the hospital where he had been admitted, is that correct?"

"Yes, that's correct."

"While at the hospital, you signed some paperwork with the social worker and then you went home. You did not stay with your father."

"That is also correct."

"Then you dropped him off at Peaceful Pines, and that was the last time you ever saw your father."

"Yes, sir."

"So, my question was: when is the last time you spent meaningful time with your father? When was the last time you actually visited with him; talked to him?"

Monica's face blushed at the question.

"Ms. Thomas?"

Monica closed her eyes. "It had been probably at least thirty years. Not since I was a teenager."

Wright let the answer hang in the air for the jury.

"So in over thirty years you had not seen your father, even on holidays, and had not called him even one time?"

"I know it sounds awful. I know it sounds like I was a terrible daughter," began Monica. "But my father was a complicated man. When I was a child, what I remember most is his drinking. And he was a mean drunk. He beat my mother. He beat me. One time, when I was a teenager, he got so mad at my mother he put her in the hospital. She divorced him, but somehow he got split custody. And when I would be forced to go see him, he would take his hatred for my mother out on me. I begged her to not make me go, but she said there was nothing she could do because that was the court's order on child custody. So I ran away. I kept in touch with mom, but I never spoke to him again."

The smug look Wright had on his face moments before began to fade. He realized his mistake immediately and cursed himself for it. He had been so concerned with the few helpful facts in this case that he had never bothered to explore the reason behind those facts in Monica's deposition. Wright glanced at the jury and saw some of the sympathy that had been eroded begin to return.

"The next time I saw my father was when the social worker contacted me," said Monica. "And I knew I couldn't take care of him, not after what he did. His disease made him more combative. His disease kept him from even recognizing his own daughter. He didn't know who I was, so I put him in a facility immediately because that was what was best for him.

"Despite our history, he was still my father. I still loved him on some level. And, frankly, Mr. Wright, no one deserved to go through what happened to him in your client's facility. No one deserved to suffer like that. He may not have had his memories, but he still had his mind. He still had his emotions. He still could feel the pain that was inflicted on him. No one deserves that."

Wright sat staring at Monica a moment, unsure of where to go next for the first time in a very long time in his career. Monica gave him the answer without realizing it.

"It absolutely broke my heart the way he died. The way he was killed."

"It broke your heart?" asked Wright, recovering quickly.

Monica nodded in response.

"I'm glad you brought that up, Ms. Thomas." Wright pushed a button on the laptop in front of him, and a projector displayed the first frame of a video on a screen set up on the opposite side of the courtroom from the jury.

"Objection!" yelled Everett as he rose from his chair. "We weren't provided a copy of this video in discovery."

Wright rose confidently from his chair and replied, "Your Honor, the video was not relevant until Ms. Thomas testified on the stand a moment ago that she was heartbroken. This video is being used solely to impeach her testimony."

"Overruled," said Judge Clement.

The video that began playing showed Monica walking through Crabtree Valley Mall visiting all the high-end stores available. Coach. Apple. Arhaus Furniture and Pottery Barn. Brooks Brothers. Her arms became more weighted with packages as the edited-for-time video played. She was smiling and jovial during the entire clip.

"Ms. Thomas, was that you in the video?" asked Wright.

"Yes," Monica whispered.

"I'm sorry, Ms. Thomas. I didn't hear you."

"Yes, it was me," Monica said with a shaky voice.

"And what does that say in the date stamp on the video?"

Monica read the date aloud to the jury even though they could see it for themselves. Wright wanted the words to come from Monica's mouth.

"That was the day after your father's death?" asked Wright.

"Yes," Monica answered while looking down.

"And the time on the video?"

Monica read the time.

"That was less than a full twenty-four hours after you were called and notified of your father's death, was it not?"

"Yes," said Monica.

"You had a life insurance policy on your father?" asked Wright.

"Objection," said Everett. He was again overruled.

"Yes, I did," testified Monica.

"And what was the payout from that?"

"A million dollars," said Monica.

"Just so I understand," continued Wright, "you hadn't seen or spoken to your father in over thirty years but still kept a one million dollar life insurance policy on him, and then in your heartbreak over his death you went on an expensive shopping spree less than twenty-four hours after he died?"

Monica could only manage a nod in response.

A tear fell down her cheek for the first time since Harry Thomas had died.

Chapter Thirty-Two

" Why are you still here?" Everett asked.

Dayna sat across from him at his desk, her hands folded calmly in her lap and her legs crossed. Her face was stern, but there was sympathy in her eyes. She watched Everett take another sip of the whiskey he kept in his bottom desk drawer.

"I'm concerned, and want to make sure you're okay," replied Dayna.

She had been scanning in the day's mail when she heard a commotion and a door slam shut. The force had knocked one of the art prints off the wall outside of Everett's private office.

"I'm fine," said Everett.

"You don't look fine."

Everett glared at his assistant.

"What happened? I thought Monica was all set." she asked.

Everett took another long sip of his whiskey and drained the glass. He poured himself another, and then began relaying the day's events to Dayna.

"The shopping video was bad enough," said Everett, "but then she started crying when Wright caught her in her lie, and there were more videos. Expensive furniture being delivered to her house. Her getting on a flight to the Bahamas. Then, after the lawsuit was filed they have her driving home in a brand new Mercedes. She didn't tell me any of this. They didn't turn this over in discovery and Judge Clement overruled the objection. I was ambushed."

Dayna pursed her lips.

"What?" asked Everett.

"Nothing," said Dayna, glancing away at the floor.

Everett knew when she was lying. "What?" he asked again. His voice was more stern this time.

"She did tell you," Dayna said.

"What do you mean she told me?"

"Remember? She called here before her deposition and said she thought someone had been following her. You told her the defense wouldn't waste their time on a private investigator in a case like this."

Everett stared at Dayna with a mixture of embarrassment and hatred. Dayna stared back at him, holding her ground. She didn't need to say the words the two were both thinking: *This is your fault because you got sloppy and over-confident.*

Everett drained his glass of whiskey and poured a third.

"Are you going to do this all night?" asked Dayna.

"Maybe I am," said Everett.

"You should go home to Olivia, and get some rest for tomorrow."

"Seeing her is the last thing I need tonight."

Dayna glanced down at the floor again. She had been Everett's right hand since he opened the law office and knew him better than anyone except perhaps Olivia. It was common knowledge around the office that he and Olivia were once in love but that the flame had been burning down and close to extinguishing for a long time.

"So what are you going to do? Just sleep here tonight?"

"Maybe I will. I have an extra suit here, and I can shower at the gym. Wouldn't be the first time I pulled an all-nighter."

"Everett, you need to get some rest. Sleeping on the couch here isn't what you need in the middle of a trial."

Everett took another sip of his whiskey.

Dayna waited for Everett to say something; he continued to ignore her.

"Jesus, Everett," she said while rolling her eyes. "So you had a bad day in court and Monica shit the bed. Big deal. She's one witness, and you knew her testimony was going to be problematic."

"It was more than problematic," Everett growled.

"Again, so what? She's one witness. By the time you get through with the others, most of the jury won't care about Monica anymore.

Is she a greedy bitch? Yes. But what Tyndall did to that man was reprehensible. Don't you think a jury will want to punish that? Don't you think they're going to want to make Tyndall pay, regardless of who is getting that money once it's all said and done?"

Everett set his whiskey glass down and stared at Dayna. She stood from her chair and crossed her arms, meeting his gaze.

The silence grew between them until it was almost unbearable and the tension was palpable in the air.

"I guess you have a point," said Everett.

"I'm sorry, did you say something? It was hard to hear with you mumbling."

Everett sneered but said more loudly, "I said you have a point."

"Yes, I do. This case is not over, so you need to stop wallowing over a bad day. You've had bad days before, and you will have them again. But I can promise you, the day this jury reaches a verdict is going to be a good day. A very good day."

Everett nodded in agreement as he looked down at his whiskey glass.

"That is, of course, if you don't decide to throw in the towel tonight and lose this case."

Everett scowled as he picked up his glass and took another sip. "You know, a lot of bosses would fire an employee who talked to them the way you talk to me."

"A lot of employees aren't near as good at their jobs as I am."

Everett tried to hide a smile but failed.

"Face it, Everett. You would be lost without me, and probably bankrupt too."

Everett turned to face the desk clock and saw that it was well past closing time.

"Dayna, go home and leave me alone."

"Only if you promise you're not going to drain that bottle and be hungover for court tomorrow."

"I promise. I'm going to finish this glass while enjoying the quiet, and then I'm going home so I'm fresh for tomorrow." Everett opened the bottom desk drawer and placed the bottle back in its place.

Dayna uncrossed her arms and softened her expression, but didn't leave.

"Go home, Dayna. I'll be fine. I promise. And I'm not paying you overtime."

Dayna turned to leave and walked out of Everett's office.

"And lock up behind you," yelled Everett.

Everett took another sip of his whiskey and looked at the photograph of Olivia he kept on his desk.

He pulled the phone from his pocket and texted his wife: *Long day in trial. Need to prepare for tomorrow due to developments today. Will sleep at office. Love you.*

Everett threw the phone back on his desk without waiting for a response, and turned in his chair to face the floor-to-ceiling windows overlooking the city. It wasn't long before he drifted away into his own thoughts.

A noise from down the hall startled him back to reality.

Chapter Thirty-Three

E verett turned from the window to face the doorway. The noise had sounded like a door opening, but there should have been no one else in the office once Dayna left.

"Hello?" he called out. "Dayna, is that you? I told you to go home."

Silence was the only response he received.

The hairs on the back of Everett's neck rose and the bourbon-induced fog lifted from his mind with a surge of adrenaline.

"Hello?" he called out again.

This time he heard the soft, slow patter of footsteps, as if someone were creeping down the hallway toward his office.

Everett picked up his desk phone and began to call building security, but realized that they would never make it to his office in time. He replaced the phone in its cradle and took the keys out of his pocket instead. The sound of the steps in the hallway were getting louder.

Bending down, Everett inserted the key held in his trembling hand into the lock on the top right desk drawer. He heard the lock click, and then slowly opened the drawer. Sliding his hand underneath a stack of blank legal pads and empty manila folders, his fingers wrapped around the butt of his Glock 9mm. Everett pulled the gun out of the drawer and raised it toward the threshold.

"Dayna, if that's you out there you better say so right now. This is not funny."

The sound of the steps halted.

Everett tried to steady his aim with his shaking hands. He took several deep breaths and began slowly inching his way around the desk while keeping the muzzle of the pistol pointed at the doorway.

As he rounded the desk, he could hear a soft rustling sound and the soft chime of metal against metal. Everett saw in his mind the image of an intruder removing his own gun from his waistband and clicking off the safety.

"I know someone is out there! I have a gun and I'm not afraid to use it."

There was no response, but Everett could feel a tension rise in the air of the office. He grasped the butt of the gun a little tighter, anticipating the force of the recoil should he have to fire.

"Don't shoot," said a man's voice.

It sounded familiar, but Everett wasn't able to immediately place it.

"I want you to slowly come to the door," commanded Everett. "Do it with your hands up above your head or I will shoot you. You're trespassing and I have every right to defend myself."

The silhouette of a man appeared on the floor outside of the doorway as the intruder passed underneath the hallway's fluorescent lights. Everett double-checked to make sure his safety was off.

The man appeared with his hands high above his head.

Everett was unable to think or form words while he processed what he was seeing.

Beginning to regain his composure, Everett wondered how it was possible to feel both terror and relief in the same moment. He clicked the safety back on and set the Glock on the desk behind him.

"What the fuck are you doing here?" demanded Everett. "I could have shot you!"

The man just smiled in response.

"And where are your damn clothes?" asked Everett.

Jake stood before Everett completely naked, with a smile still on his face. He slowly lowered his hands and took a step inside the door.

"I know you had a bad day in court, and I wanted to surprise you and make you feel better."

"Are you crazy?" replied Everett. "What are you thinking? We're blocks from the courthouse. What if someone saw you? What if my staff was still here?"

"Relax. You and your assistant were in here talking when I snuck in and I hid in one of the empty offices down the hall. As far as getting to the building, it's downtown Raleigh. There were a ton of people coming and going at the end of the workday and I was careful. No one noticed a thing."

Everett gave Jake a doubtful glare. "You can't be sure of that, Jake. This is too risky."

"Riskier than anything else we've done? Having sex in the gym shower? You coming to my apartment all those times?"

"Yes, because we're right near the courthouse. Hell, Wright's office is just above us in the building. What if some of those lawyers saw you and recognized you?"

"They didn't."

"How can you be so sure?"

"Because I'm good at sneaking into places unnoticed."

The coy smile on Jake's face indicated this was meant to be half-truth and half-joke, but it startled Everett and reminded him how many bad decisions he had made over the course of the last several months. He really knew nothing about the man he had been having an affair with; the man for which he had begun to develop feelings. Everett didn't even know his real name until the start of the trial.

"I sure as hell hope not or we're both done for. You never did answer of the question of where your clothes are." Everett took a moment from scolding Jake to admire his body.

"It's part of the surprise. I figured you'd have a hard time saying no if I was already in your office naked."

"Say no to what?"

Jake stepped forward and grabbed Everett's loosened tie, pulling him into his body. His soft lips met Everett's as his hands moved up Everett's back, pulling him in closer. He could feel Everett harden against him.

Jake began moving forward and backed Everett up until they ran against his desk. Everett relaxed deeper into the kiss and his hands moved around Jake's small waist to grab the firm, tight muscles of his ass.

Jake's hand deftly unbuckled Everett's belt and unbuttoned the top of his pants, unzipping them. Jake took both hands and forcefully pushed the pants and Everett's boxer briefs to the floor, lowering himself with them.

Jake took Everett into his mouth and began moving his soft lips and tongue up and down the length of him as Everett moaned. Jake moved slowly, then fast, then slowed down again, taking Everett at varying lengths.

Everett ran his hands through Jake's thick, soft hair and cradled the back of his head while thrusting deeper and deeper into Jake's mouth. Jake reached up and ran his hand up Everett's chest while he did so. Everett's moans grew louder and louder.

Jake pulled back right before Everett finished and stood up.

The suddenness of the movement startled Everett and Jake took advantage of the moment to grab Everett's shoulders to spin him and bend him across the desk.

Everett gasped at the pressure of Jake entering him. Jake paused for a moment before placing his hands on Everett's hips and slowly beginning to move deeper inside.

The rhythm of Jake's thrusts became faster and faster, and his grip tightened on Everett's waist. Everett looked across his desk to the window. The interior lights of the office created a mirroring effect that allowed Everett to watch Jake make love to him with the lights of the city laid out beneath them. Everett met Jake's gaze in the reflection and the two smiled at each other.

Once Jake was finished, he smacked Everett playfully on the ass and pulled out of him, backing away slightly as Everett stood upright and pulled his pants back on.

"Did that make you forget about your bad day in court?" asked Jake.

Everett smiled at him. "I think so. Much more fun that sitting here drinking bourbon by myself too."

"Good," said Jake. He moved in for another kiss then said, "I know you'll do better tomorrow."

Jake turned and walked out of Everett's office. Everett followed him to the door and watched him get dressed in the hallway before leaving for the night.

Once Jake was gone, Everett walked back to his desk and looked out at the city before turning his gaze to the picture of his wife on the desk.

"I remember when you used to make me feel that way," he said to the picture.

Chapter Thirty-Four

Everett walked into the courtroom the next morning and tried to remain calm and collected. Several members of the defense team were already assembled at their table and glanced toward him with scowls.

Everett's hands started to sweat and his heart beat faster when he saw the looks on their faces. His irrational mind made him think they knew he and a member of the jury had made love on his desk several floors beneath their own offices last night.

Monica was already seated at plaintiff's table. Her carefully applied makeup failed to hide the bags under her eyes. She looked up at Everett as he set his briefcase down on the table and pulled out his chair. She nodded a hello but didn't speak, her cheeks beginning to flush as she met her lawyer's gaze.

"Morning," Everett muttered as he took his seat and began setting out his papers for the day.

Everett glanced back over at the defense table, where more lawyers had now assembled and were whispering back and forth to each other. Some glanced in Everett's direction, a stern look on their faces. Everett could feel some of the color drain from his complexion and he turned away from them, hoping they wouldn't notice.

He looked back at his client and saw Monica staring down at folded hands in her lap, her shoulders slumped. She closed her eyes and appeared to be silently mouthing a prayer. Everett softened toward her when he realized how much she was beating herself up because of her testimony. He knew Dayna had spoken the truth last night.

Everett placed a hand on Monica's shoulder and leaned toward her. "Forget about how yesterday went," he whispered in her ear. "It's not going to make a difference. We are going to win this case and justice will be done. Take a deep breath, relax, and be strong until it's over."

Monica drew in the deep breath, and then another. Everett could see relief wash over her face at his reassurances.

The door to the courtroom opened again and Everett looked over his shoulder to see Wright, Tyndall, and Sloan march into the room. Wright had a dour look on his face, but the other two seemed relaxed. Sloan met Everett's gaze with a smug look on his face.

Everett turned back around and a few moments later the bailiff stepped into the courtroom commanding everyone to rise. Judge Clement came in after the call to order and took his place on the bench.

"Is there anything from the plaintiff that needs to be addressed before we bring the jury back in?" asked Judge Clement.

Everett stood and said, "No, your honor."

"And from the defense?"

Wright stood at his table and cleared his throat.

This is it, thought Everett. *I'm toast.*

"No, your honor," said Wright.

"Very well then. Bailiff, bring in the jury."

Everett let out a sigh of relief and his heart rate began to return to normal as the twelve members of the jury shuffled into the box and took their seats.

"Mr. Stone, call your next witness," said Judge Clement.

Everett stood once more and said, "Your honor, at this time we call Joseph Redfield to the stand."

Redfield, who had the physical features of a Hollywood leading man, took the stand in a bespoke suit without the tie. The courtroom clerk administered the oath and he glared at Tyndall as he sat down. Tyndall returned the icy gaze.

Everett began his examination with questions about who Redfield was and his background so the jury could get to know him.

Redfield lived in Raleigh. He was the owner of a technology start up in Research Triangle Park, Duke educated, and by all accounts successful. He was happily married to a beautiful wife and lived with her and their two precious children in a suburban home in an exclusive neighborhood inside Raleigh's beltline. The only downside in his life was his wife was the daughter of Ross Tyndall.

"What is your relationship like with your father-in-law?" asked Everett.

"It's cordial, but we're not particularly close. We don't have much in common."

"Do you know anything about his businesses?"

"I know what he does for a living, but that's the extent of it."

"Do you work for Peaceful Pines in any manner?"

"No."

"Have you ever worked for any of his companies in the past?"

"No, I have not."

"Have you ever acted as a consultant or adviser to your father-in-law?" asked Everett.

"No."

"Have you ever been an investor in one of his companies?"

"Again, no."

Everett reached for a stack of exhibits on his table and approached the witness stand. He handed the documents to Redfield and returned to the table to continue his questioning.

"Do you recognize those documents, Mr. Redfield?" asked Everett.

"Yes, I do. It's the articles of incorporation for my father-in-law's company."

"That's the document that basically created Peaceful Pines?"

"That's my understanding."

"Whose name is listed at the bottom of the document?"

"Mine."

"And the signature above the name, is that yours?" asked Everett.

"It's my name, but it's not my signature."

"And what about the other documents?"

"They appear to be the annual reports for each year Peaceful Pines has been in business."

"And what name is on the annual reports?"

"Mine."

"And the signatures?"

"No, they're not my signature."

"I want to make sure we all understand," continued Everett. "All of these corporate documents filed with the Secretary of State have your name listed as the owner of Peaceful Pines, but the signatures are not yours and you have never had any involvement with the company?"

"That's correct," said Redfield.

"When did you first learn about this?"

"Not until after you contacted me following Mr. Thomas's death."

"What did you do when you found out?"

"At first I was shocked and didn't believe you," said Redfield. "But, then I got ahold of the documents and sure enough someone had forged my signature. Then the shock wore off and I realized this was exactly the type of thing my father-in-law would do."

"Where was your father-in-law when you found out?"

"He was in prison for tax evasion."

"What did you do?"

"I went to see him at the Federal Correction Center up in Butner. I had the papers with me and confronted him with them."

"What did Mr. Tyndall say in response?"

"Objection," said Wright.

"Overruled," grumbled Judge Clement.

"He said not to worry about it and to not say anything if I wanted my wife—his daughter—to ever see any inheritance. He said just go along with it and everything would be fine. He said if I tried to do anything about it, he would make life difficult for me; that anyone who crosses him always loses."

"Did you do anything about it?"

"Initially, no. I wanted to protect my wife. Not because of the inheritance—we're well off in our own right—but because she loves her father and family is important to her."

"But you're here today?" asked Everett.

"After our conversation at the prison, I started doing more digging into my father-in-law's background and what was going on at Peaceful Pines. I didn't like what I saw, and couldn't sit back."

"Did you ever ask him why he listed the company in your name instead of his?"

"Taxes and liability. He only received a year on the tax evasion charges because the amount of money wasn't that much. He tried to blame it on an accounting error, so the prosecutors cut him a deal. Turns out the rest of money was used to fund Peaceful Pines, but by using someone else's name on the forms he avoided scrutiny, although for all intents and purposes he owns all the shares of the company and is the true owner."

"Thank you, Mr. Redfield. I have no more questions," said Everett.

By the time Redfield stepped off the witness stand following an ineffectual cross examination by Wright, the looks on the jurors' faces seemed to signal to Everett that they were done. Not just with Redfield, but with Tyndall and his shady practices too.

They hadn't heard the half of it yet.

Chapter Thirty-Five

E verett watched the throng of people walk up and down the street through the large windows of Beasley's Chicken + Honey restaurant a block from the courthouse.

After a few minutes he became bored and began scrolling through his emails. He recalled when he was a child and signed up for his first email address how excited he was when the robotic voice would announce "You've got mail!" Now, he received so many emails an hour keeping up with them felt like playing the world's worst game of Whack-a-Mole.

Movement from across the table broke his concentration on an email Dayna had sent him summarizing the day's developments in his other cases. Everett looked up and a frown crossed his face.

"What the hell do you want?" asked Everett.

"Hello to you too," replied Sloan.

Everett glared across the table. He hated this man, and everything he stood for. Lawyers like Sloan were an embarrassment to the profession, and Sloan was a particular pain in the ass. Everett wished he could punch the smug look from his plump face.

He didn't bother responding to Sloan. Everett had grown accustomed to silence in his experience at a litigator and was content with letting Sloan make the first move since he had brazenly interrupted Everett's downtime during the lunch recess.

Sloan broke the uncomfortable eye contact and reached into his own suit jacket with his small nubby fingers, pulling out a plain white envelope. He placed it on the wooden table and slid it across to Everett.

"What's that?" asked Everett.

"Open it and see," replied Sloan.

Everett slowly picked up the envelope, and took his time opening the flap. Once he had seen the contents, he looked up at Sloan with a face that looked both amused and annoyed.

"What's this?"

"Is it not obvious?"

"I mean, I can see what it is, but why are you giving this to me?" asked Everett.

"For your own good."

Everett's brow furrowed and his face flushed red with anger.

"For my own good? Sloan, get the fuck out of here and leave me alone."

Everett slid the envelope containing a check for five million dollars back across the table.

Sloan slid it back into the center.

"Don't be so hasty, Everett," began Sloan.

"Go screw yourself, Sloan."

An arrogant smile crossed Sloan's lips.

"As I was saying, don't be so quick to give this back to me. This is a lot of money. Most attorneys would jump at it"

"I'm not most attorneys. And if I recall correctly, at mediation your last offer was five million and one dollars, so we're to not off to a good start beginning negotiations at less than what was offered before."

"I'm sure I have a dollar in my wallet. I'll add it to the envelope if we have a deal at that amount. I can email you the settlement agreement and release before you even get back to the courtroom."

"No deal, Sloan. It wasn't enough at mediation. It's not enough now. But, in the name of professional courtesy, I'll make you a counter-demand: you pay me twenty million dollars and your client agrees to never operate any type of residential care facility again until the day he dies, and we have a settlement."

Sloan tapped the enveloped with his index finger. "This is the extent of my settlement authority and the most money you'll ever see on this case."

"What are you going to do, Sloan? Send your guy in the BMW again? That didn't work out for him so well the last time did it?"

"I don't know what you're talking about," said Sloan.

"I'm sure."

"It's in your best interests to take this money and settle before you wind up losing this case," said Sloan.

Everett started to laugh. It was several minutes before he regained his composure.

"Lose this case? Sloan, I don't think we've been watching the same trial. I'm not going to lose this case and the verdict is going to be a hell of lot more than the amount in that envelope."

"Don't be so sure," said Sloan.

Everett could think of nothing to say and instead looked at Sloan with confusion and pity, trying to determine if Sloan actually believed what he was saying or whether he was somehow an excellent actor.

"No deal," said Everett.

Sloan shook his head and picked the envelope up off the table. Just then, a waiter arrived and placed Everett's order in front of him.

"Can I can get you anything else, sir?" asked the waiter. "Or perhaps something for your friend?"

"He's not my friend," said Everett, "and I'm fine, thank you."

The waiter hurried off as Sloan stuffed the envelope back in his suit jacket.

"You're going to regret this decision, Everett."

"Sloan, you're the last person to lecture me about anything given the man you work for. Tyndall is going down, and you'll just be one of the many rats trapped on the sinking ship in the aftermath of this verdict."

Sloan chuckled and shook his head.

"Get the hell out of here, Sloan. You're ruining my appetite," said Everett as he took a bite of his chicken sandwich.

Sloan stood and said, "See you around."

Everett chewed and watched Sloan walk out of the restaurant. *If there's any justice in this world, he'll end up in a place like Peaceful Pines*, thought Everett as Sloan climbed into the passenger seat of a gray BMW pulling up to the curb out front.

Chapter Thirty-Six

I t is never a good strategy to bore a jury. They have been conditioned for action and suspense by legal dramas on television and in the movies. Jurors want an all-out brawl and battle of the wits between attorneys with high drama. Lawyers believe that if they bore a jury, the jury will hold it against them in deliberations. Most of the time, real trials never resemble the entertaining fictional ones and boredom cannot be avoided.

Everett's next witness personified monotony and academics. He would have normally considered it a bad idea to call the witness after the lunch recess, but the testimony was legally necessary for the case and Everett would reward the jury for their patience with the coming witnesses.

Dr. Edward Mason took the stand dressed in a modest corporate gray suit with an out-of-style tie straight from the 1990s. His hair was silver and he wore wire-rimmed glasses. He sat with the confidence of a witness who had testified many times before, and with the added arrogance inherent in medical doctors.

"Dr. Mason, can you please tell the jury your occupation?" began Everett.

"I'm currently employed as the medical examiner for the State of North Carolina."

Everett walked Dr. Mason through his education and training, as well as his extensive experience before tendering him as an expert witness without objection from the defense. He glanced over at the jury when that portion of the examination was complete, and saw that half of them were already fighting off sleep. Jake was the only one that appeared fully attentive.

"Doctor, I want to talk to you about your involvement in this case. Did you perform the autopsy on Harry Thomas after his death?" asked Everett.

"I did, yes."

"Can you please walk us through your findings?"

"The body was in severe shape when I examined it," began Dr. Mason. "One of the first things I noticed was the skin appeared dirty and unwashed, and the hair was matted and nails overgrown. It appeared to me that the subject's hygiene had been severely neglected.

"The body was also malnourished. Most of the bones were visible through the skin due to a severe loss of body fat and muscle. The abdomen was also distended, which is an indication of kwashiorkor."

"Doctor," interrupted Everett, "for those of us who aren't medical experts, can you explain what that term means?"

"Yes, of course," continued Dr. Mason. "That term is used to describe a severe form of malnutrition. It occurs when a person does not consume enough protein, and the severe absence of protein in the body causes fluid retention which makes the abdomen look bloated, or distended."

"Just so we understand doctor," said Everett, "the condition would cause someone to look like a skeleton with a pot belly?"

"Exactly."

Everett glanced over at the jury and saw that more than half now appeared to be fighting off sleep. Three of them had their eyes fully closed and had given up. Even Jake looked bored now. It was time to wake them and regain everyone's attention.

He approached the witness stand with large poster boards and asked Dr. Mason to step down to illustrate the rest of his findings for the jury as Everett set up an easel.

Once everything was in place, Everett placed the first exhibit on the easel and turned it around.

"Doctor, can you please identify what this is?"

"This exhibit is the diagram I drew of the body during the autopsy. It's common practice to make a diagram to illustrate the location of any unique markers, like tattoos, or any wounds and other abnormalities."

"What are these circular spots all over the front of the body and this one on the face?"

"Those are bruises."

"Based on your examination of the body, were you able to determine what caused the bruising?"

"To some extent, yes. Due to the severe malnourishment the subject had also developed anemia, which is a deficiency of iron in the body. It causes the skin to turn pale and yellowish, and also makes the skin more susceptible to bruising."

Everett continued: "Thank you, doctor. I think we understand now the medical causes of the bruising, but were you able to determine how the bruises actually got there?"

"It's difficult in some cases to tell; anemia and malnourishment cause fatigue and weakness, so the subject could have fallen at some point or dropped something on themselves, like a TV remote for instance."

"You said in some cases. What about the others?"

"This one here, on the face, and these two here, across the upper chest, are of a size, shape, and severity consistent with blows."

Everett glanced at the jury and saw he had all of their attention again, and they did not look pleased by what they had heard.

"When you say blows, doctor, what do you mean?" asked Everett.

"I mean someone hit him. Likely with their fists."

Everett paused and let Dr. Mason's testimony sit in the courtroom for a few seconds before removing the diagram and placing another exhibit on the easel.

"Now, doctor, I want to talk about the backside of Mr. Thomas's body."

Kenneth Wright rose to his feet and objected as Everett suspected he would. "Your honor, this exhibit serves no purpose except to try to inflame the jury and is overly prejudicial to the defense."

Everett smiled at the objection. If any member of the jury was still not giving their full attention to Dr. Mason's testimony, that was about to change by Wright highlighting how harmful the exhibit was about to be.

Judge Clement glared in Everett's direction.

"Your Honor," said Everett, "these photographs are clinical photographs from the autopsy. They show only the outside of the body and the condition of the skin on Mr. Thomas's back. It is important for the jury to see the condition Mr. Thomas was in so that they can make an informed decision on whether Mr. Thomas's death was attributable to the actions, or inactions, of the defendant."

Wright opened his mouth to say something more but Judge Clement raised a hand to stop him. "Overruled," said the judge.

Everett moved on to his next question, "Doctor, what did you find when you examined the back of Mr. Thomas's body?"

"It was covered in bed sores and necrotic tissue."

"What does necrotic mean?"

"Dead. It means the healthy tissue had died and become dehydrated."

"What causes that?"

"It can be caused by several different things, such as diabetes. But in this case, it was due to pressure ulcers."

"Explain that, please," said Everett.

"Pressure ulcers result from unrelieved local pressure that compresses soft tissue between a surface and underlying bony prominences. In other words, it's a breakdown of the skin that occurs when someone is in one position for an excessively long time. It's a common concern with those who are bedridden. The pressure between the surface of the bed and the bones underneath the skin and muscle cause the soft tissues to break down."

Everett turned the poster board around and the jury let out an audible gasp. He made a quick study of the shock and disgust on their faces, and fought to suppress a smile. The only juror who seemed stoic in the face of the high-definition photograph in front of them was Jake. Everett's gaze lingered on him for moment but the look was not returned.

"Doctor, is this a photograph you took of Mr. Thomas, and if so, can you please describe what we are seeing?"

Dr. Mason explained in starkly clinical terms the graphic image on display. Black, dead tissue occupied most of Harry's upper back, and stretched in patches to the lower back and buttocks. Some of the wounds were fresher than others, and appeared to ooze a pus-like substance.

"Is this level of necrotic tissue unusual?" asked Everett.

"Yes, most definitely."

"And what happens if it's not treated?"

"Infection, which can ultimately result in death. You can see in the lower wounds here evidence of obvious infection."

"What are the presence of these wounds indicative of?"

"Neglect. It's standard protocol in health care to turn and move patients on a regular basis to prevent these types of sores. The need for this, and the consequences of failing to treat them, would have been obvious to anyone with even the slightest bit of medical training."

"Were you able to determine a cause of death, doctor?" asked Everett.

"Based on the severe level of malnourishment, the signs of the infection, and the necrotic tissue, I ruled the death a homicide due to institutional neglect."

• • • •

Wright tried his best to soften the blow of Dr. Mason's testimony on cross-examination.

"Is it not true that malnutrition can affect people with dementia?" he asked.

"That is true," conceded Dr. Mason. "However, in a facility such as Peaceful Pines, measures could and should have been taken to prevent the condition to begin with despite Mr. Thomas's diagnosis of dementia."

"Doctor, is it not also true that liver disease can cause malnutrition?"

"Yes, that is also true."

"Mr. Thomas had liver disease, correct?"

"Yes, he did," responded Dr. Mason.

"And that liver disease was due to years of alcohol abuse?" asked Wright.

"That is the history that was provided to me," said Dr. Mason.

"Doctor Mason, you also testified a few moments ago that in your opinion the bruises that were found on Mr. Thomas's body were the result of blows."

"Correct," said Dr. Mason.

"But that is just opinion—you don't actually know what caused the bruising?"

"That is a fair statement," conceded Dr. Mason.

"It's possible that Mr. Thomas could have caused the bruising himself, is it not?" asked Wright.

"That is possible, yes," said Dr. Mason.

"For example, he could have dropped something on himself, such as the TV remote?"

"Yes."

"Or, he could have hit himself in a state of delirium caused by his dementia?"

"Yes, that is also possible."

Wright didn't bother touching the subject of the wounds on the back; there was nothing he could do mitigate the power of the photographs.

Everett watched the jury carefully during Wright's cross examination and studied their faces for any sign that Wright was actually scoring points. Most of the jury appeared indifferent to the testimony, including Jake. Some jurors began to fall back asleep. Others rolled their eyes.

Everett knew the defense team would also be studying the jury's reaction, and stole a glance at their table. Sloan turned his head toward Everett and met his gaze. He gave Everett a smirk as the cross examination ended and court went into recess for the day.

Chapter Thirty-Seven

The hands around his waist startled him. Everett stood in his walk-in closet undressing from his suit, only the pants remaining to be dealt with.

"I've missed you this week," Olivia whispered in his ear, hear breath tickling the back of his neck.

Everett wondered whether she was telling the truth, but returned the expected lie anyway. "I've missed you too."

"How's your trial going? You've worked late every night this week."

"We had a hiccup or two, but overall it's going well. We should finish by the end of next week."

"Hopefully you can take some time off once it's over," Olivia replied.

"We'll see. You know that while I'm in trial my other cases are being neglected so there will be a lot of digging out afterward."

Olivia unwrapped her arms and stood behind him, waiting for him to finish hanging up his suit. Everett turned to face her in nothing but his boxer briefs and socks, suppressing a cringe at the pouty look she had on her face. It made her look child-like and weak, something he detested in his partners.

"What's wrong?" he asked.

"I've just missed you is all. I understand you have to work late but you've spent a lot of over-nighters at the office. I'm just lonely and want to spend some time with you."

Since when, he thought.

"I understand. But, you know all those hours are necessary to be able to provide our lifestyle since I'm the only source of income for the house."

Olivia furrowed her brow and her body tensed.

"You always bring up the income," she said. "I can go back to work if you want. You're the one who wanted me to be a stay-at-home spouse."

That was when we first got married, thought Everett, *before you got lazy with the house and started spending money as a hobby.*

"I know. I didn't mean it like that," he said.

"Dinner's almost ready," said Olivia. "I'll meet you downstairs."

Everett watched as she walked out of the bedroom and then he went and laid on the bed for a few minutes, scrolling through his phone and building up the fortitude to suffer through another awkward and mostly silent dinner with his wife.

• • • •

"Are you ready for next week?" asked Olivia as she took another bite of her steak.

"I think so. As ready as I'm going to be," said Everett, taking another sip of his wine.

"That's good. Maybe you can get some rest and we can spend some time together this weekend."

"Yeah, that's fine," said Everett. "What would you like to do?"

"I don't know. Just spend time together." Olivia took a sip of her wine and frowned down at her plate.

"What's wrong?" asked Everett.

Olivia continued looking down at her plate and pushed around a few of the roasted potatoes.

"I just feel like we never spend any time together. Like we've grown apart the past few years."

The yard boy isn't enough to satisfy you anymore? he wanted to ask. Everett withheld the question to keep the peace. He didn't particularly care, and picking the fight would be hypocritical at this juncture since he was having his own affair. More importantly, he didn't have time for that level of fight during trial.

Everett took another sip of his wine. "I'm sorry you feel that way. I think we spend quite a bit of time together. I understand I work a lot, but that's what comes with this profession and owning your own firm."

"It's not exactly quality time though, is it?" asked Olivia. "Sure, you're home at night and on the weekends, but you're at the gym most mornings before I get up and then we just sit on the couch once you get home. We don't talk as much as we used to. We don't touch each other like we used to."

Everett took a deep breath and leaned back in his chair.

Why does she need to do this now? he thought. *I don't have enough to worry about with this case than for her to bring up this problem right now? It's been this way for years, and now is when she wants to talk about this?* He took another sip of his wine to try to tamp down the anger bubbling in his chest.

"What do you want me to do?" he asked, perhaps a little sharper than he intended. "It's not like I'm the only one in this relationship. You could make an effort sometimes. But you're on your phone just as much as I am, or have your face buried in your books. And never once have you tried to initiate any intimacy between us, at least not anytime I can recall."

"I just feel like I'm losing you," she said. "I love you and don't want to lose you."

Olivia looked toward him, her eyes glistening with percolating tears. She blinked and one fell down her cheek, rolling off her jaw into her lap. She picked up her napkin and dabbed the rest of her tears away, before returning to her meal without saying anything more.

Everett felt the tension in his muscles release, his shoulders lowering themselves to a normal position and his face reclaiming a neutral expression. Olivia's statement and the emotion she showed were an unexpected gut punch. It was true that their romance had cooled and the flames were gone, but he could see now that there was still an ember in her. The small one that remained in him flamed up.

"I'm sorry," he said with a slight crack in his voice as the stress of everything in his life reached a boiling point. He took another, longer sip of wine before continuing. "I love you too. I really do, and I'm sorry we've gotten to the point we have. After this trial is over, let's resolve to do better. Both of us. I promise I'll try if you will."

Olivia continued looking down at her plate and nodded in response. Everett could see the tiny droplets of her tears falling onto her steak.

Chapter Thirty-Eight

E verett felt her presence behind him as he loaded the last dish into the dishwasher. As soon as he had closed the door and stood back up, her hand grasped his rear through his joggers. He turned to face a naked Olivia.

"What are you doing?" he asked, a smirk appearing on his face.

"Initiating," she said as she took a step forward, sliding her hands under the waistband of his boxer briefs. She leaned up and pressed her lips to his.

Everett could feel the warmth of her breasts though his t-shirt, and felt himself becoming hard as their tongues massaged each other. One of her hands grasped him and slowly moved up and down his shaft. He moaned with anticipation.

His fingers gently brushed the outside of her thigh and moved to the interior. He gently pressed his first two fingers into her, feeling warm wetness. Olivia's hips drew forward and she pressed into his hand as he massaged further into her.

As they continued to kiss, Everett removed his fingers and reached around with both hands and took firm hold of Olivia's ass. He lifted her up and sat her on the island counter. Olivia lowered the rest of herself onto the cold marble.

Everett pushed down his pants and exposed his throbbing cock. Gently he moved Olivia's legs wider, leaning forward and entering her. He bent over and kissed her deeply, enjoying the sensation.

He stood back up and began to thrust, slowly at first and then building into a steady rhythm. They both moaned with a pleasure.

"Fuck me harder," moaned Olivia.

Everett increased the speed and intensity of his thrusts, his cock driving deep into Olivia. She screamed in ecstasy as she finished.

Everett's body shuddered with his own climax before falling forward and catching himself with his arms. He looked down at Olivia, their eyes locking before he leaned in for a long, slow kiss.

"I love you," said Everett.

"I love you too," said Olivia.

• • • •

They continued to drink wine and make love well into the evening. Later, they lay in bed together, covered only with the sheets. Olivia's back was turned to Everett on the spacious king-sized bed and she was breathing softly. Everett lay awake staring at the ceiling, his hands behind his head.

He smiled as he reflected on the evening. It was the happiest he had been at home in years, and it was remarkable to him that there had been a spark of passion. Perhaps the relationship could be salvaged. It was a thought that kept colliding violently with another ricocheting in his mind like a pinball.

Everett had meant it when he told Olivia he loved her. But Everett couldn't deny the flutter in his chest when he saw Jake, and his happiness when the two were together. It was the same feeling he had with Olivia when he knew he wanted to marry her someday.

He kept trying to convince himself the feelings for Jake were not love, but rather adrenaline from the adventure of their affair. Jake was new and forbidden. He was the fulfillment of a side of Everett that had never been acknowledged before. The satisfaction of fulfilling a lifetime of desires: the taste of another's man's lips, the embrace, the sex.

Jake brought a turmoil with him, however. Fear and anxiety mixed with happiness and attraction. Everett was risking a lot by continuing the affair. Everett's entire life would be ruined if anyone ever found out.

Could he trust Jake? Could this continue long-term? Everett knew the answer to the latter question was no, and was unsure of the former, which is what bothered him the most. At the end of the day, his and Jake's relationship was nothing more than a tryst. Everett barely knew anything about him, and what he did know he learned mostly from jury selection. Their relationship outside of the courtroom had been based on lust, and there was little pillow talk.

Everett wasn't ready to end things with Jake. And certainly wouldn't before the trial ended so as not to compromise the verdict with a jilted lover. The side of him that wasn't controlled by logic wanted the relationship to continue beyond the trial—for years to come. If Olivia could have her so-called secret affair, why couldn't he? For a lifetime. He was falling in love with Jake, and it terrified him.

Everett glanced over at Olivia, who was still sound asleep. He then reached over onto his night table and grabbed his cell phone.

You up? he texted.

He stared at the screen, his heart racing.

Yeah, replied Jake.

I need to see you this weekend.

Chapter Thirty-Nine

" How did you explain where you are today?" asked Jake. "I didn't think you could get away on the weekends because of your wife."

"The trial gave me a good excuse. I told her I needed to clear my head, and go into the office afterward."

"She's okay with you being gone so much?"

Everett looked over at Jake. "Yeah," he said curtly.

"So when you said you needed to see me, I assumed you meant at my place. Not... this."

The gravel crunched under their shoes as they walked along a trail flanked on each side by pines, sycamores, and birches. It was a pleasant day, but the shade from the canopy blocked most of the sun.

Everett had insisted that the two come for a hike. He didn't completely lie to Olivia; he did need to clear his head and the woods were the second best place behind the pool for doing so. More importantly, he needed to talk to Jake about them. And it needed to be someplace where not many people would see them together. Everett also knew that out in public he was sure to actually talk to Jake rather than immediately jump into bed with him.

"What's the matter?" asked Everett. "You can't handle a little exercise?"

Jake smiled. "You know I can. I mean, we met in the gym. I just thought when you said you needed to see me you meant see me naked, not going for a walk."

Everett looked down at the trail as the two took a couple steps in silence.

"I wanted to talk to you about some things."

"Uh-oh," replied Jake.

Everett shook his head slightly. "No, it's not bad. At least I don't think it is. We just need to figure some things out."

"This is how most break-up conversations start," said Jake.

"Jake, I have no intention of breaking off our... our thing. I enjoy your company too much."

"Oh I know you do. You make that clear every time I'm inside you with how loud you get and the look on your face."

Everett felt his face flush and he looked around even though they hadn't seen another person on the entire hike.

Jake chuckled. "I'm kidding. Why are you so embarrassed right now?"

"I don't know," said Everett. "I'm still pretty new to all this."

"Affairs? I thought those were pretty common among lawyers."

"No," said Everett. "Well, yes. The affair. But I meant mostly the other stuff."

"The other stuff?"

"The... the gay stuff."

Jake laughed. "What do you mean the gay stuff?"

"I mean what we've practically spent all our time doing. The sex."

Jake hesitated mid-stride before recovering. "I know what you meant by that. I'm just confused. You're gay, right?"

Everett was quiet for a long time.

"Right?" asked Jake again.

"I would label myself as bisexual. If I had to label myself at all."

"Well, that still makes you a queer. I was afraid you were about to say you were straight—then I'd be really confused."

Everett gave a nervous chuckle. "You know, I've never said that out loud."

"What?"

"I'm bisexual."

Jakes stopped walking and looked at Everett. "So when you say you're new to all this..."

"I mean all of it. I've never had a relationship with a man. I've never said out loud who I really am."

Jake's jaw dropped.

"So..." began Jake before pausing again to collect his thoughts. "Is that what this is about? You brought me out here to come out to me? Because I hate to tell you, but I already kind of figured you were into men." Jake winked at Everett.

Everett smiled a nervous smile in return.

"No. Yes. I just need to figure out what is going on."

Jake stood looking at Everett, saying nothing.

"Why me, Jake?"

"I don't know, Everett. We're just born this way regardless of what the bible thumpers say."

"No. I mean, why did you come up to me in the gym that first morning?"

"I liked what I saw."

"I doubt that."

"Why?" asked Jake.

"You're so much younger than I am. I'm in shape, but not a model by any means. You're gorgeous. You can have anyone you wanted."

"And I did. I wanted you."

They continued to walk down the trail in silence for several minutes as they both became lost in their own thoughts.

"It's just weird," said Everett.

Jake said nothing as the crunch of gravel filled the space between them.

"I guess I can accept you wanted me, but the way you did it was... very forward."

Jake smiled. "It got your attention didn't it?"

It was Everett's turn to smile.

"Look, Everett, I'm not sure what this is all about. But, I did what I did because I thought you were hot. I wanted to get your attention, so I did it in a way I knew you couldn't ignore."

"That was a big risk. What if I turned out to be some homophobe and beat you up?"

"I've known who I was for a long time, Everett. My gaydar is rarely wrong."

Everett glanced over at Jake who returned the look. The two shared an awkward smile.

"Why are you on my jury, Jake?"

"I supposed because the lawyers didn't dismiss me." Jake smirked at Everett.

"I was going to. I was seconds away from it. But I know what I saw—you warned me off. I should have done it anyway, but I was panicked."

"Why were you panicked?"

"Oh, maybe because the man I'm having an affair with showed up in the jury box in the biggest case of my career and that threatened to derail my entire life if anyone found out."

"Fair enough."

"You didn't answer the question," said Everett.

"Yes, I did—the first time you asked it when you confronted me all freaked the hell out thinking we were going to be sent to jail."

"We could have been sent to jail. Still could."

"No one is going to find out."

"You don't know that." There was an edge in Everett's voice.

"It's a risk I'm willing to take."

"It's a risk you forced on me without consent," said Everett.

"You did consent. You could have dismissed me, but you didn't."

"Because you shook your head right before I was going to."

"That's not the same as holding a gun to your head."

"Jake, please answer my question."

"I already told you, Everett. I didn't want jury duty—no one ever does—but when I got in that courtroom and saw you in there I knew I wanted to be on your jury because I wanted to see you in action. More importantly, I wanted to be around you more. It's not easy having a boyfriend marred to a woman—too scared of ruining his straight man image and perfect facade of a lifestyle to be seen in public with me. When I got called into the box, I wanted to stay. I wanted to see my lawyer boyfriend in action. I wanted to be in that room with you. To see you where you're happiest."

"No offense Jake, but that sounds a little like bullshit to me. You could have just as easily come to the trial and sat in the gallery rather than trying to get on the jury."

"So you would want me to come every day to trial and sit in a mostly empty gallery and have all those people wondering who I was and what I was doing there?"

Everett thought for a moment and shook his slightly. "No, I suppose not. But, what you did is kind of stupid and has put us in quite a predicament."

"No one needs to know, Everett. No one is going to find out. We've been very careful."

Everett considered Jake's response and thought of how naive it was. It was easy for him to forget how much younger Jake was and what it was like to be in one's twenties. Everett had probably been naive when he was Jake's age too. Of course, the predicament they were in couldn't fairly be blamed on Jake. It was mostly of Everett's own doing; he should have dismissed Jake from the jury. He should have been thinking clearly. He never should have started this affair begin with. Everett was glad he had though, despite the risks.

The crunch of gravel had been replaced by the soft swish and crumple of fallen leaves as they continued walking further into the woods.

Clearing his throat, Everett considered his next move. He knew what he wanted to ask, but didn't know if he should. It was like cross examining a witness. Was he about to ask one question too many and have everything blow up in his face?

"Why did you lie to me?"

"I didn't lie to you," said Jake, an edge to his voice. "I've told you that twice now. If you don't believe me that's on you."

"No, I mean why did you lie to me about who you are, Jeremy?"

Jake stopped walking and turned to face Everett. His shoulders were tense, and anger flashed in his eyes.

"Did you not think I would find out?" continued Everett. "Did you not think that when they used your real name calling you into the box I wouldn't try to find out as much as I could about the man who had been fucking me? Who instead of saying hello started off our interactions by kissing me in the shower? How could you possibly not think I would look into your background? You'd have to be stupid to think I wouldn't find out."

"I'm not going to be lectured about lying by you of all people."

"What is that supposed to mean?" asked Everett through a clenched jaw.

"It means you have spent your whole life lying about who you are too. You put on this image that you think means success. A lawyer with a trophy wife he despises, and desires he won't even acknowledge to himself. Refusing to acknowledge to anyone who you are. Well, I know who you are. I know what you are. I've seen it in the look of ecstasy on your face when I'm inside you. You're a faggot. Just like me."

Everett clenched his fists, and the muscles in his arms tensed. Before he knew what he was doing, he took a swing.

Chapter Forty

Jake ducked the blow just before it landed. He had had his share of beatings by Johns over the years, so was no stranger to fighting. None had been as bad as the ones his father had given him when he had discovered Jake was gay.

Everett stumbled as his right hook met the air, but was able to shift his weight before he fell to the ground.

"Why didn't you tell me your real name?" he screamed.

"I did. Jake is my middle name."

Everett took another swing, which Jake blocked.

"Or that you were a prostitute?"

"Something tells me that would not have been a good way to start our relationship."

"Don't get cute with me," Everett said through gritted teeth.

"I was born cute," said Jake with a smirk. His legs tensed, ready to dodge another swing.

"Fuck you," said Everett as he rushed forward.

Jake side-stepped and extended his leg, tripping Everett. He chuckled as he watched Everett stumble forward and face plant into the grass. Jake took the moment to look around.

"So where do we go from here?" asked Jake.

"What the fuck do you mean?" asked Everett getting back up to his feet.

"I mean where do we go from here?" said Jake, motioning with his hand. "We're at a dead end."

The two had walked off the trail while they were lost in conversation and were now in a small meadow surrounded by trees and no trail ahead of them.

Everett glanced around; his breathing was heavy. Anger still burned in his eyes.

Jake returned Everett's stare. "Look, I'm sorry I didn't tell you everything. I liked you. And after we starting hooking up more and became more of a thing, I wanted to tell you, but by then it seemed like it was too late. I didn't want to ruin things between us or scare you off."

Everett unclenched his fists and relaxed his shoulders as he considered what Jake said. The cynical part of him that made him so good at his job wasn't sure if he believed the words Jake had uttered. His heart wanted to believe and was currently winning the debate.

Jake smiled at Everett. "But, I'm not going to apologize for calling you a faggot. Because you are—whether you want to admit it or not." He smiled at Everett.

The anger that was beginning to dissipate within Everett returned with the slur and he rushed toward Jake to tackle him.

Bracing himself, Jake waited until Everett was inches away before spinning on the balls of his feet and hip checking him. He grabbed Everett's shoulders and lifted Everett off the ground, slamming his back into the grass. Everett exhaled a soft grunt of pain.

Jake jumped on top of him before Everett could make to get up again, his strong thighs straddling Everett's torso and squeezing tight to hold him in place. Jake reached out and grabbed each of Everett's wrists in his hand, pressing them firmly into the ground. He leaned over Everett, staring into his eyes.

The tension lingering in air between the two turned from anger to desire as they both continued to breath heavily and stared into one another's eyes. Jake leaned forward and kissed Everett, who after a moment of refusal gave in to the feel of Jake's soft lips. He allowed the tension in his body to release and submitted to Jake's advances.

The mid-morning sun shone brightly on the two as they kissed on the grassy floor of the meadow. The beams of light coming through the canopy warmed both of them. Jake released his hands from around Everett's wrists and straightened to a sitting position before removing his shirt.

Everett stared up at Jake and his bare chest. He allowed a smile to cross his face as he took in Jake's defined torso. He reached out with his hand and ran it over the contours of Jake's smooth skin. Everett felt himself harden.

Feeling the same, Jake smiled down at Everett before sliding his body lower over him toward his legs. He gripped both sides of Everett's waistband and with one smooth motion yanked the athletic shorts down to his knees. He took Everett in his hand and applied a firm yet gentle grip before lowering himself and taking Everett deep into his mouth.

Everett moaned as Jake worked his shaft while cradling his balls. The contrast between the warm wetness of the blowjob and the gentle breeze blowing through the trees and over his skin only made him harder.

Jake's tenderness vanished and he violently flipped Everett onto his stomach, ripping his shorts the rest of the way off and tossing them aside in a crumpled pile. Jake forced Everett's legs open with his knee and leaned over the top of him, pressing the side of Everett's face into the ground with his hand.

Everett gasped and felt a momentary pressure as he gave in to Jake. A long, low moan escaped his lips when Jake entered him. Everett could feel Jake's breath on his ear as he lowered his face toward his.

"Faggot," Jake whispered. Everett smiled and moaned louder as Jake pushed deeper inside.

The two laid naked side-by-side in the grass after Jake was finished. They kissed and embraced each other, running their hands over one another's bodies and through their hair and then they made love again.

Once they were both completely spent and exhausted, Everett and Jake lay on their stomachs allowing the sun to warm their skin. Everett admired the beauty of Jake's nakedness, head on crossed arms and a sleepy look in his eyes. *It's like looking at Adam in the garden*, he thought. *The closest to heaven I'll probably ever get.*

Jake caught Everett's gaze and smiled at him. "What are you thinking about?" he asked.

Everett held Jake's eyes but didn't say anything in return. Just as the silence was becoming unbearable and a concerned look began to cross Jake's face, Everett said the words he had felt for weeks but had been too afraid to say.

"I love you."

Chapter Forty-One

The scalding water flowed down his neck and back as he rested his head against the tile. Everett was relieved to find Olivia was out when he came home from his hike with Jake. He needed time to himself. To think. Too sulk. To cry.

I love you, he had said as they both lay naked under the sun, spent from their fight and the make-up sex.

What had Jake said back?

Nothing.

Jake stood and walked toward his pile of crumpled clothes amongst the grass and leaves. He got dressed in silence then looked at Everett and said with a somber face, "We should probably get going."

Everett had laid there looking at Jake in stunned silence. He couldn't move. The air had been knocked out of him no differently than had Jake actually punched him in the gut. The meadow tilted and then spun, and Everett felt the color drain from his face before it came rushing back all at once in embarrassment, making his cheeks and ears feel like they were on fire.

Everett rose up on his elbows and opened his mouth to speak. Perhaps Jake hadn't heard him. Maybe Jake misunderstood what he had said. He knew that was a lie. He could see it in Jake's face. The face that was turning away from him and walking toward the trail they had arrived on.

Everett rose to his feet and called after him, "Jake. Wait."

Jake kept walking and was almost out of the meadow.

"Jake!"

"I need to go, Everett. I'm sorry. I'll talk to you later."

Everett stood there paralyzed and overcome with emotions as he watched Jake begin jogging down the trail and out of sight. He felt his knees go weak and his stomach churn, and Everett sat back down in the soft grass. He stared down the trail after Jake for a long time, his mind numb and uncomprehending.

It was a half-hour before Everett had recovered. He stood and quickly got dressed, then walked the long trail back to the parking lot where Jake's car had long since departed. On his walk, his embarrassment and bewilderment turned to anger. By the time he had reached his car, the anger had given way to dread.

Everett slid behind the driver seat wondering what this meant for he and Jake. He wondered what it meant for his case. The nausea returned to his stomach and his heart rate increased.

Now at home, his back was almost fire engine red from the water as he stood in the shower lightly banging his head on the tiled wall. He replayed the events of that afternoon over and over in his mind. Everett couldn't believe he had gotten himself into this situation in the first place. He had shown incredibly poor judgment, and hadn't thought about the endgame and how any of this may affect his life. He was unsure what would happen, how the pieces would continue to move on the board and that made him worry the most. What was worse is he could confide in and seek advice from no one. He would have to suffer in silence.

"Are you okay?"

Everett jumped and opened his eyes. He turned to face the door of the master bathroom where Olivia now stood in the threshold with a puzzled look on her face.

"I'm fine, "Everett said, though it was barely audible under the din of the flowing water.

"You don't look fine," said Olivia as a concerned expression moved over her face. "Are you sure everything is okay?"

Everett opened his mouth to speak and but closed it quickly. In his heart he wanted to confess. He wanted to tell someone what was wrong and what worried him. To tell someone what he had done.

To tell someone who he really was. His mind pushed those emotions away as it so often did, and he simply turned and shut off the water.

"Yes, everything is fine," he said as he stepped out of the shower and grabbed a towel from the rack. "I was just running through the case in my mind. Replaying the testimony and thinking of next moves."

Olivia's lips pouted. "That's too bad. I know you wanted some respite from that case and to clear your head today."

"It's okay. I was fine until I got in the shower," lied Everett. He managed a half-smile and said, "You know how I get my best ideas in the shower. It was bound to happen."

"Was the hike at least enjoyable?"

"It was great, until the end when it got a little rough."

Olivia looked poised to ask a follow up question, but Everett changed the subject. "Where did you go?" he asked.

"Just ran some errands and went to the bookstore to find something to read."

"Let me guess: another romance novel?" said Everett with a smirk.

"Well, I have to get my romance from somewhere," chided Olivia.

The smile vanished from Everett's face.

"I didn't mean it like that," said Olivia. "It was just a joke."

"I know. It's okay," said Everett flatly.

"Besides, I don't really need these books—I got my hot man right here in front me," she said as she gave him a playful nudge to his chest.

Everett faked a smile the best he could in return. He worried he may have lost his hot man.

Chapter Forty-Two

The courtroom was silent as the jury shuffled into the box early Monday morning. Everett fought to keep his hands still and display confidence. He watched the jurors; some looked around the room, some made eye contact with him, others gave a polite smile.

Jake was the last juror to take his place in the box. Everett stared at him intently. He hadn't spoken to him since Jake abruptly left him in the woods two days before, and he was hoping to get a read on him.

Jake took his seat and kept his eyes downcast. Everett felt his heart sink as he turned his attention back to his legal pad on the table.

"Good morning," Judge Clement said to the jury with a slight smile before turning his attention to Everett. "Call your next witness, Mr. Stone."

"Your Honor, we call Annie Smith to the stand," announced Everett.

As she climbed the witness stand and placed her hand on the bible to swear her oath, Annie held her head high with her shoulders back. She stared at Ross Tyndall as the clerk asked if she promised to tell the truth and nothing but. Annie held her gaze on Tyndall as she said she did with resolve in her soft voice.

"When did you begin working at Peaceful Pines?" asked Everett.

"About two weeks before Mr. Thomas died."

"Did you meet Ross Tyndall at that time?"

"No," replied Annie. "I met with Bill Tremaine, who was the manager. I never met Mr. Tyndall."

"Why not?" asked Everett. He wanted to remind the jury as many times as possible where Tyndall was while one of his residents died in his facility.

"He was in prison when I worked there."

"Why did you apply for a job at Peaceful Pines?" asked Everett.

"I went into nursing to help people. I wanted to work with dementia patients because you can make a real difference in their lives. You can help them feel better, give them consistency, and, more importantly, give them companionship in their later years since family tends to abandon them once they're in a facility like that." Annie gave a quick glance toward Monica.

"How would you describe working at Peaceful Pines?" asked Everett.

"My initial impression was it was going to be great. Mr. Tremaine discussed during the interview about the pride they placed in the care they provided to their patients and the quality of their staff. It sounded like a sales pitch, and a compelling one at that. I was excited to join the team when he offered me the job at the end of the interview."

"Did you find anything odd about the interview?"

"He asked very few questions of me. And I didn't receive a tour of the facility, which was somewhat odd."

"Did your excitement about your position last once you started?"

"No, not at all," replied Annie.

"Why not?"

"When I walked in that first day, I was immediately taken aback. When you walk in past the lobby, you get to the dining area where most of the residents were eating breakfast. The first thing that hit me was the smell. It wasn't the food—that was just oatmeal for every single patient. There was a strong odor of urine and fecal matter in the room, as if many of the residents who had incontinence issues hadn't been changed.

"And there was just a general lack of staff around. There was a single staff member in the dining hall to cover a dozen residents."

"What did you do next?"

"I was assigned my patients. I recall being assigned to Mr. Thomas. And then I looked through their patient charts to familiarize myself with them in terms of their medical conditions, routine medications, and other pertinent information."

"How was Mr. Thomas the first time you met him?" asked Everett.

"Not good."

"How so?"

"His dementia was advanced. He didn't have a good grasp of where he was, or even who he was. But, that's not uncommon. It was the rest of it that made me gasp when I first walked into his room," testified Annie.

"Can you please tell the jury what you saw?"

"The first thing that hit me again was the smell. It was clear his adult diaper had not been changed in a while. Then I noticed how frail he looked. Not just weak, but emaciated. You could see his bones through his skin. His face had an expression that appeared to me that he was in pain.

"As I got closer, I noticed his skin was covered in grime and it looked like he hadn't been bathed in a while. Then I noticed his skin looked flaky and his hair looked like straw. His nails appeared brittle."

Everett paused. He glanced at the jury box and noticed many of them glaring at the defense table. Jake was looking down at his feet. Everett glanced the other way at his client and noticed she was looking ahead at Annie with a stoic expression. *Would it kill her to show some emotion for her own father?* he wondered.

"What did that indicate to you?"

"Objection," said Wright standing to his feet. "This witness is not a medical doctor. She's merely a nurse."

"Overruled," snapped Judge Clement.

"What did that indicate to you?" Everett asked again.

"The smell and his dirty appearance indicated to me that he had been neglected. That the nurse who was assigned before me had not taken care of his hygiene properly. More importantly, the condition of his skin, hair and nails told me that he was severely malnourished."

"What did you do next?"

"I introduced myself and tried to talk to Mr. Thomas, but he seemed completely out of it and not even aware of my presence. I next double checked his patient chart because I just could not believe what I was seeing. The level of neglect was something I had never encountered before as a nurse."

"What did the chart tell you?"

"The opposite of what I was seeing."

Annie paused for dramatic effect. She had worked hard when going over her testimony with Everett leading up to trial. Everett gave a slight nod signaling that she should continue.

"The chart indicated he had been receiving all his medications as scheduled. It showed regular bathing and hygiene care. It showed he had regularly been taking his meals. That was not consistent with what I was seeing with my own eyes."

Annie next told the jury about how she had cleaned Harry up; changing him for the first time in what she thought had been days. Bathed him with a sponge, which took considerable effort to get all the grime off him while at the same time taking care not to cause him too much pain. She told the jury about how he flinched at even the slightest touch because of his malnutrition and lack of medication. Annie told the jury about how tears welled up in her eyes as she bathed him and noticed the numerous bed sores on his back, buttocks and legs. How it was clear to her that Harry had not been out of bed for a long time, and that no one on staff had bothered to rotate him to keep his skin from breaking down.

Everett kept glancing toward the jury as Annie told her story. The men either crossed their arms in disgust and stared angrily at

Tyndall and his table full of lawyers. The women stared down at the floor to try to hide tears that were forming in their eyes. Even Monica had retrieved a tissue from her purse and was dabbing the corners of her eyes as Annie recounted in graphic detail what her father had gone through.

Everett next glanced at the defense table and saw several of the junior lawyers with uncomfortable expressions on their face. Even Wright's practiced poker face cracked and Everett could see the slightest traces of worry and concern.

Judge Clement's typically serious and sour expression had softened as he listened. Perhaps he was thinking of Harry; or, Everett suspected he may be thinking more of himself and what may await him in only a few short years.

The only people in the courtroom who seemed unaffected by Annie's testimony were Tyndall and Sloan.

Chapter Forty-Three

Annie returned to the witness stand at the conclusion of a much-needed morning recess. She looked at Tyndall directly with the same fiery determination in her eyes as she had when the day began. *Fuck you*, her eyes seemed to say.

During the recess, Everett had remained in the courtroom standing next to counsel table, stretching his legs and gathering his thoughts for the remainder of her testimony. If the jury thought what they had heard so far was shocking, they were in for a surprise for the second half.

When recess was called, Jake had gone immediately to the jury room and Everett hadn't seen him come out. It felt like Jake was trying to torture him by avoiding any kind of eye contact the entire day. Everett had let Jake know how he felt in the woods, and he was beginning to feel nauseous at the thought that Jake might be sending him a message concerning how Jake felt about him.

With recess over and trial resumed, Everett stole another quick glance at the jury box before he asked his next question. It was time to get his head back in the game and focus on finishing Tyndall once and for all.

"I was screamed at," said Annie as she began recounting for the jury her attempts to give Harry the care he needed. "Mr. Tremaine refused to allow me access to Mr. Thomas's medications. Said it cost the company too much money. I pointed out that, according to the chart, he had been getting his medications and he told me not to worry about that."

"Do you know what he meant?"

"Not at the time, no, but I have since found out."

"What do you mean?"

Wright rose to his feet and objected, but Judge Clement quickly overruled him.

"The medications reflected in the electronic chart were a lie."

Everett stood from his seat and approached Annie, handing her an exhibit. She told the jury the documents were copies of Harry's electronic medical record. Everett then walked back to counsel table and projected the records on a screen for the jury to see.

Annie quickly walked the jurors through how to read the records and what they showed. They were textbook perfect: medications delivered on time and in compliance with physician's orders; regular bathings and hygiene work; and regular meals.

"How do you know these were a lie?" asked Everett.

"Because I found the paper flow sheets before they fired me. Flow sheets are what we use to keep track of what is going on during our rounds before we enter the information into the electronic medical system. Once the information is entered, the flow sheets are kept in the chart, but because there are so many they usually get thinned out regularly and placed in storage. Although no one showed me where they were located, I happened upon them during my time there and checked Mr. Thomas's records."

Everett projected another record on the screen, and left it side-by-side with the electronic version. Annie explained what the notations on the flow sheet meant, although she didn't have to because anyone could easily see the electronic record had been altered. The handwritten record told a story of incompetence and neglect.

Everett walked Annie through several more records for dramatic effect. The jury's scowls were growing deeper, and Wright shifted uncomfortably in his seat.

"Where did you find these records, Ms. Smith?"

"I found them in the storage room. They were hidden behind some of the cleaning supplies along with some trash that needed to be taken out. It looked to me like they were going to get rid of them."

"Are these all the records you found?"

"No, there were several boxes. You need to understand that in an inpatient setting, the amount of paperwork generated per patient is enormous. It would be tens of thousands of pages for a patient admitted as long as Mr. Thomas."

"Where are the rest of the records then?"

"These were just the ones I could take with me on short notice," said Annie. "I don't know what happened to the rest of the handwritten, original records."

Everett did, and soon the jury would know too.

"Why did you take the records?"

"I knew something was seriously wrong when I found the records. I took what I could sneak out for evidence. I wanted to protect my patients."

"Was Mr. Thomas the only patient whose records you found?"

"No, the handwritten records were there for most of the patients."

"You were eventually fired from Peaceful Pines, is that correct?"

"Yes."

"Do you know why they fired you?" asked Everett.

"They said it was because I wasn't doing my job."

"From your perspective, was that true?"

Wright lodged another objection that was quickly overruled.

"Absolutely not. In fact, they fired me for doing my job how I'm supposed to do it under the standard of care. As the days went by, I realized that when Mr. Tremaine had told me not to worry about things that I absolutely needed to worry about them. I noticed the nurses on the other shifts weren't doing hygiene and medication administration. But the charts kept saying they were. I talked to some other nurses to try to find out what was going on, but they told me to keep my mouth shut and do whatever Mr. Tremaine said if I wanted to be able to make my rent.

"That didn't sit right with me. I needed the job, but I'm not going to do anything unethical or illegal. I'm not going to put my license in jeopardy. I can always find another job, but not if my ability to do so is taken away by the State. I told Mr. Tremaine I was going to do proper patient care and document the charts accordingly. He told me if that was the case, then I could go home and not come back. So that's what I did."

• • • •

Wright did his best on cross examination to undo the damage. Annie faced his questioning defiantly and answered in short, matter-of-fact sentences to show him and the jury she was not afraid of him or the truth.

"You didn't have permission to remove the medical records?" asked Wright.

"No."

"So you stole them?"

"That's one what of putting it."

"An accurate way?"

"Yes, I suppose."

"Now, Ms. Smith," said Wright as he moved to another line of questioning, "is it unheard of for changes to be made when transferring data from a flow sheet into an electronic medical record?"

"It's not unheard of, no."

"That's because sometimes in the moment a nurse can record the information on the flow sheet wrong, and then go back and change it in the EMR."

"That's correct."

"Kind of like a typo?"

"Yes."

"And you would agree, it's entirely possible these entries in the EMRs were corrections of errors on the flow sheets?"

"No."

"No?" scoffed Wright.

"Sir, perhaps a small handful of entries could account for that possibility. But every single entry was changed that I saw. That indicates to me, in my experience, a deliberate attempt to change the substance of the records."

"But you don't know that for certain. You didn't speak with any of the nurses who wrote that material on the flow sheets."

"I couldn't. They no longer worked there."

"And you didn't speak with anyone who entered the information in the EMR."

"That's correct, sir," answered Annie.

"Ma'am, you were upset when you were terminated, correct?" asked Wright.

"Yes, I was upset. I think anyone would be."

"And you were angry."

"Yes, I was. I was doing my job properly and was fired for it."

"So angry you stole documents from the facility."

Annie didn't respond to the statement disguised as a question.

"Ms. Smith?" prompted Wright.

"Yes, that's correct."

"And you ran straight into the arms of plaintiff and her attorney."

"Because I wanted to help stop what was going on there."

"The facility had a five star rating, did it not?"

"Yes, that's true."

Wright continued with his questioning and even went so far as to try to suggest that nothing could have been done to save Mr. Thomas, despite what the records showed. To Everett, his theme seemed to be "old people just die sometimes."

Everett watched the jury closely during the cross examination and saw most of them rolling their eyes or looking around the courtroom. Wright was doing a decent job with the cards that he had been dealt, but he was holding no cards of any use. The jury didn't care about a single point he made. Since the cross had been so ineffective, Everett decided not to redirect once Wright was finished. There was no need wasting the jury's time.

Everett watched as the jurors shuffled out of the courtroom at the end of the day. Jake was the first one out of the door and vanished down the stairwell. Everett finished packing up his briefcase with his materials and offered reassuring words to Monica before turning to leave himself.

Tyndall caught Everett's eye as he walked past the bar and toward the doors at the back of the courtroom. Tyndall winked in Everett's direction.

Everett kept walking and didn't react. Still, the bravado Tyndall was showing in the face of this trial confused Everett.

Something felt wrong.

Chapter Forty-Four

E verett stood in his office before the large windows. He took another sip of his whiskey while he waited, the ice cubes clinking against the thick glass as he raised it to his lips. The office was silent this late in the evening, the staff having left long ago.

A text message had come through on his phone as he was stepping onto the elevator in the courthouse. *I need to see you*, it read. *Come to my place.*

After reading it, he fired off a text to Olivia and told her that he would be working late that night getting ready for the next day of trial.

No, not your place, he typed to Jake. *You can meet me in my office in an hour.* That had given him enough time to pour himself a whiskey and to try to calm his nerves.

Everett took another long sip, the glass now half-empty, as he looked at his watch. He took a deep breath. Anxiety buzzed within him; hope and anger competing with each other for dominance.

The faint echo of a door closing traveled down the hallway. Everett turned to face his office door, bracing himself for... what? He didn't know what to expect.

Jake appeared in the threshold as Everett took another sip. He was still dressed for court in a pair of tight fitting chinos and a tapered dress shirt, his blue eyes sparkling under blonde hair.

"Hi," Jake said with a faint smile.

"Hello," Everett said with as much chill in his voice as he could muster.

The two stood looking at each other as an awkward silence settled in the room. Jake stepped though the threshold.

"Thanks for letting me see you," he said.

Everett said nothing in return.

"Are you sure it's okay for me to be here?" asked Jake. "I know last time I came you were a little upset, given the trial and all." A flirtatious smile crossed his lips.

"It's fine," said Everett. In truth, he wasn't sure it was or that even meeting Jake was a good idea. But, Everett wanted his office to be the setting of whatever this was about. He wanted to be on his own turf, where he had the power.

Jake hesitated before speaking again, shoving his hands into his pockets as Everett stared him down with a practiced poker face.

"Look," he said drawing a deep breath, "I just wanted to say I'm sorry."

He met Everett's cold eyes and waited for a response that seemed to take an eternity to arrive.

"That's it?" asked Everett.

Jake opened his mouth to speak but was cut off by Everett's anger, which had boiled to the surface with the apology.

"That's all you have to say? 'I'm sorry?'," demanded Everett. "I trusted you, Jake. You came on to me in that gym. In a moment of weakness, I let you. I should have shoved you away and never let any of this happen but I stupidly didn't. I trusted you with my marriage. I trusted you with my career when you got in that box and stayed there. With my reputation. Then, after all the time we spent together, all those moments of what I thought was reciprocal passion and affection, I trusted you with my heart while we were both in that field. And you just walked away. No, not walk. You literally ran away."

Jake looked down at the floor, his cheeks reddening.

"And you expect to come in here and apologize with a smile and... and what... what are you really doing here, Jake? What do you want from me? Because all you have done is taken from me. You took my body. You took my peace of mind. You took my heart. What could you possibly want now?"

Everett didn't give Jake a chance to respond before continuing.

"What do you want? Money? That's what you do, right? Seduce men with your smile and looks and then take off your clothes for some cash? You finally want your payday for all the sex?"

Jake raised his head, glaring at Everett. "Fuck you," he spat.

"You already did," Everett sneered. "In every way possible."

Jake took a step forward, removing his hands from his pockets. They were now clenched into white-knuckled fists.

Everett took a step forward in response, setting his drink down on his desk and bracing himself.

The two stood staring each other in the eyes. Their bodies rigid and breath heavy, like two fighters in a ring ready to start a match.

"I didn't know what to do," said Jake after a few more tense moments. His hands unclenched and his voice broke as he spoke.

"I'm sorry. I didn't know what to do," he repeated, shaking his head. Tears were welling in his eyes. "I was scared. I was scared of letting you in. I was scared of what I was about to say to you in that field. I felt trapped, and my instincts told me to run. Because that's what my life has always been. Running. Running from home when my parents beat me because they found out I was gay. Running from the law because the only way I could make a living on the street was turning tricks and breaking other laws. Running from the shame of how I made my money back then. Running away from being hurt. Again."

Everett felt the tension release from his muscles and his face soften. "What were you going to say?" he asked.

"What?" Jake asked though tears.

"You said you were scared of what you were going to say in that field. What was it?"

"That I love you too."

Chapter Forty-Five

"Are you stupid?" screamed Wright as he slammed his hand on the conference room table.

Tyndall stared defiantly into Wright's eyes from across the expansive table. Between them, the army of associates had their eyes downcast. Sloan sat next to Tyndall with a smile on his face.

"Don't speak to me that way," sneered Tyndall.

"I don't know how else to speak to you at this point," said Wright. "You haven't listened to a damn word I've said this entire case. It's time you start listening."

"I have listened," countered Tyndall. "It's just you've been wrong this entire time."

The veins in Wright's neck bulged and his face turned a dark crimson. He stood from his seat and walked to the windows, taking in the same view of the state capital as Everett.

"You know," began Wright, "part of me wishes I could just throw you right out this window. I have never in my life met someone so obstinate and arrogant and fully entrenched in an erroneous position"

Several of the other attorneys looked up with startled expressions. One of the more senior members of the team pushed his chair a few inches from the table and tensed; ready to intervene in the event his boss made good on his threat.

Tyndall chuckled. "I'd like to see you try."

Wright took a deep breath as the room descended into silence.

"We need to settle this case. Now," said Wright. It was at least the fifth time he had made the comment since the meeting started after court.

"No," said Tyndall.

"Help us understand then, Ross, why you don't want to settle. You have an entire room full of lawyers and every one of them is is advising you to do so," said Wright.

"I'm not," said Sloan.

Wright and his underlings all glared at Sloan in unison. They looked upon him the same way they might a smear of dog shit on the bottom of their designer shoes.

"He's right," said Tyndall with a chuckle. "Sloan's the only lawyer here that has some sense."

"We'll have to agree to disagree on that," said Wright.

"Look, gentlemen," said Tyndall. "I understand you believe what you are saying. I understand all the experience in this room. But, please understand that I also have experience. This is not my first rodeo either and all of you know I've been sued by families chasing the ambulance before. I am not willing to offer what Stone wants. I am not willing to offer money out of my own pocket to settle—that's my money."

"It could be a lot more of your money when this verdict comes down. It could, in fact, be all of your money," countered Wright. "How many times do I have to say that?"

"I doubt that. In fact, I don't think it will even get to a verdict."

It was Wright's turn to chuckle. "What makes you think that?"

"I am confident Stone will come to his senses. He will settle the case."

"You're delusional," said Wright. "If this was a criminal trial, I would be demanding the court order a competency test. Sloan, he listens to you. Surely you must see how hopeless this case is. Talk some sense in him."

"I agree with him," replied Sloan. "Stone will end up taking the insurance money before any verdict is returned in this case."

Wright's jaw dropped once more.

"What makes you so sure of that?" said one of the other lawyers.

"Because it's a win-win for everyone," said Sloan. "He gets his money, his client gets her money, and we keep our money."

"Sloan, it's not just about the money," said Wright. "He's out for blood. He wants to shut you down. And in the process, he'll make a hell of a lot more than the insurance coverage."

"You let me and Sloan worry about that," said Tyndall. "I'm telling you, this case will go away before it ever gets to verdict. At the end of the day, Stone will play it safe and take the money."

"Based on what, Ross? We have nothing to defend this case with. The only thing we have going for us is that Monica Thomas is not a sympathetic witness. But, a jury's going to look past that. Records were altered, and worse. A man was killed. This is as close to a slam dunk case as you can get as a lawyer. So tell me. What makes the two of you so sure Stone is going to settle?"

Tyndall and Sloan looked down the long table at Wright and smiled.

Chapter Forty-Six

Jake's tears bled though Everett's shirt. After his confession, Everett enveloped Jake in his arms, squeezing tight. The two stood in the middle of the office and said nothing for the longest time.

"It's okay, Jake," said Everett fighting back tears of his own. "I understand now. It's okay."

Jake continued sobbing against Everett's chest, his shoulders shuddering.

"I'm sorry I hurt you," Jake said. "I'm so sorry."

"It's okay. It's alright now. I understand," repeated Everett.

"But it's not, is it?" asked Jake as he stepped out of Everett's embrace. "It's not okay."

"What do you mean?"

"What happens to us from here?" continued Jake, choking back more tears. "We both said we love each other, but how can we possibly make it work?"

"We'll figure something out," said Everett.

Jake let out a chuckle. "I don't think you believe that."

Everett took a deep breath to steel himself against the truth of Jake's statement. He loved Jake. He loved what they had. But, Jake was right. How could they possibly make it work? Everett was a married man. On some level, he still loved Olivia. Although their marriage was on life support, there was still a chance things could turn around. Things had been better recently. Even still, a split from Olivia would invite too many questions. Questions about why. A divorce involves litigation and he had no doubt Olivia would make things difficult for him. Those lawyers would do investigations. Send people to track his movements and look for dirt that they could use against him. Everett couldn't risk it. He couldn't risk anyone finding out and potentially risking his image and reputation. He couldn't risk people knowing who he really was. He didn't want to be out, and didn't think he ever would be ready.

"Jake," began Everett. "I do believe it. Because we've already figured something out. We've already got all that we need."

"You mean keep sneaking around? Fuck sessions in private places and nothing more? Everett, I don't think I can do that long term. You're not a hook up to me. This is the first time I've felt something real for a man in a long, long time. We love each other—we've admitted that. I want to go to dinner with the man I love. To the movies. Hold hands in the park. We can't do that."

Everett's heart broke at the thought of what could be. He took an unsteady step back and sat calmly in his desk chair, resting his elbows on the arms rests and raising his fingers to massage his temples.

"Jake," he said, "I was wearing a ring."

"What?"

"I was wearing a ring when you came on to me. I was wearing a ring that first time in the gym shower. You knew I was married, or should have known."

Jake took in a sigh. "I know. But at the time I just wanted to have some fun. I didn't... I didn't expect to develop feelings for you. But, I did."

Everett allowed a smile to cross his face. He had wanted nothing more than sex at the beginning and then the same thing happened to him. The irony of their situation would be comical if it wasn't also tragic.

"I know," he said. "I think both of us wanted the same thing at first, and now we're both stuck in this problematic situation."

The conversation paused as the two stared toward one another but not at each other, looking beyond and lost in their thoughts.

Everett stood from his chair and walked over to Jake, taking him in his arms once more.

"Give me some time. We'll figure this out," he whispered into Jake's ear.

Jake's blonde hair tickled the side of Everett's cheek as he nodded in agreement.

"Let's get through this trial. It's not just Olivia we have to worry about. We're in a much more precarious position because you're on my jury and we need to continue to be discreet for both our sakes until that's over. Once it's safe, we'll figure something out. I promise."

Jake lifted his head off Everett's shoulder and looked into his eyes. "Everything will work out," Everett said with a reassuring half-smile. "I'll figure it out. I always do."

Jake returned the half-smile and nodded as Everett's hand rose and caressed the side of Jake's face. The delicate touch traveled toward the back of his head as Everett ran his fingers through his blonde hair and pulled him in close. Their soft lips touched in a long slow-burning kiss.

"You know what the best part of a fight is?" asked Jake, moving his hands down Everett's back and gripping his ass.

"What?" Everett said with a smile.

There was a metallic clink between the two as Jake's hands moved to Everett's front and undid his belt.

"The make-up sex."

Chapter Forty-Seven

The ding of the elevator and soft *whoosh* of the door opening prompted Everett to walk forward into the car. He didn't bother looking up from his phone as he scrolled through his emails.

He couldn't erase the smile on his face after seeing Jake again, who had left thirty minutes before him.

The doors closed and Everett glanced quickly to the control panel and saw the light for the lobby was already illuminated. He was aware of someone's presence in the car with him, but paid them no mind as the elevator began its slow descent down the tall building.

Everett switched from email to scrolling through the headlines. He didn't particularly care about the news any longer. For the past few years it seemed nothing good was happening in the world. He scrolled anyway to avoid making awkward small talk with whomever was on the elevator with him.

The car came to a lurching halt as a hand reached out and pressed the stop button on the control panel. The elevator's alarm began to blare.

Everett slid his phone in his pants pocket and looked up for the first time. His mouth fell open in surprise.

Tyndall stood against the elevator wall with his arms crossed over his broad chest. Everett had never noticed how tall and imposing he was until this moment in the confined space. Tyndall was giving Everett a menacing smile.

"Mr. Stone, I was just talking about you upstairs."

"Mr. Tyndall, I can't ethically speak to you without your attorney present."

"Well, according to what I've been hearing in this trial I'm an unethical murderer, so why should the rules matter to me now?" Tyndall chuckled.

"I'm not going to have a conversation—"

"What exactly is your problem?" asked Tyndall as he cut Everett off.

Everett blinked in silence as he considered the audacity of the question.

"My problem?" asked Everett with a sharp tone in his voice.

"Yes. Your problem. You've been a real pain in my ass and I can't figure out why. Most attorneys would have taken the money and called it a day. I understand greed, as you know. But five million dollars is five million dollars, and you don't have to worry about getting nothing if you just take it and end this charade of a trial."

Everett stared at Tyndall for a few moments in stunned silence. He was used to ego and hubris in this profession, but he had encountered nothing as brazen as what he just heard. He let out an incredulous chuckle as the anger began to build in him.

"First, I'm doing this because I care," replied Everett. "I'm not in this profession just for the money. That's a part of it, I won't lie, but, I became a lawyer to help people and I can think of no better group of people that need help more than the patients you allow to suffer and die in your incompetently run facility.

"No, incompetent isn't the right word. That implies someone who doesn't know what they are doing. And you, Ross, know exactly what you're doing. Because you've done it before. And if someone doesn't stop you you'll do it again. You'll allow vulnerable, trusting people to suffer and die so you can get rich. I'm doing this with justice in mind. And that involves one of two things. Either you settle and give me so much of your own money it makes you think twice about your shady practices and you clean up your act, or a jury is going to give me a a hell of a lot more and I'll take everything you got and then some."

The two men stared at each other under scowls as Everett paused.

"Second, I'm not going to lose this trial," seethed Everett. "If you believe that then you're just as demented as your poor patients."

Tyndall slammed his fist into the start button on the elevator's control panel with such force that it shook the wall of the car. Everett flinched and took a step back.

"You act so brave, but you're really just a scared little shit," laughed Tyndall. "You can think you're a do-gooder all you want and that justice will prevail, but I'm telling you now, Stone, there is no justice. There's just us. And I'm going to win this fight. I win all my fights."

The car stopped and the doors chimed open as Everett was about to respond. Tyndall stepped off the car and yelled over his shoulder, "Get a good night's sleep, Stone. You're gonna need it."

Chapter Forty-Eight

Tyndall's threats turned out to be empty. The following days had been filled with more witnesses laying out the atrocities committed at Peaceful Pines: a former nurse Everett had found that corroborated Annie's testimony; families of residents who actually visited; doctors who had once made rounds at the facility until Tyndall realized they could not be paid off.

The defense scored few points on the cross examination of these witnesses. Everett had left court with a smile on his face.

This evening, he was smiling for a different reason. Everett thrummed along with the music on the steering wheel as he drove away from downtown and toward the suburbs. He drove past the turn that would weave him through the city's streets to his own neighborhood. Olivia had given him no resistance when he said he needed to pull another all-nighter. Everett would need to deliver big on all the promises of quality time he had made to her after the trial. His smile faded a little at the thought.

His heart fluttered as he neared his destination and the palms on his hands moistened. His smiled grew so wide in his head he imagined the comical Cheshire Cat. Everett felt like a high school senior on his way to pick up his prom date.

He whipped the Lexus into a parking space and strode quickly across the lot. He bounded up the steps to the apartment he had come to know so well, ready for a night of celebration and the first sleepover with his boyfriend.

Boyfriend. Such a simple word that for so long had been taboo for him. He now had one. It was messy and came with complications, but he would figure all that out later. Jake had asked him to spend the night by text over the lunch recess, and Everett didn't think anything could make him feel as happy has he did right then.

Pausing at the apartment door, Everett took a deep breath and tried to get ahold of himself. He wanted to make sure to act like a normal person, and not jump into Jake's arms gleefully and out of control in his love. After another deep breath, he rapped on the door and waited.

Everett knocked again. The butterflies in his stomach turned to knots, then back to butterflies again as the anticipation grew. It wasn't like Jake to keep him waiting. Perhaps he was preparing a special surprise for tonight and finishing preparations. Everett bounced on the balls of his feet. He fought the urge to kick the door in and run to Jake.

A few seconds later, Everett leaned his ear to the door as he debated whether he should knock a third time. It had been a long day in court, and a long trial, so perhaps in the two hours since court recessed Jake had accidentally fallen asleep. Everett was the lawyer, driven to stay awake by the adrenaline that came with the high stakes of the courtroom. Jurors had the harder job of sitting stoically and silently in their seats listening for close to nine hours a day without very many breaks. He could understand how it could be exhausting.

He could now hear Jake's heavy footsteps coming from the back of the apartment faintly through the door. Everett straightened himself and took a final deep breath as he heard the turn of the deadbolt and click of the lock. The door squeaked open on old hinges.

Everett's smile diminished as Jake stood before him with a dour look on his face. The look reminded Everett of the day in the woods. Jake stepped aside in the gloom of his apartment without a word and Everett followed him in.

"Is everything okay?" asked Everett.

"Yeah," Jake grunted in return. He walked from the entry way and hooked a sharp left at the living room toward the kitchen. Everett followed a few steps behind.

Jake reached into a kitchen cabinet and pulled down two whiskey glasses. He grabbed a bottle of bourbon from the counter and poured two fingers neat into each glass. Swallowing his in one gulp, Jake thrust the other glass forward in one hand while pouring himself a second round with the other.

Everett took the glass and considered the scene in front of him. Jake gulped the second glass of whiskey and began filling a third. His mood had not changed at all since opening the door. If anything, the creases in his brow only deepened and the corners of his mouth downturned further.

"Jake, what's wrong?" he asked.

"Drink your whiskey, Everett. I think you're going to need it."

Everett 's breath caught in his chest.

"You're not trying to break up with me again, are you?" asked Everett with a forced chuckle. It was a vain attempt to break through the tension.

Jake shook his head. "I think you're the one that's probably going to be breaking up with me tonight."

"What? Jake you're crazy. We've talked about this. I love you and would never break up with you."

"We'll see," said Jake as he shotgunned his third whiskey.

"Jake... just tell me. What's wrong?"

"Nothing's wrong," came a voice from down the hallway. "Everything's going quite well."

Chapter Forty-Nine

The glass shattered on the kitchen floor. A chill of recognition ran down Everett's spine. He stared straight ahead at Jake, confused and hurt. Jake stared into the empty glass in his hand and avoided Everett's gaze.

"Have a seat on the couch, counselor. We have a lot to discuss."

Everett turned toward the hallway. His empty hand trembled as he faced the man in front of him.

"What the fuck are you doing here?" he asked.

Everett hoped the tone of his voice sounded menacing, but knew it betrayed the fear running through him.

"Please, have a seat," said Sloan, gesturing toward the couch in the living room.

"Just take a seat, Everett," said Jake.

Everett turned to look at Jake, a questioning look on his face.

"Please... just do it," Jake said.

"Better listen to him, Stone. It's his house and you wouldn't want to be rude to your host, would you?" said Sloan.

Everett walked over to the couch as he locked eyes with Sloan. Rage began to simmer as he took in the smug look on the shyster's face.

"I'm glad you came," said Sloan after all three were seated around the coffee table with Everett on the couch and Jake and Sloan in the two chairs opposite. "We need to talk."

"About what?" asked Everett as his mouth ran dry.

"About settlement, of course," said Sloan.

There was a long silence between them as Everett willed himself to regain control of his emotions. His heart beat intensely and his hands continued to shake. He gripped his knees to make the fear less obvious. Everett drew long, deep breaths with nostrils flaring. His eyes were downcast at the coffee table.

As his nerves calmed and the rational part of his mind regained control, Everett glanced up at the two men across from him. He first looked at Jake, who was seated, hunched over his thighs and staring at the floor. His face was pale and he looked sick. Everett's flicker of pity for him was replaced with the crushing disappointment of betrayal.

Sloan met Everett's gaze with a large smile on his round face beneath slicked back black hair. His eyes were bright and he was clearly enjoying this moment. The moment Everett hoped to avoid forever, and his biggest fear. Everett wanted nothing more than to leap across the coffee table and strangle Billy Sloan to his deserved death.

"I told you, there's not going to be a settlement," said Everett, almost in a whisper.

Sloan guffawed in response before stating, "Yes, there is, Stone. I tried to get you to see reason before, but I guess my advocacy skills aren't as good as yours. So I'm here to take what I think will be a more persuasive track. I have to protect my client, as a lawyer as good as you knows."

"Your client is scum, just like you, and is going to get what he deserves."

"Those are some pretty mean words from a lawyer sleeping with one of his jurors. I wonder what Judge Clement and the State Bar will say about that?"

Everett went pale, but kept his composure. "What do you think you have here, Sloan? Nothing that's what. You go to the judge, and all you get is Jake kicked off the jury and replaced with an alternate. At worse, a mistrial and we'll just start this all over again with the same evidence. As far as the Bar, that's an empty threat and you know it. You're here too, Sloan, which means if they come after me for communicating with Jake they come after you too. Plus, it's my word against yours that this is even happening, and I'll put my credibility against yours any day of the week."

Sloan leaned forward, a wicked smile crossing his lips. "You're doing a lot more than 'communicating' with young Jake here."

Everett's stomach lurched, but he forced himself to swallow it down.

Sloan began speaking again. "You didn't think we were going to let you put us out of business did you? We've been doing this too long. There's too much money involved. Others have come before you, as you know, and tried to stop us, but they failed just like you're about to fail.

"You're persistent. I'll give you that. And that's something Ross and I admire so we'll give you one final chance at the five million dollars as a consolation prize. Take the insurance money, have your client sign a release, and call it a day. It's for your own good."

"And if I don't?" croaked Everett.

A chuckle ripped through Sloan's bulbous belly. "We ruin your life."

A soft moan escaped Jake as he raised his hands to his eyes and buried his face.

"How do you propose to do that?" asked Everett in a whisper.

"Did you not think we would do our homework on you, Stone? Maybe you did. But, I guarantee you never considered how deep we would dig. We knew exactly what that Thomas woman would do once her old man passed. You could smell the greed coming off her and we knew she would hire an attorney as soon as possible. And once she hired you, we knew we would need insurance. I'm not talking about the policy. I'm talking about insurance for this very event right here: a greedy ambulance chaser who considers himself to be fighting a righteous fight against evil and wrongdoing. I read you like an open book. No matter what you tell yourself, it's about money with you but you have to cling to this notion that this case is about principal to help you sleep at night."

"It is about the principal," snarled Everett.

"Sure it is. Why don't you look me in the eye and tell me you haven't been salivating over the thought of all the money you would get out of this case. Spending the money in your mind before the check even arrived. I'm right, aren't I?"

Everett glanced away, which provoked another chuckle from Sloan.

"Of course I'm right. But you would never admit it. Instead, you hide behind your lie of principle and fighting the good fight that all the ambulance chasers out there clutch onto to make themselves feel like respectable lawyers."

Sloan stared down his thick nose at Everett, waiting for him to speak.

"So what?" said Everett. "None of that changes what Tyndall did, nor does it change the evidence in this case."

"Oh, I know it doesn't change the evidence in this case. We tried to, as you know, but that bitch got the real evidence out of the facility, which only strengthened your resolve as she went running to you. That's what brings us here."

"I'm not letting this thing go for the policy limits, Sloan. Nothing you say is going to change that. Tyndall is going to pay. I'm putting him out of business."

"You haven't asked me what we found when we did our homework yet."

"I don't care. I've done nothing wrong."

"Do you hear yourself right now?" laughed Sloan. "We didn't just Google you. We didn't use a private investigator. We found your deepest secrets."

"What do you think you found, Sloan?" asked Everett with a sigh.

"When Ross was unjustly spending his time in the penitentiary he met some folks that have skills we knew we could use down the road. We added them to our payroll. I'm not exactly sure how they do what they do, but I know they are good at what they do."

"And what exactly do these men do?"

"They're hackers."

Everett took another deep breath and braced himself for whatever Sloan was about to say next.

"It took us awhile. You're careful online, but they were eventually able to break into your email account and from there we got access to well, pretty much everything. Most of it I admit was pretty boring, but you do enjoy going to the darker and more adult-oriented areas of the internet from time-to-time."

Everett thought his heart might stop beating at any moment.

"We found the porn sites you like to visit," continued Sloan. "Bisexual male porn. Gay porn. Some kinky shit. It's not my thing, but to each his own, I guess. But we also found out you like to scroll personal ads for men seeking men. Spent a lot of time on those sites, didn't you?"

Silence filled the room. Everett couldn't answer even if he wanted to in that moment.

"Yeah, you did. It's okay. I don't care what people do behind closed doors. Our problem was you weren't doing anything. Try as we might, we couldn't find any evidence that you had ever contacted anyone from those sites. Never tried for an anonymous hookup despite all that pent up desire. I have to confess, I admire that. It's rare to find someone so committed to their marriage vows nowadays. Unfortunately, we had to change that to protect ourselves."

Everett clenched his fists so tight his knuckles blanched. He stopped breathing altogether and, while he wasn't a religious man, he prayed to be anywhere other than that living room. Whether his conscious mind had processed what was coming next or not, his gut knew what was about to happen.

"Please don't," said Jake with a soft sob.

"Yes, we had to do what we needed to do to protect ourselves," said Sloan while ignoring Jake. "So we decided the best insurance policy would be to help you live out your fantasy. Give you the little push you needed to fulfill your deepest, most secret desires. That's where young Jake comes in."

Sloan reached up and patted Jake on the shoulder. "We found a former escort and paid him a handsome amount of money to give you what you've always been wanting."

Everett wanted to look at Jake, but couldn't. He felt the tears welling up in his eyes and it was taking every ounce of his strength to fight them back.

"But that wouldn't be enough would it?" asked Sloan. "People have affairs all the time. A queer being in the closet ain't no big deal. Pretty normal, actually. We may have ruined your marriage, but that doesn't impact the case does it?"

Another silence.

"Does it?" asked Sloan more sharply as Everett said nothing.

A shake of the head was all Everett could manage.

"No. It sure doesn't. So, we had our hacker friends break into the Clerk's system. Jake here gets in the jury venire. Now you have a problem that becomes our solution. Now you're not just having an affair, but having an affair with a juror. You're doing something illegal and something that will get you disbarred. Ta-da!"

A stray tear fell down Everett's cheek. He still couldn't bring himself to look at Jake. "You still have nothing," he managed to say. "You can't do anything with this information without implicating yourselves."

"I thought you might say that," said Sloan with a smile. "The thing is our hacker friends can send an email to anyone anonymously.

I'm quite certain no one will ever trace it back to us. We paid a premium for complete anonymity."

Sloan paused and leaned back into his chair.

"So here's the final settlement offer counselor: you are going to accept the five million dollars and dismiss this case. Tomorrow. First thing in the morning."

Everett spoke but none of the three men could hear it.

"What was that?" asked Sloan.

Everett cleared his throat and spoke again, his voice shaking. "And if I don't?"

Sloan leaned forward and grabbed the remote off the coffee table. He pressed a button and the screen cast its soft glow over the room.

"If you don't, then this gets emailed out far and wide," said Sloan.

Everett recognized the setting of the movie that was now playing. It was right down the hall from him in Jake's bedroom. Everett's face was centered in the frame, his eyes closed and his tanned face resting against the white sheets. His mouth was open and the surround sound speakers projected his moans through the room.

He was naked, his knees raising his ass into the air above his head. Jake was behind him, and his hips were thrusting his cock deep into Everett.

"You like that?" Jake asked on the recording.

"Yeah," moaned Everett. "Fuck me harder."

Smack reverberated through the speakers as Jake's hand connected hard with Everett's ass. The tempo of Jake's thrusts intensified as the video continued playing.

Everett felt the room start to spin.

Chapter Fifty

A numbness settled in every cell of his body. Everett felt paralyzed. He stared out the windows of his office toward the city lights below, seeing nothing except his own reflection.

He didn't remember coming to his office or how he got there. All he could think about was seeing the video of Jake fucking him while sitting in the darkened living room. He remembered Sloan laughing and then leaving. He remembered Jake crying and apologizing and speaking, although Everett had heard none of it. Everett remembered the room spinning and waves of nausea rising as his world tilted and threatened to fall apart.

The next thing Everett knew, he was standing here. The whiskey glass dripped condensation onto his shoes and the soft tap of water on leather was the only sound in the room. His hair was disheveled from running his hands through it; his eyes red from the tears. Everett saw the paleness of his face in the reflection and wondered if he was a ghost. If the shock of what had occurred in Jake's apartment had killed him.

Perhaps being dead would be better. Everett contemplated whether that was the solution to his predicament. This was the rare problem he wasn't sure he could solve, so why solve it at all? Why deal with the pain and hurt and shame and the fallout from the biggest regret of his life?

Only it wasn't a regret. He knew what he was doing that first day in the shower, and his heart had blossomed at how right it felt. Everett knew he loved Jake just as he had once loved Olivia, and as much as he wanted to, he couldn't regret what he had done. He regretted that he got caught. He regretted that someone had found out. That he could no longer hide behind his ability to pass as straight and the privileges that had always brought him.

216

A persistent buzzing brought Everett out of his head and back into the office. He turned toward his desk and saw the soft light of his iPhone's screen indicating an incoming call. The number on the screen wasn't assigned a contact, but it was familiar. It was a number he had once been excited to see whenever it came up on his screen. Everett let the call go to voicemail and noticed the same number had called him a half-dozen times.

A single buzz alerted him that he had a text. Everett glanced down at the screen again as he took another long pull of his whiskey.

Please talk to me, Everett. Let me explain.

Everett's free hand reached for the phone and then stopped. Jake had broken his heart twice. This second time worse than the last. There was nothing for the two to talk about. He felt tears building in his eyes again.

Another buzz. *Everett... I'm sorry. Please answer me. I know you're getting these because you're never far from your phone.*

"Fuck you," Everett muttered.

A third buzz. *I'm so sorry, Everett! I can't say that enough. I wish you would believe that.*

Everett took another sip of his whiskey and pushed his free hand into his pocket. His resolve not to engage with Jake was weakening.

The phone buzzed with yet another text.

We can figure this out. This can all be okay. Just take the money like Sloan said and we can go back to how things were. I know I screwed up, but I can make things right. Take the money and let me try.

Everett grabbed his phone and threw it; whiskey sloshed over the rim of his glass and fell to the carpet. He watched as the phone traveled across the room, through the threshold, and into the hallway wall opposite the door. He stared at the dent left in the drywall as the phone fell to floor and the screen spider-webbed.

He set his glass on his desk and fell into his chair. He brought his hands to his eyes as he rested his elbows on his desk. Everett's body shuddered as he began to sob once again.

Chapter Fifty-One

S loan winked at Everett as he walked into the courtroom. Tyndall sat beside him, looking as nonchalant as ever. The rest of the defense team had their typical dour expressions, no doubt oblivious to the events of the night before.

Everett averted his gaze from their table as he walked to his own. His head pounded from the hangover. His heart pounded with fear. His stomach turned but there was nothing left in it to give, the unpleasant taste of the morning's vomit still coated his tongue.

Everett's life would be ruined today. He had slept very little as he tried to decide what he should do. He had drank to the point of almost passing out, but the gravity of his predicament had kept even his drunken mind awake. Every conceivable way out of his situation had been thoroughly examined and weighed. There were not many options to choose from. Images of the aftermath of each decision played out in his head over and over until the fog of intoxication lifted. Pure exhaustion eventually overtook him in the last hours of night, only for him to be jarred back to consciousness by his alarm blaring from the hallway floor two hours later.

Everett's hand shook as he placed it on the back of his chair. He placed his briefcase on the table and sat down with as much an attempt at normalcy and confidence as he could muster. Everett pulled out his materials and stared at his legal pad.

"Everett?" whispered Monica.

He turned to look at his client.

"I said good morning," she said. "Are you okay?"

Everett met her eyes. He wanted to tell her that he was not okay. He wanted to scream and throw something and cause violent harm to the sons of bitches sitting at the next table over.

"I'm fine," he replied. "Just lost in thought. Sorry." He managed a small smile, which took every ounce of his strength to conjure.

Monica gave him a worried look when he startled as the bailiff yelled out the call to order.

"Is there anything we need to address before we get started today, counsel?" asked Judge Clement. It was a question that Everett had been asked many times before. All judges asked it each day of a trial. Never before had the routine question caused Everett's palms to dampen and his mouth to run dry.

"No, Your Honor," said Wright, breaking the momentary silence.

Everett tried to speak but couldn't.

Judge Clement glared at him from the bench. "Mr. Stone?"

Everett could feel the stares from every set of eyes in the courtroom. None burned into him more than those he knew came from Sloan and Tyndall.

"N-no, Your Honor," stammered Everett.

Judge Clement gave Everett a look that seemed at once both inquisitive and annoyed before turning his attention to the bailiff.

"Very well, bring in the jury."

· · · ·

Everett stared unblinking as the twelve men and women began filing into the jury box. Some looked bothered. Some look tired and ready for the case to be over so they could go back to their lives.

Everett didn't notice any of them while he was lost in his thoughts. His focus bounced back when the last juror filed into the box. Dread filled him.

Jake looked panicked. His eyes were wide and his face pale. If Everett didn't know him better, he would have thought he was strung out on drugs. Everett tried his best not to look at him. The pain of the betrayal, and the anger it stoked, was still all too strong and Everett was afraid of how he would react in the courtroom if they made eye contact. Jake leaned forward in his seat, trying to get his attention.

Everett glanced at him and their eyes locked for no more than a second or two. Jake's soft lips moved so subtly that most people would not have noticed, if they were looking at Jake at all. The message was intended only for Everett, and Everett knew what he had said with the minuscule movement: *take the money.* Instead of an apology, Jake was making one last plea with Everett to get them both out of the mess they had created. Everett looked away when the sting of tears started in the bottom of his eyes.

"Mr. Stone, call your next witness," ordered Judge Clement.

Everett spoke, but his voice caught as if he had just hit puberty again and he stopped.

"What?" asked an annoyed Judge Clement.

Everett cleared his throat and tried again. "The plaintiff calls Randy Montague, Your Honor."

Randy looked every bit the part of the seasoned former cop as he made his way to the witness stand. He was broad shouldered with a square jaw, salt and pepper close-cropped hair, and intelligent eyes that had seen too much.

Randy shot a quick glance toward the defense table as he crossed the bar of the courtroom from the gallery. He shot Everett a glance as well and a look of concern crossed his face at Everett's appearance.

After swearing to tell the truth, Randy sat down with a ram-rod posture and nodded to the jury. Everett began his questioning and focused on Randy's credentials and work history to create credibility and impress the men and women in the box.

Everett next walked his witness through his involvement in the case and his digging into Ross Tyndall. Randy talked about the background information he found; he talked about how he had led Everett to Joseph Redfield; and how he found Annie Smith, who then led him to the rest of the former employees who had testified during the trial.

The dirt on Tyndall was piled high, and Randy's testimony stretched on for over two hours. Just before the direct's grand finale, Judge Clement called the morning recess.

• • • •

Randy was slow to step down from the witness stand after the jury had exited the courtroom. He had watched them leave, and saw the urgent look Juror Number twelve had given to Everett. The same juror seemed to mouth something at Everett, but Randy was unable to make out what was said. He saw Everett's reaction though.

Randy also saw the moment when Everett's eyes met those of Billy Sloan. Sloan had made a crude gesture toward Everett when their eyes met. His cheek had puffed out, pushed by his tongue. Everett had blushed, his shoulders sagging. He had retreated quickly as Sloan grinned in his direction. Randy paused and made note of the exchange.

Randy glared at Sloan. His investigation had shown him and Everett the ease with which Sloan seemed to slip through the fingers of every law enforcement agency and disciplinary board that had come across him. Most people thought he was an ineffective attorney and an idiot, but it was obvious that was only because Sloan wanted them to think that. He was in reality highly intelligent and slippery, like a fish coated in oil.

• • • •

Outside of the courtroom, Randy was unable to find either Sloan or Everett, who had walked out before him. Most of the jurors were milling about in the hallway. Some were chit-chatting about nothing in particular, and others were waiting for the restroom to open up. Randy didn't see Juror Number twelve.

He ducked into the stairwell while pulling out his phone.

. . . .

In a conference room, Everett stood opposite Sloan, trying to quell two competing urges. Part of him wanted to break down and relent to Sloan's demands. The other part wanted to take the conference room chair and beat Sloan to death with it.

"What do you want, Sloan?" Everett's voice was just above a whisper.

"I'm just trying to figure out what the hell you're doing," said Sloan.

Everett didn't speak. He didn't have an answer to the question. Over twelve hours since the ultimatum was delivered, he still could not decide what to do.

"Do you want the world to know you're a faggot?" asked Sloan. "Do you want them to know you're fucking a juror? Do you want your life ruined?"

Everett placed his hands on the back of the conference room chair to steady himself. His knees were shaking as he tried to speak. His mouth failed to form words as Sloan stared at him from across the table.

Sloan crossed his arms over his bulbous belly and smirked. "You're lucky we're charitable people, Stone. Lesser people might have already ruined your life. But, we understand that this is a big decision with big consequences. You can choose to do the right thing by your client, and by you too, or you can fly this plane straight into the side of a mountain. To me, the choice seems obvious, but I've been married five times so I understand matters of the heart make simple things complicated.

"Ross wanted me to press send on the video as soon as you called Montague to the stand, but I persuaded him to wait. To give you a chance. As you know, the law allows you to take a voluntary dismissal at any time before you rest your case. I suspect you're getting close to that point anyway, but you have until the end of today to take the money and dismiss this matter, or until the point you rest your case, whichever comes first. If you don't, you know what happens."

Sloan stepped around the table and patted Everett's arm. "Do the right thing, Stone."

The conference room door shut softly as he left the room.

Everett rushed to the corner, grabbed the trash can off the floor, and filled it with his vomit.

Chapter Fifty-Two

R andy was back on the stand after the recess and was staring straight at Billy Sloan as the jurors shuffled into their seats. Sloan stared back with indifference on his face.

Everett for his part looked calm and composed for the first time all day. It wasn't because he had made a decision about what he should do, or had come to terms with his predicament. Exhaustion had set in, and Everett was too damn tired to care what happened to him at the moment.

The more Everett had thought about it, settling the case was the only option that made sense to him. The smaller amount of money he would receive for his fee, while nowhere near the size he could get by finishing the trial, was still well into the seven figures and nothing to sneeze at. Monica would get even more. More importantly, his life would be preserved. He would still have his marriage. He would still have his reputation. Protecting the image of Everett Stone was his primary concern.

Now the jury was back in their box and Randy was back on the stand. Everett focused his attention on the case, but time was running out. Randy was his last witness and he still had more than an hour before the lunch recess. Everett would have to stretch out time.

· · · ·

The majority of the jury struggled to keep their eyes open, and a few had already succumbed to a bored sleep. The only juror who looked wide awake and alert was Jake. His knee was bouncing up and down while he fidgeted with his hands.

"Mr. Stone," sniped Judge Clement. "While this is all very fascinating, your questioning of Mr. Montague is becoming extremely repetitive. I believe we all get the point. Move on."

Everett had been spending a great deal of time covering details with Randy he had already gone over during his earlier testimony, and was hyper-focusing on the minutiae of Randy's investigation. He checked his watch and had managed to burn a little over thirty minutes of the time remaining before lunch. With any luck, things would work out how he hoped.

"Yes, Your Honor. I understand."

Everett turned his attention back to Randy. "Mr. Montague, I would like to turn your attention now to the last time you were at the Peaceful Pines facility. Can you please tell the jury what you found?"

"Sure. As I've stated several times now, Annie Smith was instrumental to my investigation. After speaking with her, we knew that the leadership at Peaceful Pines was altering records, but we weren't sure what was happening to the originals or how the process was escaping detection. I, therefore, kept the facility under closer surveillance at more regular intervals watching for something that appeared unusual or out of the ordinary. It wasn't too long before that day came."

"How long were you at the property that day?"

"Several hours. I arrived late in the afternoon on a hunch that the facility would not destroy the records in the middle of the work day to avoid any visitors or vendors seeing what they were doing and asking questions."

"What did you see over the course of those hours?" asked Everett.

"Not a whole lot of anything, actually, at least during the day."

"What happened at the end of the day?"

"That's when things got interesting," said Randy. "Once the staff was gone and twilight set in, I noticed the administrator, Bill Tremaine, was still at the facility. I didn't see much movement in the front of the building, so I repositioned myself in the woods out back."

"What did you see from that vantage point?" asked Everett.

"There was a large yard out in back surrounded by a fence. There was a small garden that you could tell some of the residents tended, and a few benches scattered about. For the most part, though, it was just a wide area of unkempt grass surrounded by cheap chain link fencing. It reminded me kind of a prison yard."

"Was there anything unusual that you saw?"

"Yes, there were four large metal drums in the center of the yard."

"Like the kind you put oil in?"

"Yes," said Randy, "that or some chemical. They were about the size of a garbage can and metal. They were uncovered."

"Could you see what was inside of them?" asked Everett.

"I didn't need to."

"Why not?"

"As I was sitting there taking photographs of the yard and just trying to see if anything was going on, the back door of the facility opened and out walked Bill Tremaine."

"What was Mr. Tremaine doing?"

"He was pushing a dolly with banker boxes stacked on it."

"Could you read what was on the boxes?" asked Everett.

"Not with my naked eye. However, I took out my camera with the telephoto lens and zoomed in. Once I saw what was written on the boxes I started clicking the shutter."

Everett stood from counsel table and approached Randy with a large poster board, which he took care to keep facing away from the jury. He asked the questions required for the exhibit's admission into evidence, and then turned the exhibit to face the jury box. He took a step forward so they could get an even better look.

The jurors by this point seemed to wake back up and Everett made sure to make eye contact with all of them as they took in the picture. He refused to look at Jake, though. He needed to keep his cool. Several jurors scowled as they read what was written on the box: *Thomas, Harry.*

"Did you take pictures of what you saw next?" asked Everett as he returned to counsel table.

"No, what I saw next warranted a video."

Everett once again laid the legal foundation for his next exhibit and introduced it into evidence. He projected the video onto a large screen so it was visible to the whole courtroom.

Bill Tremaine could be seen pushing the dolly across the grass yard and toward the barrels. One-by-one, he removed the boxes from the cart and tipped them upside down. The jurors watched as thousands of pieces of paper cascaded into the steel containers.

Tremaine could then be seen walking back into the facility and a few minutes later returning to the yard. This time there was something in his hand, and the video zoomed in so it could be clearly seen. It was a bottle of lighter fluid. The sun had finished setting and it was now almost fully dark outside. The building's flood lights provided just enough lighting to make out what was happening.

Whoosh. The sound of the fluid igniting in the barrels was loud enough to be heard on the video. Randy had been hiding in the woods several hundred yards away. The flames shot up several feet in the air and lit the area like the sun.

Tremaine could be seen stepping a few feet back from the blaze and pulling his cell phone out of his pocket. The lights came back on in the courtroom as the video ended.

"Mr. Montague," continued Everett, "were you in the courtroom earlier in this case when Charles Reed, the state inspector testified?"

"Yes, I was."

"Do you recall Mr. Reed saying that he never found anything out of the ordinary or against guidelines at the facility?"

"Yes, I do."

"Do you recall him saying that there was never any evidence to substantiate the complaints made against the facility"

"Yes, I do."

"Mr. Montague, was that the first time you had ever seen Mr. Reed?"

"No, Mr. Stone. It was not."

"On what other occasion had you seen Mr. Reed?"

"I happened to be surveilling the property on one of the days that he came to do an inspection," said Randy.

"What did you observe?"

"I actually have a video of it," said Randy.

Once more the lights were dimmed and a video began to play on the screen for the jury. It showed the front parking lot of Peaceful Pines from afar. Charles Reed could be seen pulling into the lot in a white state-issued sedan, park, and begin walking toward the facility. Before he could reach the door, Bill Tremaine walked outside and shook Reed's hand before passing him a thick envelope. Reed was then seen walking back to his car, and then driving off.

"What happened after this?" asked Everett.

"I followed Mr. Reed."

"To where?"

"You'll see that in the next video," replied Randy.

One of the jurors let out an audible gasp as Reed's white sedan was next seen pulling into the parking lot of a local bank. Reed could be seen on the video carrying the thick envelope Tremaine had given him into the bank. A few moments later, Reed walked back out of the bank without the envelope. He crumpled up a small sheet of paper and threw it away, climbed into his car, and drove off.

"After Mr. Reed left," said Randy, "I walked up to the trashcan and took out the paper that Mr. Reed had tossed in. It was a receipt showing a cash deposit into a savings account owned by Reed in the amount of ten thousand dollars."

"No more questions, Your Honor," Everett said.

Judge Clement leaned forward from his reclined position in the plush leather chair. "Ladies and gentlemen," he said, "that brings us to our lunch recess. Court will resume in ninety minutes."

They would be the most important ninety minutes of Everett's life.

Chapter Fifty-Three

M onica and Everett managed to get a table in the back corner of Gravy restaurant located a few blocks from the courthouse. The dining area was crowded and conversation echoed off the walls. It was the best they could hope for in terms of privacy, and for what Everett was sure would be a difficult conversation.

Everett took a sip of his water and looked at Monica after they placed their order, welcoming a break from the awkward small talk the two had been engaged in while they waited.

"I just wanted to say thank you," said Monica before Everett could speak again. "Thank you so much for all the work that you have done on this case and for trying to get justice for my father. I can't tell you how much I appreciate it."

What little appetite Everett had diminished even further.

"It's been my pleasure," he replied with only a faint trace of sincerity. The truth was it had been, until the case became his nightmare.

"So what's the next step?" asked Monica.

Everett went through a recitation of the upcoming stages in the trial and told Monica that he thought they had at most a day or two left, depending on whether the defense attempted to put on any evidence in the case.

Monica nodded her understanding and then asked the same question she asked in every conversation: "So, how much do you think we'll get from the jury?"

Everett took a deep breath and another sip of his water. The waiter, a cute blonde female in a black skirt, brought their food at the same time and Everett waited on her to leave before answering the question.

"It's hard to say, Monica," said Everett. "Juries are unpredictable."

"You've said before it could be in the tens of millions of dollars. Perhaps one of the largest verdicts in the state. Do you still think that might happen?"

Yes, thought Everett. He took a bite of his pasta and tried to think of a response he could give to the question that would accomplish his goal for the conversation. If he was going to get what he needed from Monica, then he could not tell her the truth.

"Maybe." He took another bite and tried to stall for more time.

"Trial has gone well, hasn't it?" asked Monica.

Had it ever. Everett was convinced the jury was firmly with him and ready to ruin Ross Tyndall and put him out of business once and for all. The evidence he had presented over the course of the trial left little room for doubt that Tyndall's management of the facility had created a culture of willful neglect, and that Tyndall had then tried to cover it up to save his own skin. Everett was also confident he had proven Peaceful Pines was birthed from fraud. It was more of a question of when, not if, the jury agreed with their side.

That was before it all went to hell, of course.

"I think so," said Everett. "But, perhaps not."

Monica looked up at him from her plate and set her fork down.

"Perhaps not?" she asked. "What do you mean?" She took a sip of her water and looked like she was trying not panic.

"It's hard to explain," began Everett. "Listen, I've tried a lot of cases in front of a lot of juries. There were some I thought I would lose, but I won. And there were some that I thought I would win, but I lost. Juries are inherently unpredictable. You can drive yourself crazy trying to scrutinize every movement their body makes and every facial expression to try to speculate as to what they are thinking and how the case may turn out. The truth is there's really no way to tell what they are going to do. It's the same as going to Vegas and throwing a pair of dice down the craps table—you may hit sevens, but you may hit snake eyes."

Everett paused to take another bite of his food and Monica filled the momentary silence. "But this isn't going to be one of those cases you lose? Right? I mean, the evidence is pretty damning. I'm no lawyer, but I think even I can figure that out."

"Maybe," continued Everett. "Like I said there's no way to tell. You're right in saying that our case has been strong, but it hasn't been perfect."

"What do you mean?" asked Monica.

Everett put his fork down and took another sip of his water. He had only finished about half of his plate, but he had lost all appetite.

"Well, your father already had a lot of health problems before his death. That's why he was in Peaceful Pines to begin with. Certainly the nature of some of his care would be enough for the jury to overlook that, but you may have some more conservative jurors that take that into consideration when determining an amount. More importantly, you were not the best witness on the stand. While I'm sure the jury doesn't like Ross Tyndall, I'm not sure they like you either. That may depress the amount of the verdict."

Monica's face flushed and she downed the last of her water. Everett took another sip as well, and then continued with his sales pitch.

"Listen, we've tried the best case we possibly could have. You did the best job you could have on the stand. We may very well get that huge, record-setting verdict."

"It sounds like there's a 'but' in there somewhere," said Monica.

"There is. The law is a profession based on reason and common sense. Jurors are supposed to decide a case on the evidence and the law as the judge gives it to them. But, we know sometimes that doesn't happen. Jurors are people and they aren't infallible. Sometimes the best thing a lawyer can do in a trial is get out of their head, step back from the evidence no matter how well in their favor it may be, and listen to their gut."

"What does your gut say?"

"It's nagging at me. There's something that gives me some pause. I can't articulate what it is. All I can tell you is after trying as many cases as I have that something feels off."

Monica looked at Everett and considered his response. The color had drained from her face and her hand shook against the table.

"So what are you saying?" she asked.

Everett swallowed and wiped his sweaty palms on his pant legs under the table.

"Taking the settlement offer may be the best approach."

Chapter Fifty-Four

It did not take long for Wright to cross-examine Randy. There wasn't much to cover when most of the testimony was backed up by photographs and the damning video. It took even less time for Everett to rehabilitate what little damage Wright had done.

Randy stepped off the witness stand and immediately left the courtroom. Everett looked at his client and Monica gave the slightest shake of her head.

They had argued intensely at the restaurant when Everett suggested a settlement. Heads had turned in their direction from other diners when she had yelled, "Are you kidding me?" at the mere suggestion.

Everett had tried everything he could think of to get Monica to take the money, but in the end it was impossible to convince her to accept the offer when for months he had filled her head with dreams of much more. Everett began to wonder whether that was Tyndall's plan all along—not to get out of the lawsuit, but to ruin Everett's existence.

The truth was, Everett had underestimated the amount of greed in the case. He had assumed Tyndall would fight dirty to save his skin, but he hadn't expected for him to commit more crimes fresh out of prison. He hadn't expected Monica's level of greed either. Every plaintiff in any lawsuit is at some level motivated by money, but most are looking for some form of justice and tend to listen to their lawyer's counsel. Monica was motivated solely by profit. Everett knew when he signed her that she didn't care about her father or putting Tyndall out of business, she just wanted the riches.

Everett had fooled himself into thinking that the two of them were out for justice and pursuing a righteous cause. Everett had wanted the money as much, if not more, than his client, however. He had to admit that now, and now it could very well slip from his grasp.

He had been greedy in other ways too, and that had been his worst sin. Everett had everything he needed: a nice home; a wife; a thriving career. He hadn't been satisfied. He had an affair with a younger man, who was on his jury, no less. Everett hated himself for it.

"Any further evidence?" asked Judge Clement from the bench. His ornery tone brought Everett back into the moment.

Everett rose from his seat. He gripped the table with his hands as he did so to avoid falling over. His legs were shaking. He could feel Monica's eyes on him. He could feel the jury's eyes on him. Everett glanced quickly over at Jake, who looked like he was on the verge of tears. Everett could feel Sloan's stare on him strongest of all. He didn't have the strength to glance over at him.

"Well?" bellowed Judge Clement.

Everett's knuckles turned white as he continued to grip the table for support. He looked at the judge and said the words that would ruin his life: "No, Your Honor. The plaintiff rests."

· · · ·

"Are you okay?" whispered Monica into Everett's ear.

Everett looked around and saw that the jury and most of the defense table had cleared out of the courtroom. Judge Clement had also left.

"What's a charge conference?" asked Monica as Everett turned to look at her.

"It's... um..." Everett cleared his throat and gave his head the slightest of shakes to try to clear the disorientation he was feeling. "It's when the lawyers discuss with the judge what law the jury should be instructed on before closing arguments."

"Okay. So then since he sent the jury home for the day that means that we do closings in the morning because the defense said they were not calling any witnesses?"

Everett was finding it hard to comprehend what Monica was asking. It's not that he didn't know the answer to her question, it's that he had no recollection of Judge Clement sending the jury home for the night. He wasn't sure whether he had actually fainted or not. Everett assumed not, but all he could remember were horrible visions of the future flashing in his mind after he rested his case.

"Yes, we do closings in the morning," replied Everett.

"Alright. Well hopefully we'll both be rich tomorrow then," said Monica with a smile. "I'll see you after the recess."

"Yes," said Everett. He couldn't muster the strength to return her smile.

Monica walked out of the courtroom and Everett followed behind her at a distance. He immediately walked into the conference room off the hallway and locked the door. Sitting down, Everett loosened his tie and tried to breath normally. His hands were clammy. Closing his eyes, Everett took deep breaths and tried to return his heart rate to normal.

Then his phone buzzed.

Chapter Fifty-Five

The call went to voicemail again. Dayna slammed the handset into the receiver so hard it cracked the plastic casing. She had called Everett's number six times in the past five minutes, and each time it had been sent straight to voicemail. He never had his phone off, and Everett always answered her. Until now.

Dayna stared at her computer screen, still numb from the shock of opening the email. She thought it was a scam at first. Some phishing attempt and she almost didn't open the attachment, but something compelled her to double click. Dayna glanced around and saw the small team of professionals that made up The Law Office of Everett Stone had done the same from their facial expressions.

The "To:" field on the email was blank. The sender had used the "Bcc:" field to populate the recipients. But who received the email? Was it just their law office? Dayna had an uneasy suspicion that it wasn't. That would be good news, and it was clear this day was going to be one for horrible news.

The sender was suspiciously named "Lawyers' Daily" and had an official looking logo that was similar to the local bar's weekly newspaper. The subject line was little more than clickbait: *Breaking: Local Attorney Caught Tampering With Juror in Multi-Million Dollar Trial.*

When Dayna had opened the email, it was well-crafted to appear legitimate. Below the main headline, which featured the headshot of Everett from their website, were other articles that had clearly been pulled from a wire service. The email had a gossip rag feel to it.

Underneath Everett's photo was a short paragraph intended to bait readers into clicking a link to an exclusive video proving the allegations. The message read:

Everett Stone, managing partner of The Law Office of Everett Stone, is in the middle of a jury trial in which his client seeks a multi-million dollar verdict after rejecting reasonable attempts at settlement from the defense. An anonymous source has come forward with evidence that Stone has been tampering with the jury during the trial in the hopes of securing a favorable verdict for his client. Click here to read more on this developing story.

Dayna clicked the link and her internet browser opened automatically. An embedded video began to play and sound erupted through her speakers.

She exited out of the video after a few seconds, her computer going silent and her hand still covering her mouth. Dayna blinked her wide eyes and shook her head. She deleted the email from her inbox as if willing it out of existence.

Soft groans drifted to her ears from nearby. She turned her head and yelled at the rest of the staff, "Turn that shit off and delete that email now or you're fired!"

"Like any of us will have jobs much longer anyway," said one of the legal assistants.

"Get the fuck out! Now!" screamed Dayna.

Dayna grabbed the phone off her desk and dialed while the assistant grabbed her purse and walked out of the office.

Chapter Fifty-Six

Tyndall turned the water to the sink off and tore some paper towels from the dispenser. After he was finished drying his hands and tossing the spent paper into the trash bin, he pulled his phone out of his pocket and checked his email.

A smile crossed his face when he saw the message at the top of his inbox.

Great job, once again! he texted Sloan.

Tyndall looked in the mirror and smiled at himself. He straightened his tie and smoothed the front of his suit jacket.

"Time to go home," he said to himself.

He turned the lock on the bathroom door. Before he could pull it open, the door rushed forward and slammed against his body, knocking him back a few steps.

"What the fuck?" exclaimed Tyndall.

The door slammed and the lock engaged. A hand grasped Tyndall by the tie and pushed him into the counter with a loud thud.

"I am so sick of you, you know that?" asked Wright through clenched teeth.

"I suggest you take your hands off me, Ken. It's not a good look for such a distinguished attorney to assault his client in a public restroom."

Wright loosened his grip on Tyndall's tie and took a step back before dropping his hand completely. He glared at Tyndall.

"You're responsible for this," said Wright.

"Responsible for what?" asked Tyndall.

"Don't play dumb with me. You know exactly what I'm talking about."

"I'm afraid I don't."

Wright shoved his phone in Tyndall's face. Tyndall smirked.

"Not me," said Tyndall.

"I don't believe you," sneered Wright. "And you better hope no one can prove you're behind this. But, I know it was you. This is exactly the extra-judicial gutter trash type of thing you would do to try to save your own ass."

"It worked, didn't it?" chuckled Tyndall.

"So you admit it?"

"Why not? You're my attorney. You can't tell anyone anything. Yes, we're behind the email. And we didn't do anything wrong. All we did was expose a cheat and a liar—a corrupt lawyer."

Wright shook his head. "It's despicable what you did. He didn't do anything wrong in bringing this lawsuit against you. It's his job. And, frankly Ross, you fucking deserved it. You're a guilty piece of shit that has got away with shit like this for too long. Stone is married. You've ruined his life. You've gone too far."

Tyndall took a step forward, towering over Wright by a few inches. "Too fucking bad. He shouldn't have gotten greedy and he should have taken the check and left well enough alone. He didn't want his marriage ruined? He didn't want his life ruined? That's bullshit. He wanted to ruin his life. If he didn't, he would have listened to Sloan and taken the fucking money like we told him to. Hell, he never would have had the affair to begin with—that would have been the right thing to do all along. At the end of the day, he's responsible for his own downfall."

Wright shook his head and rubbed the bridge of his nose. "How did you even arrange all this?"

"Through a better attorney than you."

Wright chuckled. "Sloan?"

"Yes, Sloan. He's my fixer, and he did exactly what I pay him to do."

"But how?" asked Wright.

"The details don't concern you. All you need to concern yourself with is doing your job, which Sloan and I just made much easier for you." Tyndall glanced at his watch. "It's time to get back to court, counselor. I expect a mistrial within the hour."

Chapter Fifty-Seven

E verett walked out of the conference room and straightened his tie. He checked his watch and saw recess was over and he was due back in the courtroom, but he stepped into the nearby restroom instead. Everett didn't care if he was late, or if Judge Clement was mad. He had bigger problems to deal with.

He walked over to the sink and splashed water on his face. Everett looked at his reflection and felt a wave of disgust wash over him. How could he have been so stupid? Why didn't he just resist Jake that first time? Why did he have to keep pursuing him? Everett went pale.

His phone buzzed. Everett reached into his breast pocket and silenced it without bothering to look at the notification. It had been buzzing non-stop since a few minutes after he rested his case. He shut it off.

Moments later, his palms were still sweaty and he thought he was going to throw up again as he opened the door to the courtroom. Everett saw Monica sitting in her seat; her face appearing normal, as if she was ignorant of what was transpiring. He thought that made sense. Why would Tyndall have Sloan send her the email? He'd rather make it a surprise when Everett was forced to explain it to her personally in court.

The defense table was crowded, and none of the lawyers from Wright & Reynolds made eye contact with him. Everett looked hard at Wright and could not decipher his crimson cheeks. Tyndall and Sloan glanced at him and nodded. If this was not a courtroom with an armed bailiff, Everett may have killed them with his bare hands right then and there.

The bailiff was standing in front of the bench, watching Everett intently as he made his way to the table. Judge Clement was noticeably absent.

Right as Everett was about to take his seat, the bailiff stepped forward and said, "Judge Clement wants to see counsel in chambers before we continue."

Wright and Sloan stood from the defense table and began walking to the door that led to chambers. Everett tried to follow, but found he could not will his legs to move. He felt light-headed, and his grip remained on the chair for support.

"Mr. Stone?" asked the bailiff. "Judge Clement needs you in chambers, sir. Now."

Summoning every ounce of strength he had, Everett walked toward the door behind which he was sure contained the death of his dreams for the future.

Judge Clement was standing behind his desk when Everett crossed the threshold, and Sloan and Wright had already taken their seats. Before Everett could take his, Judge Clement raised a spindly arm draped in the black judge's robe, pointing his bony finger at him. It looked like the arm of the Grim Reaper. Perhaps it was.

"What in the absolute hell is wrong with you, Stone?" yelled Judge Clement.

Everett didn't answer. He felt compelled to say something, but his mind couldn't find the words. For the first time in his life, he had been rendered speechless.

"Well?" commanded Judge Clement.

When Everett finally spoke, it was at such a low volume no one else could hear him. Judge Clement leaned forward and put a hand to his ear.

Just as Everett opened his mouth to repeat himself, he was cut off.

"You know what? Forget it. I don't care what you think is wrong with you. Hell, Stone, I don't even care if you are a faggot," said Judge Clement. The use of the slur made Everett flinch and turned his cheeks bright red. "What I care about is how you couldn't keep your damn dick in your pants and now you've gone and fucked up this entire trial."

Judge Clement smacked his withered hand on the top of his desk for emphasis. "Damn it!"

Every lawyer for the past forty years had a story about Judge Clement. Even in his younger days, he had a short temper and was known to inspire fear in even the most seasoned trial lawyer. His temperament had only grown worse as he reached old age, but Everett doubted if anyone had ever seen Judge Clement this angry.

The lawyers remained silent as Judge Clement finally took his seat. He continued to glare at Everett, and then shifted his gaze toward Sloan and Wright.

"Did you two have anything to do with this?" he asked.

"No," said Sloan before Wright could speak.

Judge Clement stared a Sloan for a few uncomfortable moments while Wright stared into his own lap. "It's not like you to be so quiet, Ken."

"I'm sorry, Your Honor," said Wright. "I... I don't know what to say. These revelations have been shocking to say the least."

"What do you have to say for yourself, Stone?" asked Judge Clement.

Everett took a deep breath. What did he have to say for himself? How could he possibly excuse what had happened? There was no excuse. It was time to own his truth.

"I'm bisexual," he said, his voice shaking. "That's only the second time I've spoken those words out loud, although I've known the truth of them for as long as I can remember. It's a part of me that for the longest time I felt shame about, and hid. I would still be hiding it had that email not been sent."

Everett exhaled, perhaps the first full exhale of his adult life.

"I didn't seek out a relationship with Mr. Phelps. In fact, he's the one that approached me before this trial even began. He initiated the relationship. I've been unhappy in my marriage for a long time, and had always denied my feelings toward men, so when this younger, attractive man took an interest in me I surrendered to what my heart was telling me to do. It was a mistake. It will cause many people pain, but that's what happened.

"When I saw Mr. Phelps called into the box, I panicked. I knew I should have disclosed that I knew him, but I was too afraid of being asked how I knew him. I was too afraid of people finding out what I am and what I had done. I didn't want anyone to know, and that's how I intended to keep it until the choice was stolen from me."

Everett took another deep breath and wiped his eye with the back of his hand. He didn't look up, but knew all eyes were still on him. He could sense the tension in the room.

"Mr. Stone..." Judge Clement began.

"That's not all of it, Your Honor," said Everett, cutting him off. "Once Mr. Phelps was empaneled as a juror, we never discussed the case. We continued our affair largely at his insistence, which I should have resisted but didn't. I learned later during this trial that it was no accident Mr. Phelps came on to me initially. He was paid to seduce me. He was paid to have sex with me. It was all caught on film without my knowledge, some of that footage you have now seen. Mr. Phelps's actions were part of a scheme to pressure me into getting my client to accept a settlement and drop this case altogether."

Everett looked up and met Judge Clement's wide eyes before continuing. "It was an extortion attempt orchestrated by the defendant."

Judge Clement stared unblinking for a brief moment before he turned to face the defense side of the room. "Is this true, Ken?" he demanded.

"It's absolutely false," said Sloan again before Wright could speak. "We had nothing to do with this, and there's not a shred of evidence connecting this to us. This is a now-admitted liar's attempts to smear the defense and take the focus off of his own unethical—and indecent—actions."

"You know exactly what you did, Sloan," sneered Everett. "You know it's the truth."

"If you're so sure it was us, then prove it," dared Sloan. The statement was made with such confidence and defiance that Everett wondered if he would be able to. Sloan was smart enough to probably use a burner phone when contacting Everett during his blackmail attempts. There were no identifiable witnesses to the meetings they had had. The only one that could definitively tie Sloan and Tyndall to this whole thing was Jake. Would he do the right thing? Everett felt sick as he considered the question.

"We'll find out soon enough," said Judge Clement as he interrupted the exchange. "This whole mess is bad enough. God help you if I find out that the defense had anything to do with this and what Mr. Stone says is true. I can assure you we will get to the bottom of this as soon as the jury returns in the morning, and I'll also be requesting a formal law enforcement investigation of this whole incident."

Judge Clement removed his hands from his desk and leaned back into his chair. He looked at Everett, and then the defense, appearing to size up the situation. "The more pressing question this afternoon is where do we go from here gentlemen?"

"I think the only appropriate thing to do is to declare a mistrial," said Wright.

"I bet you do," said Judge Clement. "What about you, Stone?"

"I'm... I'm not sure judge. I've obviously never been in this situation before. What I can say is my client has waited a long time for justice to come. Nothing about what happened changes the evidence or impacts the facts of this case. Jake... I mean, Mr. Phelps... and I never discussed the case."

"Are we supposed to believe that?" asked Wright. "We've all seen the video. Are we supposed to believe that two lovers didn't talk about their shared day in court while twisted up in the sheets after they were done with their fun?"

Everett felt the heat rising in his cheeks. He was able to calm his mind enough to develop a proposal that might persuade Judge Clement.

"Judge, poll the jury," he said. "You're already going to speak with Mr. Phelps in the morning. We know he's going to be dismissed from the jury—that's a given. Ask him to verify what I've been saying. Then ask the jurors, separately, whether any of them have discussed the case during recesses and specifically with Mr. Phelps. If they say yes, then declare the mistrial and this case can start back at square one just to return to this point again in another year. If they say no, and it's clear they are still impartial, then empanel one of the alternate jurors and let it proceed to verdict."

"Your Honor," began Wright, "That would be entirely too prejudicial to my client. We have one juror already lying to the court and having an affair with plaintiff's counsel without telling anyone. How can we be assured the others would tell the truth? To not grant a mistrial when plaintiff's counsel is sleeping with one of the jurors would be reversible error. I don't see how it couldn't be, judge."

"I guess we'll find out, Ken," said Judge Clement. "I'm sorry, but you know how I'm loath to have delays on my docket and Mr. Stone makes a compelling point. If I can be assured that this jury remains impartial without Mr. Phelps then I see no reason to stop this trial from moving to a verdict. We can sort out the rest of it later."

"Judge..." began Wright before being cut off again by Judge Clement.

"Save it, Ken. If you don't like whatever ruling I make then you are free to make your objection on the record and appeal it. I don't really care. I've made my decision and that's final. We are all going to go back out in that courtroom, go back on the record, and conduct the charge conference. We're already going to have a delay in the morning while we poll the jury and talk with Mr. Phelps so we may as well continue with getting that out of the way as planned this afternoon despite this damn mess."

Judge Clement leaned forward in his chair again and stared directly at Tyndall. "And so help me, you better pray that what Mr. Stone claims happened is truly the lie you claim it to be."

Chapter Fifty-Eight

Wiping his mouth, Everett stood straight on the edge of his driveway and hoped his stomach and nerves would settle. He was surprised that he was still alive. Between having to give a closing argument in the morning and the events of the afternoon, he thought he would have had a heart attack or stroke. There was still time for both, of course. If Olivia didn't murder him first.

He turned to face his home and stared at the stately colonial for a long while. Olivia's car was still in the driveway. Did she know what was happening? Everett assumed she did. If by some miracle she didn't, there was no question he would have to tell her. Everett had been trained in the art of storytelling and advocacy and thinking on his feet. Despite that training and years of practice, he wasn't sure how he would begin to explain things to his wife.

Stepping through the door, Everett felt the silence envelope him. It was not a peaceful quiet. It was the type of quiet that feels heavy; full of unspoken rage.

A wine bottle sat empty on the kitchen counter. *She knows*, he thought.

Everett walked around the downstairs as if he were a burglar. He wasn't sure what to expect. Would Olivia be crying or having a breakdown? Would she immediately demand a divorce?

Ascending the stairs, he felt like a man walking to his execution. The weight of the silence was crushing and ominous. The door to the master bedroom was shut, and he let his hand linger on the knob before turning it and walking into the room.

The tip of his ear was cut by a shard of the wine glass that exploded on the wall next to his head. Olivia was standing in the middle of their room on the opposite side of their king-sized bed. A suitcase was laid out across the duvet, stuffed with clothes haphazardly thrown inside. It was Everett's suitcase.

"You lying son of a bitch!" screamed Olivia. "How could you?"

"Olivia..."

"How could you do this to me!" she screamed again before Everett could finish speaking. "All these years together! And you cheat on me? With a fucking man!"

Olivia picked up the book that was on her nightstand and hurled it at him. The book left a dent in the drywall where the wine glass had struck.

Everett raised his hands in front of him defensively and said, "I know. I was wrong. And I'm sorry."

"Sorry? That's all you have to say for yourself? You have humiliated me!"

He swallowed hard and fought the urge to remind his wife that it was not a video of her in the middle of sex with the landscaper sent to all their friends and colleagues. "I'm sorry," he said again.

"Get the hell out! I can't have you in this house tonight. I refuse to sleep under the same roof as you."

"Olivia, please," implored Everett. "Let's both just calm down and talk about this."

"Calm down? Don't you tell me to calm down! How am I supposed to calm down when a video of my husband getting fucked by another man is circulating around online? A video all of our friends have seen?

"I loved you. I put up with your long hours and your shit for all these years and how do you repay me? You cheat on me! But you couldn't even do it with a younger woman like most husbands, you did it with a man!"

Olivia drew in a deep breath and Everett could see tears welling up in her already blood-shot eyes.

"Are you gay?" she asked.

"No."

Olivia shook her head and wiped a tear falling down her cheek.

"I'm not gay," continued Everett. "I'm attracted to both women and men. I'm bisexual." The words were still strange to say out loud.

The room fell into silence as Everett watched Olivia try to stop crying.

"All these years," Olivia said. "Why didn't you tell me? Why did you keep your sexuality from me for all these years?"

Everett looked down at his feet as he tried to find the words to answer the question.

"I don't know," he said. "I really don't. I think I've known my whole life, but I refused to admit it to myself. I denied it to myself. Tried to rationalize it and explain it away. I didn't—don't—want to be like this. It's not how I imagined my life turning out."

"You should have told me," Olivia sobbed.

"I know. I'm sorry. I don't know what else to say."

"How many others?"

"What?"

"How many others have there been since we've been together? Men and women," she asked again.

"None," said Everett. "There have been none."

Olivia shook her head. "I'm not sure I believe you."

"I understand," replied Everett. "But I'm telling you the truth."

"The truth. Would you even know the truth, Everett? You stretch and bend the truth for a living. You've been lying to me our entire relationship. You've been lying to yourself your entire life."

He stood there, stung by the truth in Olivia's words. Everett swallowed and clenched his jaw as he felt his eyes begin to sting and moisten.

"You're one to talk," he said after a pause.

Olivia went rigid. "What's that supposed to mean?"

"I'm not the only one with secrets, or the only one who has been lying in this relationship. You don't think I know about your affair?"

Olivia stood mute for a moment, her cheeks flushing. "You don't know what you're talking about."

"The hell I don't. I saw some messages between you two while you were in the shower a long time ago."

"You expect me to believe you knew all this time and didn't say anything?" asked Olivia.

"I don't care if you believe it or not. It's the truth. I just didn't care." Everett inhaled deeply and let out a long sigh. "We haven't been in a good place in a very long time, Olivia. You have to see that."

Olivia glanced down at the floor, but Everett could see the tears building in the corner of her eyes.

"I'm sorry for what I've done," he said. "But I'm not the only one to blame for this marriage falling apart. However, I'm willing to try to work through some of these problems if you are."

"I can't talk to you anymore about this. I can't look at you right now," said Olivia. She closed the suitcase and zipped it up.

"Olivia..." Everett said, his voice cracking.

"Get out," she said.

Chapter Fifty-Nine

" Are all my jurors present?" Judge Clement asked the bailiff.

"No, Your Honor. We're still missing one."

"I bet I can guess which one," the judge replied.

"Yes, sir. I bet you can."

Judge Clement turned his attention to Everett. "Where is your boyfriend, Mr. Stone?"

Everett rose to address the court. "I don't know, Your Honor."

He wanted to argue with Judge Clement, and point out that Jake wasn't his boyfriend. He was his lover. His biggest mistake. Everett resisted the urge. It had been a hard enough morning, and he worried the day was only going to get worse. Could a day get worse when you started it at rock bottom?

Everett had awakened in a cheap hotel as it was the only place he could find a room without a reservation. Olivia hadn't bothered to pack a suit for him, so he was still wearing the one from the day before except for the spare tie he kept in his car. Half the night had been spent working on his closing; a closing he still wasn't sure he would be able to deliver, depending on what the jury said this morning.

The other half of the night had been spent dealing with the fallout of his doxxing. He had spent over an hour on the phone with Monica, trying to explain what had happened and what it meant for her case. She had wanted to fire him on the spot, not because of his sexual relationship with another man, but because he may have jeopardized her winning the lawsuit lottery. He was still her lawyer, only because he had been able to convince her that if she fired him mid-trial it could cause bigger problems for the case if the jury was ignorant as to what had transpired. What little sleep he was able to get was spent tossing and turning on the bed and crying into his pillow.

His thoughts returned to the courtroom as Judge Clement began shouting orders at the bailiff.

"Have a deputy go find Mr. Phelps and make sure he gets an escort to this courtroom," commanded Judge Clement. "He's not going to lie to this court and compromise the integrity of this trial and then run away with no consequences."

"Yes, sir," said the bailiff. He spoke into his radio to relay the orders to dispatch.

"Bring the rest of the jury in," Judge Clement instructed.

The remaining eleven members of the jury and the two alternates began shuffling into the courtroom a few minutes later. Everett watched them intently, and glanced around the room to see the others doing the same. Some of jurors seemed normal, like they had every other day of the trial. A few glanced Everett's way in a manner that made his stomach sink.

"Good morning, ladies and gentlemen," said Judge Clement.

A half-hearted murmur came from the jury in collective response.

"Normally we would go right into closing arguments of counsel this morning, but some things have been brought to my attention that I need to address with all of you before we continue with this trial."

A few of the jurors nodded their heads up and down. Several glanced at Jake's empty seat. Everett felt like running to the window and throwing himself out of it.

"Have any of you received and seen a... how should I put this... unusual video since court adjourned yesterday? If you have, please raise your hands for me," said Judge Clement.

All the jurors raised their hands.

"I was afraid of that," said Judge Clement. "But, I need to make sure we're talking about the same thing, since everyone these days spends their life pointlessly scrolling through social media. Let me rephrase that question. How many of you saw a video in the past day that depicted Mr. Stone and one of your fellow jurors engaged in... a physical activity together?"

All the jurors again raised their hands.

"This video, I presume, raises some questions for you. First, I want to say that this court does not know who is behind this video, or how it was obtained, but we are currently looking into that.

"I want to make clear that there is currently no evidence whatsoever that either side in this case was responsible for the filming of that video or its dissemination. Do you understand that?"

The jury nodded.

"This is obviously an awkward situation," continued Judge Clement. "It's a first for me as a judge, and I've been on this bench a long, long time and have seen many things that would shock you. But this trial is not about what Mr. Stone may do in his private life, and it's not about what Mr. Phelps may do in his private life. What two consenting adults do in their own time is no one's business except their own. Do all of you agree with that concept?"

All of the jurors except one nodded their heads.

"Mrs. Lawrence, you did not nod your head. May I ask why you disagree with what I just said?"

Mrs. Lawrence was juror number six, and had a close-cropped perm and wide-framed eyeglasses. Her face was wrinkled from a long life, and her hair was a shimmering silver. She was dressed as conservative as her beliefs. Mrs. Lawrence cleared her throat and shifted in her seat as she began to speak.

"Judge, I'm sorry, but I just don't agree. I'm a Christian. And the Bible teaches that homosexuality and sodomy is a sin. I cannot support the people that choose that type of lifestyle."

Everett was not surprised at Mrs. Lawrence's statements. Although Raleigh was a progressive and inclusive city, it was a dot of blue in the sea of red that is rural North Carolina.

"I see," said Judge Clement. "I can understand that view, Mrs. Lawrence. Do any of you other jurors agree with what she just said? If so raise your hands."

None of the other jurors raised their hands, which Everett found to be a bit surprising.

"As I was saying," Judge Clement continued, "This case is not about the private lives of the attorneys. It's not about what occurred on that video. This trial is about the evidence, and judging that evidence by the law, as I will instruct you at the conclusion of closing arguments. Can everyone agree that they will follow the law, and only consider the evidence, and not allow what you may have learned about the private lives of Mr. Stone and Mr. Phelps influence your decision? If so, please raise your hands."

All of the jurors raised their hands once more.

"Equally as important, I need to ask all of you whether you have discussed this trial or Mr. Stone with Mr. Phelps? If so, please raise your hand."

None of the jurors raised their hands.

"This is extremely important, so I want to ask it again. If you answer truthfully that you have discussed the case, I give my word there will be no consequences under the circumstances. Have any of the eleven of you mentioned or discussed any of the evidence, any of the testimony, or anything relating to this case whatsoever with Mr. Phelps."

All of the jurors shook their heads and kept their hands by their sides.

"Ladies and Gentlemen, I need to discuss some things outside of your presence with the lawyers. Please be patient just a little longer and I promise we will get things moving this morning very soon. Bailiff, please escort the jury back to the jury room."

Once the all the jurors were gone from the courtroom, Judge Clement turned his attention back to the attorneys. "Do either of you have anything you wish to say?"

Wright rose to his feet and in a confident voice said, "Your Honor, while I appreciate that the jury just committed to following the law and the evidence, I must move for a mistrial once again. That video was seen by every one of those jurors, and it clearly depicts a member of the jury sleeping with plaintiff's counsel."

"They just said they didn't talk about the case amongst themselves," said Judge Clement."

"Yes, that's true, Your Honor. However, can we really believe that? They know, or at least strongly suspect, that Mr. Phelps is in some hot water right now for not following the court's instructions. Can we trust that they would admit to violating the instruction not to discuss the case? Are we really supposed to believe that Mr. Phelps didn't try to influence at least one of those jurors back there to benefit his lover?"

Everett could feel his face flush with the comment, and he shifted lower in his seat.

"I just told them there would be no consequences if they admitted to it, Mr. Wright. Mr. Stone?" asked Judge Clement.

"Your Honor," Everett began after rising to his feet on shaky knees, "on behalf of my client we would object to a mistrial. The jurors have indicated that they can disregard this event, and decide this case on the evidence and the law. In fact, they are under an oath to do so. I realize that the video is a complicated issue, but I can swear as an officer of this court that what I told Your Honor regarding the relationship between myself and Mr. Phelps and the reasons for our non-disclosure is the truth. I can also swear that at no point did I ever ask or intimate to Mr. Phelps that he should try to influence this jury, and at no point did he ever indicate to me that he had attempted to do so."

Everett cleared his throat.

"Your Honor," he continued, "what should not be lost here is that a man is dead. My client has waited a long time for justice, and that justice should not be delayed due to my personal failures and shortcomings. The jurors swore an oath, and they have assured this Court that they will follow that oath. Mr. Phelps is not here, and we have alternates that can fill the empty seat. This trial should proceed."

Wright began to stand up again as Everett sat down, but Judge Clement raised his hand, indicating the conversation was over.

"The defense's motion for a mistrial is denied. We will empanel one of the alternate jurors and continue with closing arguments."

A loud *snap* in the courtroom caused everyone to turn toward the defense table. Tyndall was red-faced and holding a broken pen in his hand.

Chapter Sixty

" Any word from Everett?" asked Randy as he walked up to Dayna's desk.

"None," she said. "He's been radio silent since that video was sent out. I've tried calling, texting, and emailing and he hasn't responded at all. I thought maybe he would come back to the office last night or even this morning and I could catch him then, but he hasn't shown up here either."

"Maybe you should go down to the courthouse and check on him?"

"No, that's the last thing I should do. Everett always responds, especially to me. His silence means that he doesn't want to be bothered, and doesn't want to see anyone. I can understand that, under the circumstances. It's best to let him focus on the trial as best he can, and he'll get in touch when he's ready."

"I suppose I would want to be left alone for a while too if my biggest secret were broadcast to the entire legal community and my wife in that way," said Randy.

"Speaking of which, have you found anything?"

"Nothing," said Randy. "I've done everything possible since you texted me yesterday to find out who was behind it, but whomever did it was too good and too clean to trace. It was someone was impressive computer skills, and while I'm pretty good at cyber forensics it's beyond my abilities. It would probably take the NSA or CIA to figure it out."

"What about the boy?" asked Dayna.

"He's disappeared too. I can't trace his phone; he was using a burner. Credit cards haven't been used. His apartment is empty, and the landlord and neighbors have no idea where he has gone or if he'll ever be back. No known relatives to contact, and no forwarding address. He's disappeared physically, and all online traces of him have also disappeared. I don't have hope he'll ever surface."

"We have to keep trying," said Dayna, "Either we need to find out who was behind the video or we need to find the boy. He set Everett up and I won't stand for that. He knew exactly what was going on and knew they were being filmed, you can see it in the way he looked directly into the hidden camera's lens during the video."

"I'll try, Dayna. You know I'll try. Everett's a good guy and this shouldn't have happened to him. You and I both know that Tyndall is probably behind this, but I have to be honest with you and say that I don't have a lot of hope that we will ever get the evidence we need to prove it. The kind of cash Tyndall has buys a lot of resources to pull something like this off. I just want you to be prepared that we may not get what we need on this one."

Dayna stared at Randy for a moment, considering the truth of what he had just said. She knew in her heart that Tyndall was behind the ruination of Everett's life but she had to admit that proving it would be almost impossible. The police were looking for the missing juror but it didn't seem promising. Randy was better at finding things and people than the police, and if he couldn't find the missing juror or any evidence of him or who sent the video, then it was probably a lost cause. Still, Dayna had to keep trying for Everett's sake.

"Why are you still standing here?" she asked Randy. "Go back out there and keep looking until you find something."

Chapter Sixty-One

" Harry Thomas died alone while surrounded by dozens of other people. Confused because of his disease, he lay in a bed dependent on others to take care of him. People who worked for Ross Tyndall and that he should have been able to trust. That trust was betrayed."

Everett's nerves had settled and the fog dissipated from his thinking as he began delivering his closing argument to the jury. He hadn't rehearsed it for hours the night before like he normally would, but he knew this case in-and-out and had no trouble giving the performance he had been waiting for since he first heard about Harry Thomas.

"When Monica Thomas selected Peaceful Pines as the caretakers for her father, she did so based on the promise that they would take excellent care of him. It was a promise that not only Mr. Tyndall made to her, but a promise the State of North Carolina made with their five star rating.

"But all of that was a lie. Peaceful Pines began with a lie—a fraud committed by Tyndall in forging his son-in-law's name on the corporate paperwork and funded with money that was hidden from the IRS. The lies continued as ill-equipped nurses and staff were hired. They continued again when medical records were falsified. And the lie of five stars was bought with an envelope of cash."

The scandal that had enveloped his life left his mind entirely as he went through every bit of evidence demonstrating Tyndall was responsible for the death of Harry Thomas. Everett summarized the testimony of every witness called, emphasizing the most obscene details and weaving a story of horror that even Stephen King would have difficulty imagining.

His presence filled every inch of the courtroom, his cadence was measured and powerful, and his eyes were alight in passion.

Every individual watched with rapt attention as Everett delivered a masterful closing.

"No one can bring Harry Thomas back from the dead," Everett said as he began to conclude his speech. "No one can wind back the clock and take away the pain he experienced as medications and meals were withheld from him, and as he lay in that bed dirty and covered in his own filth. But what can be done—what only you have the power to do—is prevent another Harry Thomas. You have the ability to deliver a verdict that sends a message not just to Mr. Tyndall, but every other business and individual entrusted with the care of one of our most vulnerable populations, our elderly and infirm parents and grandparents. A message that says the behavior shown at this trial is absolutely not tolerated in this community."

• • • •

The chair creaked in the silence of the courtroom as Wright rose to his feet and strode to the center of the room in front of the jury box. He cleared his throat and looked at the jury, then to his client.

"What happened to Mr. Thomas was a tragedy, but it wasn't the fault of Ross Tyndall," began Wright as he turned his attention back to the jurors.

"Peaceful Pines had a long-standing five star rating from the state, and every single complaint made against it was investigated and concluded to be unfounded. Every single staff member employed was properly credentialed, and electronic medical records reveal they did their job properly.

"Mr. Thomas had a host of pre-existing medical conditions before he arrived at Peaceful Pines. And you've heard evidence during this trial that many of those conditions likely contributed to his condition at the time of his death, and, in all probability, caused his death. Dementia is a horrible disease that attacks the mind, and then begins to waste away the body."

Wright paused and took a deep breath, taking in the jurors. Many of them stared back at him with what appeared to be disgust, as if he had shoveled literal bullshit straight into the jury box.

"Where does the evidence to the contrary come from?" asked Wright.

"Annie Smith is one of the plaintiff's star witnesses. A witness who stole protected health information in violation of Federal privacy laws. A witness who disclosed that information to third parties in violation of Federal privacy laws. A witness who was fired for incompetence in her job; who ran straight into the arms of the plaintiff because she had an axe to grind."

Wright continued to do his best to spin Peaceful Pines and Tyndall as less than the embodiment of evil that Everett had made them out to be. There wasn't much evidence he could use to make his arguments, but he was a skilled litigator and played the hand he was dealt expertly. He saved his best card for last.

"Ask yourselves, ladies and gentlemen, why are we really here? Are we here to right a wrong and send a message like plaintiff and her counsel are trying to convince you? Or, are we here because someone is looking to profit from tragedy?

"Make no mistake that Monica Thomas could have cared less about her father. She had not seen him in over thirty years. Had not spoken to him. Had not sent a text, email, card, nothing. But she would have you believe she's here because she loved her father and wants justice.

"What she wants is money. She wanted that check that came from the insurance company immediately after her father passed because of a policy she kept on him even though she had been estranged from him for three decades and never once visited, called, or wrote her father. Monica Thomas didn't care about her father—she never once returned one of the many messages left by Peaceful Pines staff about him or his condition. She never once visited. She dropped him off and abandoned him. And how did she grieve after learning of her father's death? By smiling while going on a shopping spree less than twenty four hours after she learned about it.

"The real message you should send with your verdict is this: unpreventable and natural death is not an excuse to play the lawsuit lottery."

• • • •

The jury now had the case and Everett didn't expect them to deliberate long. With nothing to do but wait, he tried his best not to let his mind drift back to Jake and the problems that he would need to solve after the trial was over. He attempted to make some small talk with Monica, who had turned cold toward him. Everett suspected the affair that almost resulted in a mistrial was a small part of the reason for it; but he guessed her main worry now was how much she was about to receive and how to spend it.

Everett watched as Sloan rose from his seat and walked out of the courtroom. After a few seconds, Everett followed him out.

In the hallway, Sloan was leaning against the wall and typing into his phone. Everett walked up to him and grabbed him tightly by the arm, yanking him off the wall and dragging him the short distance into a conference room.

"I just wanted to have a quick word, Sloan," said Everett as he closed the door.

"We don't have anything to talk about," Sloan replied.

"Maybe so, but I just wanted to say that you can go fuck yourself."

Sloan smiled. "Are you through?"

"No. You and Tyndall think you were so clever with what you did. It didn't work out for you though, did it? I didn't sell out like you thought, and you didn't get a mistrial or a dismissal either. Now you're about to be out of business when this jury comes back. And, if Tyndall declares bankruptcy I won't rest until I get every cent I can. You ruined my life, and I'm going to ruin both of yours. I'm going to prove that you tried to extort me and were responsible for the leak of that video, and you and Tyndall can both rot in jail together this time."

"Is that so?" Sloan asked while laughing. "How do you plan to do that? Where's the hooker we paid to set you up? No one has found him and we've paid him enough and given him the resources so that he'll never be found. Without him what evidence could you possibly have? I'll answer that for you: none."

Everett's jaw clenched along with his fists at Sloan's arrogance.

"And this verdict?" continued Sloan, "We had hoped to avoid the headlines and negative press that will forever be online for prospective residents and their families to find. But, we ultimately don't care anymore. You know why? Because whatever amount these twelve morons give you, you'll never collect on it. And I'm not talking about bankruptcy because we won't be doing that. We'll keep right along with our business and we're going to appeal the denial of our mistrial. We'll win."

"Don't be so sure of that," said Everett.

"Oh, I am completely sure we will win, Stone. Look what we did to you. You don't think we've got the resources to ensure that we win the appeal? Hell, we'll get the three most conservative judges appointed to the panel that hears this case, and they'll side with us because all of them receive large checks from us each election year to ensure they decide cases how we want them to. So you can sit there and think you've won this case, but you haven't. Your life is ruined because you got greedy, and the shame of it is your so-called win at trial will be reversed and ripped right out of your queer little hands. So you can go fuck yourself."

Sloan brushed passed Everett and left the conference room. Everett stood there in the silence trying to resist the urge to follow Sloan and pummel him in the hallway, or to punch a hole in the wall.

Everett walked back into the courtroom and seated himself at counsel table. No sooner had he done so, there was a knock on the jury room's door. Everyone stopped what they were doing and stared motionless at the small hallway off the courtroom as the bailiff went to see what the jury wanted.

"The jury has a verdict," said the returning bailiff.

Part III

Appeal

Chapter Sixty-Two

Tyndall finished reading the letter from Wright and tore it into pieces. His face flushed and he punched the wall. He cursed loudly and sat back down on the edge of his bed, before standing again and pacing back and forth.

I wish you everything you deserve. This will conclude our representation.

Those were the words at the end of Wright's letter. A final brush of his hands from the filth that was his former client.

There had always been a next move in Ross Tyndall's past when he found himself in trouble. He had a knack for slithering out of it and moving on to his next plan. That's what frustrated him the most. There was no next move.

Tyndall let out a scream in rage.

"What's going on in here? Keep it down!" said a man from the opposite side of the door.

"Sorry," replied Tyndall after glaring at the prison guard.

It had been two years since the jury returned a two hundred million dollar verdict against Tyndall and his business. Not only did they find him liable for the death of Harry Thomas, but they found he had fraudulently set up his business and that the limited liability afforded to corporations would not protect his personal assets. He had filed bankruptcy, but had too much in assets to fully discharge the debt. Execution on the massive judgment, the largest in state history, had been stayed pending appeal. That appeal was now over, according to Wright's letter.

The Supreme Court of North Carolina unanimously found in Monica Thomas's favor, affirming the Court of Appeals. Tyndall and Sloan's plan to pack the panel with judges favorable them had failed, and indeed had backfired on them both.

Sloan could no longer help him. He had been disbarred. What was worse in Tyndall's eyes is that his long-time fixer had betrayed him. Sloan had become a cooperating witness in exchange for probation when law enforcement began to close in on Tyndall and those associated with him. The whore Tyndall and Sloan had paid off to frame Everett and ensure the case resolved in their favor had never been found, but the investigation into the video and jury tampering had been assisted with a video statement Jake emailed to Judge Clement and the investigators. In addition to his statement, he provided a trove of information proving a connection between Sloan and Tyndall and the leak of the video, as well as their payments to Jake.

Phishing. That was the word Sloan had used when the information was turned over. Jake was apparently a skilled hacker too, and had secretly uploaded a program that mined Tyndall and Sloan's devices for information when they had set up the plan. In addition to every communication and wire transfer related to the extortion of Everett, it had also uncovered the bribery of the conservative judges on the Court of Appeals and a host of other criminal offenses that had overshadowed the manufactured scandal surrounding Everett sleeping with a juror in the trial.

Even despite these developments, Tyndall had held out hope the Supreme Court would reverse the record-setting verdict. He had always believed he should have received a new trial when it was brought to light that Everett was sleeping with a juror, but the justices had disagreed and their word was final. Wright had called it a "results-oriented decision" in his letter, which Tyndall knew was legalese for "the judges determined the result they wanted and engaged in mental and legal gymnastics to justify their holding." Although the justices had not condoned any of the conduct that had transpired in the trial court, they reasoned that the verdict should be affirmed because the defendant could not benefit from his own wrongdoing.

Now, as he continued to pace his cell, execution on the judgment was beginning. Tyndall knew a receiver had been appointed and his sprawling mansion and vacation homes were currently up for sale. His bank accounts and investments were being liquidated, and his luxury cars, art, and boats were being sold at auction to the highest bidder.

He had planned for this day so long ago when he started his business empire. A nest egg of untouchable cash in Cayman and Swiss accounts under an assumed name that was untraceable. Money that he could always count on being there for him.

Until now. There is always a digital record. The secret nest egg had been discovered by Jake in the phishing attack and evidence of that existence was also turned over to investigators. That money was now gone too. Fifteen million dollars. Only Tyndall and Jake knew that the balance had been twenty million before investigators became aware it. Tyndall wondered sometimes what Jake had spent the money he stole from him on.

Tyndall was powerless and penniless for the first time since he was a young man.

Chapter Sixty-Three

Everett watched as high tide rolled up the shore and the horizon became streaked with rows of deep purple, pink, and orange. The breeze felt good against his skin and cooled him. The sand beneath him was still warm from the day's sun, smoldering like embers. Since moving to the beach town of Emerald Isle along North Carolina's coast a year ago, Everett had promised himself he would never miss a sunset.

The Thomas case had not only been the biggest case of his legal career, it had been his last. Although he evaded criminal charges, the State Bar was not as kind to his sleeping with a juror and failing to report it. The video of him and Jake having sex had been a scandal in the legal community and spread far and wide. The media latched onto it, especially with the record-setting verdict. The Bar felt an example needed to be made of him and disbarred him.

Since he was a solo practitioner, Everett had wound up his law practice. Laying off his staff, especially Dayna and Randy, had been the hardest part of the whole ordeal, but he had worked what few connections that had not been alienated during the scandal to find them jobs in other firms. Dayna was actually making more than what he could ever afford to pay her, and seemed to love her new job, according to what she told him. She was the only person from his old life that he still kept in contact with.

The Thomas case and his affair with Jake had forced Everett to come to terms with his bisexuality, and he no longer tried to hide who he was from the world. He wasn't the type to wear the rainbow, but he held his head with pride in who he was and for the first time in his life felt comfortable in his own skin.

Olivia had not been as understanding. The only contact he had had with her after she kicked him out of the house was through a divorce lawyer. What could have been a drawn-out legal battle resolved quickly, as Everett didn't retain his own counsel and didn't put up a fight. He had caused Olivia enough pain over the years, and it was time to buy peace between them and allow them both to move on with their lives. She had taken almost everything he had.

Everett smiled as he thought of the news he had received on his phone earlier in the day. While Tyndall was rotting in a jail cell after being convicted of jury tampering, extortion, bribery, and a host of other charges, Everett had been kayaking in Bogue Sound. Dayna informed him that the Supreme Court had affirmed the judgment against Tyndall. He had yelled out in joy, causing several white egrets to take flight from the nearby marsh grass.

He would see none of the money since he was no longer an attorney. That was okay with him. He still held the record for the largest verdict ever received in the state, and he had achieved justice for Harry Thomas. More importantly, Tyndall was out of business, bankrupt, and imprisoned. At one point not too long ago, thinking of losing out on an almost seventy million dollar contingency fee would have sent him into a depressive spiral. But Everett didn't need the money any longer—he had everything he needed in his life.

His swimming habits came in handy when he moved to coast. He readily found a job as an ocean rescue lifeguard, and was able to rent a small cottage not far from the ocean. He didn't make anywhere near the money he used to, but he was comfortable enough. Everett had started fresh in this coastal community three hours from Raleigh, where no one knew him and the news of the Thomas case two years ago barely registered in anyone's memory unless they were some of the handful of lawyers who practiced in the area or came down to their vacation homes. Everett was able to start building the life he wanted, rather than the life he had always felt he needed to have.

As the sun sank below the horizon behind him taking with it the last of the day's light, the ocean in front of him turned deep navy.

Everett looked at the man laying in the sand next to him. He was lean and muscular, and tan. His hair was brown and a five o'clock shadow covered his chiseled jawline. He looked like the first man he had ever loved, but was different enough where no one noticed.

Alex had walked up to Everett at the local coffee shop shortly after Everett had moved to Emerald Isle. Everett had been on break from his life guarding shift. Alex looked familiar to Everett when he walked in wearing a tank top and short gym shorts, but he couldn't place the face.

The two had exchanged flirtatious small talk before Everett excused himself to return to work, leaving the handsome stranger behind. When he was almost to his car, Alex ran out of the shop after him.

"You forgot something," Alex had said.

"What?" Everett replied.

"This," said Alex. He pulled Everett close and kissed him. It was in that moment Everett knew he loved Alex, and wanted to spend the rest of his life with him.

"What are you staring at?" Alex asked with a chuckle as he withdrew his lips.

"You. Always you. I love you," said Everett.

"I love you too," said the man once called Jake.

Share Your Thoughts!

Let others know what you thought of *Conflict of Interest*! Scan the QR code below to leave a rating and review on Goodreads. Or, leave one where you purchased your copy. Leaving an honest review is the best way to support independent authors!

• • • •

Stay in Touch!

Want to know what I'm working on next, or read my other works? Stop by my website and sign up for my newsletter. You'll get information about upcoming releases, short stories, exclusive sales and giveaways, and much more!

• • • •

www.ingramcontent.com/pod-product-compliance
Lightning Source LLC
Chambersburg PA
CBHW020419260626
47156CB00007B/2457